MW00898287

Short Short Stories

To My Friend,
Truman

by Gene Zimmerman

Gene Zimmerman

Preface

We all like stories, often the longer and more involved, the better. But sometimes we'd like something we could read in a few minutes while we are commuting on public transportation, waiting in the doctor's office, or enjoying a cup of expresso at Starbucks. This book is a compilation of seventy very short stories that I've written over the last several years and read at biweekly meetings of the San Antonio Writers Meetup group. Some of the stories may make you laugh, some may tug at your heartstrings, some may make you wonder, but hopefully all will entertain you.

I want to thank my wife, Jan Zimmerman, for painstakingly editing each of these stories. I'm also grateful to our daughter, Michelle Vieau who designed the book cover.

If you enjoy these stories, you may also want to read *Terror at Black Canyon*, a novel I wrote about terrorism in the oil and gas industry. Published by iUniverse, it is available in digital and paperback formats.

Thanks for buying this book.

Gene Zimmerman

San Antonio, Tx

Contents

Short Short Stories

A Blue Sky Day in Virginia Beach

It was one of those blue sky Chamber of Commerce Days;
the kind of day they use for shooting travel brochures that entice
tourists to visit Virginia Beach during the Cherry Blossom
Festival. Little did I know it would be a day I'd never forget, like
the day that yours truly lost his first part-time job as a grocery
store bagger, or like the day my girlfriend threw my car keys
down the storm drain to drive home her point during an
argument.

I'd decided to get out of the office for lunch and pick up a
tasty hamburger at Wendy's. On such a gorgeous day, it was hard
to keep my mind on my driving. The cherry trees along the
parkway were in full bloom and the sight almost took my breath
away. Before I realized it, the traffic light that had seemed so far
away was looming just two car lengths away, and it was red! Then
I heard tires squealing – surely not my own – and I was skidding
straight into the shiny black Lexus obediently parked in front of
the light.

"Damn, it, Jack!" I exclaimed at the sound of metal to metal
impact. Suddenly the Lexus moved forward a couple of feet as the
bumper on my old pickup slammed into that shiny black trunk.
Wouldn't you know it, but the trunk latch disengaged and the lid
flew open! "Crap," I muttered to myself, "you've really done it this
time. What a way to ruin a beautiful day."

I opened the pickup door and stepped down to access the damage and trade the requisite particulars with the Lexus driver. The car door opened and a lady turned to get out. It seemed like slow motion as I saw her left foot in gold stiletto heels emerge first, and then a long curvy calf and thigh, partly covered by a Ralph Lauren brown frilly skirt. The driver stood up in the road, tossed her long brown mane, and pulled off her sunglasses as she turned toward me. The most beautiful green eyes were staring at me and her gorgeous olive-skinned face was hardened by the scowl that was spreading across her brow. Damn, she looked beautiful, even in her obvious frustration. Something about her looked familiar, too.

"Mister, why did you hurt my car?" were the words coming out of those luscious red lips. At that point, I realized who she was, Ava Maldonado, the star of my favorite TV show, "Lusty Housewives of Virginia." I couldn't believe it! For a minute I forgot what had brought about this chance meeting, and I was mesmerized by the presence of the woman I'd secretly lusted after in my heart for the last two seasons. Then the horror of what I had done hit me again. I'd smashed up the high-priced car of this wealthy actress, who no doubt had several high-powered lawyers on retainer. The minimal insurance on my old relic wouldn't cover all the potential pain and suffering damages they could dream up. This was going to really hurt me!

"I know who you are, Ms. Maldonado, and… and," I'd stammered, "I'd never hurt you or your magnificent car on purpose. I'm Jack Slater and I'm a big fan of yours. And don't worry, I'll make it right."

I could smell the scent of her perfume (was it Allure?) as she extended her dainty hand to shake mine, which was trembling ever so slightly. "Mr. Slater, so you're a big fan of mine, and you'll make all this right?"

"Absolutely!" I exclaimed, all the time realizing that my insurance agent would be furious that I had admitted fault. "Why don't we walk around to the back of your car and check out the damage?"

"Definitely," she purred and followed me as I approached the car's rear with its crumpled back bumper and popped up trunk lid. Suddenly my eyes spied the contents of the trunk, which I'd expected to be shopping bags or something of that ilk. But no, it was a man. Or rather the body of a man, twisted in such a way I knew he must be dead. Sure enough, there in the trunk of gorgeous Ava Maldonado's black Lexus was a dead body.

"What the hell, Ms. Maldonado?" I inquired, turning toward her just as she let out a blood-curdling scream. She threw her hands up to her face in a look of shock. Either she was a really good actress off the set, or she really hadn't known about the body.

"Oh my god, it's Raul!" she exclaimed as she caught a glimpse of the face. "That's my gardener, Raul Martinez. He looked so happy yesterday when he finished pruning the roses and told me he was taking off work early to go see his son. And now he's dead! I feel faint..." she uttered as she reached out to the side of the car to steady herself.

A crowd was starting to gather at the intersection and I heard someone calling 911 on their cell phone. Everything seemed so unreal at this point I wondered if I was in a bad dream.

"Ms. Maldonado, the cops are going to be here any minute. What can you tell them about why this guy's dead body is in your trunk?" Out of the corner of my eye, I spied a long-stemmed rose clenched in the gardener's teeth. What in the heck?

"Mr. Slater, I mean Jack. I swear upon the blessed Virgin that I know nothing about this! You've got to believe me. You've got to help me!"

I turned and looked over Raul's twisted form more closely, careful not to actually touch him. Obviously his neck had been broken, but there, almost concealed by the shadows was an ivory-handled knife in his back, buried to the hilt. I pointed it out to the actress and she burst into tears.

"That's Joe's knife. You know, Joe my no-good ex-husband who was the soccer player. He always imagined there was something going on between Raul and me. The jealous bastard told me he'd kill him if he ever caught us alone together. But there wasn't!"

I turned toward the sound of the police car siren and realized that this would be a blue sky day I'd never forget.

A Cup of Cold Water

Jostling up and down in the open-air jeep on a rocky road back to the dig; Peter Rogers replayed the dinner conversation from the evening before in Cairo.

"Dr. Rogers, it's been fascinating to see your new archeological dig here in Egypt. And I've thoroughly enjoyed your company."

"Miss Saint James, the pleasure has been all mine. It's not often I get to show our work to such an accomplished – and attractive journalist." He smiled as he sipped his glass of wine and smelled the faint scent of her perfume as she sat across from him.

"What I'd like to know is why a good looking scholar who is also kind isn't married. Is that too personal? The question can be strictly off the record! I won't mention your answer in my article in the Times."

"Well. You probably don't know that I initially studied for the priesthood. You obviously learn to avoid romantic entanglements when you believe you are called to remain celibate. When I finally realized my true calling was archeology I focused my passion on those studies and I guess I never unlearned that life skill." He laughed. " Now I'm married to my work in the deserts of Egypt."

"So you didn't go into the priesthood. You seem to still be a spiritual man."

"I guess you could say that. The study of ancient cultures has a spiritual aspect to it." Looking at his watch, he added, "it looks like we need to continue this conversation on the way to the airport; otherwise you'll miss your flight to London."

The archeologist was interrupted from his reverie by a loud hiss, followed by the sight of steam from under the hood of the jeep. Raising the hood, his worst fears were confirmed: a broken radiator hose.

"Drat! Why did you have to give out on me now, old girl?" he asked the jeep. "It must be fifty miles back to civilization, and the dig is still a good twenty miles ahead. It's not going to be an easy walk in the summertime heat. But I can do it!"

Grabbing his valise out of the jeep, Peter pulled his battered fedora down to shade his face from the midday sun. After unhooking the two canvas water bags hanging on the front of the jeep, he slung one over each shoulder and set off on the long trek toward the little oasis that was the site of his new excavation.

Perspiration dripped off Peter's face and shirt after only a short time. Every half hour, he'd stop to take one small drink of cool water from one of the canvas bags to keep his head clear and yet conserve his water supply. A couple hours into the trek, he saw someone leaning against a large boulder ahead. As he got closer, he could see it was an old Bedouin, dressed in a white robe and red and white-checked head dress.

Using the best Arabic he had, Peter said, "Hello fellow traveler. Are you well?"

"No, I'm not well." He answered in a low raspy voice. "I hurt my ankle and cannot walk on it. My companions left last night to get me help. I don't expect them back until dark. My water is gone and I am very thirsty."

"I think you're suffering from heat exhaustion, my friend." Then to himself, Peter thought, *can I spare one of my water bags for this desert wanderer? If I don't he might well die out here...*

Just then, a scripture from his seminary training came to mind, "And whoever gives only a cup of cold water to one of these little ones to drink because he is a disciple--amen, I say to you, he will surely not lose his reward."

Peter gazed into the azure sky as though looking for an answer from above and felt the brilliance of the sun bake his forehead. "Okay," he muttered and turned back to the Bedouin. "Here friend, I can spare some of my water with you. Take this bag and drink from it. You can keep it, for, as you can see, I have another."

The Bedouin accepted the full bag with gratitude. "My friend, may Allah – and Jesus – bless you for your kindness."

Shouldering the remaining bag that was still mostly full, the archeologist traveled on. He continued to carefully ration his water by drinking only one swallow every thirty minutes, though his lips felt parched and his throat was dry long before it was time for the next water stop.

For a brief time a cloud came up and shielded Peter from the sun. "Maybe that's my reward," he smiled through cracked lips. *Better than nothing, I guess.*

Late in the afternoon, Peter estimated from nearby landmarks that he was still two hours away from the oasis, and started to worry that he might not make it. Suddenly he came upon a poor beggar sitting beside the road. "What in the heck is this guy doing out here?" he wondered aloud.

Conversing with the ragged and dirty beggar, he realized the man was disoriented. The beggar claimed to have come from the oasis, though Peter had never seen him there. The man was obviously lame and very old and couldn't explain how he'd gotten there or why. But he was very thirsty and Peter knew he needed water to survive until nightfall.

"Can you give me a drink of water, sir?" the old man pleaded as he gazed into Peter's face.

Lord, when did we see you hungry and feed you, or thirsty and give you drink? And the king will say to them in reply, 'Amen, I say to you, whatever you did for one of these least brothers of mine, you did for me.' The words intruded into Peter's thoughts as though they'd been placed there by an outside source. Though Peter had only a small amount of water left in the canvas canteen, he knew what he must do.

Unscrewing the cap from the bag, he bent over and let the beggar drink the bag dry. As he did, the dull look in the old man's eyes became bright. As Peter stared, he felt incredible joy and peace as the man's eyes reflected such love and compassion that Peter felt his heart leap in his chest. Suddenly it seemed that instead of looking into the visage of a dirty and weary old man, he was looking into the very face of Jesus.

"Thank you, my son" the beggar smiled and handed the bag back. As Peter received it, he was surprised that the bag had water in it. He took a long drink, screwed the cap on, and walked away in a daze.

After a hundred yards or so, Peter looked back to see that the beggar was gone. The archeologist continued on his way, full of questions, but energized for the rest of the journey. He drank more water from the bag and yet it still wasn't empty. Just as the sun set, he could see the palm trees of the oasis in the distance. Trudging toward them, he wondered, *What if I'd decided to keep all the water for myself? Would I have made it?*

A Geezer Endless Summer

I could see the summer sun glinting off the crashing waves as the tanned surfers paddled out on their boards to catch the next big kahuna. There I was, with a surf board across my shoulder on the first day of summer vacation! The damp sand felt good between my toes, the sound of the surf was music to my ears and the salty smell and taste of the Pacific was exhilarating.

"Gene, you've got that faraway look in your eyes again…" remarked Bill, as he walked up to my table on the Starbucks patio and jarred me out of my reverie.

"Yeah. It was the summer of 1963 again and I was heading into the surf just as you brought me back to reality."

"Were you really a surfer back then?"

"Yeah; if you count virtual surfing that is! But it was tough to be a real surfer in the Tucson desert. I was a huge Beach Boys fan, I loved the water, and when I was stationed in Hawaii years later, I did learn to body surf. But even then I was too chicken to try to shoot the bonsai pipeline on a surf board. How about you, Bill? Did you ever learn to surf?"

"Only surfing I've done is on the Internet, though I've lived near some good surfing spots over the years," my friend chuckled.

"What do you think it was that made surfing so appealing to us when we were young?" I asked.

"Trying to make a philosopher out of me? I guess it looked exciting, almost dangerous, and it impressed the girls. Plus it represented freedom and seemed to be a way of becoming almost one with the sun, sand, and surf."

"Yeah, freedom to do what you wanted, I think was one thing it represented. Like that surfing documentary, "The Endless Summer" where they just traveled around the world trying out all the best surfing spots."

"Chasing the idea of an endless summer! Sounded romantic, especially to those of us who had to work most of the summer back then."

"Well, it's summer again, my friend. Now that we're retired we don't have to have to work most of it away. What could we do to make this an endless summer?" I mused aloud.

"Well, I don't recommend surfing. We'd have to move from San Antonio to take it up, plus there's no way our tired old bodies could stand the beating the waves would give us."

"Let's think of something fun that we haven't ever done and go do it this week. Then next week we'll think of something else and go do it. Each week until this fall we could go do something new."

"Kind of like a geezer version of the endless summer, I guess! Let's do it, Gene."

"What should we do this first week?"

Bill thought a bit and then suggested taking a barge trip the length of the new Museum Reach section of the Riverwalk. "That's something we've never done before."

"Shucks, it's something most people in San Antonio haven't done yet. And to make it more memorable and save some cash while we're at it, why don't we ride the VIA bus system?"

The next day found Bill and me and our wives riding the express bus downtown. I had a senior bus pass that let me ride at half price, so we went by the VIA transit office on West Commerce to get Bill a senior pass for the ride back. All he had to do was show them a Texas Driver's License.

"I'm sorry, sir, but we can't issue you a senior bus pass with this driver's license," declared the lady at the window.

"Why not? What's wrong with this license?"

"Sir, it expired on your birthday six months ago!"

As we beat a hasty retreat from the transit office, I had a feeling that the day might not go as well as we'd hoped. However, soon we'd bought some all day barge passes that entitled us to travel up and down both the old and new sections of the Riverwalk and all seemed to be well. We started riding a yellow-flagged barge on the old part of the Riverwalk and Bill's wife happily snapped photos of old buildings as we drifted by.

When we came to the start of the new Rivewalk extension near the McCullough bridge our barge pilot announced, "Okay, folks, the next bridge is as far as I go. At that point one of the red flag barges will pick you up and take you through the locks and up to the end of the new section."

At that moment a barge with a red flag rounded the bend, and our driver noted that we could directly transfer from his barge to this one without the usual half hour wait. "I'll just pull up alongside Joe's barge and you can step from one to the other."

"Great!" I exclaimed and started to step from our barge to Joe's when they were still maybe two feet apart. No problem for someone who'd been daydreaming of surfing the day before, right? Wrong!

As I lost my footing, I heard the cries of everyone on the barge and suddenly I was in the river, struggling to stay afloat and spitting foul tasting water out of my mouth.

"Just relax, sir, and let your feet touch bottom. The river's only four feet deep here. Here take my hand!" The barge pilot reached down and pulled me back onto the barge, where I caught my breath and tried to regain my dignity.

"Macho man, are you okay?" my wife asked as she tried to choke back a laugh. "I wish I had some towels; you're soaking wet!"

Eventually we got on the red flagged barge and I drip-dried in the sun while we traveled the length of the new Riverwalk extension and back. We waited about thirty minutes for a yellow flag barge to pick us up and drop us off by the Lone Star

Café for lunch. The waiters looked at me strangely as they heard the squeak of my wet shoes and noted my disheveled appearance.

As we later waited at the bus stop for the ride back, a couple of drunk gang banger types sidled up to our wives and tried to pick them up. Thinks got pretty nasty for a few minutes until a cop on a bicycle showed up and arrested them for something.

Bill and I looked at each other on the long bus ride back and sighed. Somehow the idea of an endless summer had lost its appeal. Bill spoke first, "Maybe we should rethink this thing, Gene."

"Yeah, somehow it sounds like a lot more fun to daydream of an endless summer at the coffee shop than it is to live it."

"Meet you at Starbucks next week?" asked Bill as he and his wife stepped off the bus.

"Sure thing, old friend!"

A Hint of Fall

There was a hint of fall in the air and after the long hot summer, people were fleeing their houses for the great outdoors. I picked up the Saturday newspaper and savored the coolness of the morning air, as I looked up and down the street of my new neighborhood. My neighbor to the left was already on a riding lawnmower mowing his tiny yard. I smiled at my neighbor to the left, Mrs. Sanchez, who was outside in a tiny red bikini planting fall flowers. Across the street, the neighborhood geezer, Mr. Wilson, was staring through some binoculars from his front porch.

"No doubt he's studying Mrs. Sanchez' gardening techniques." I chuckled to myself. "Guess you're never to old to learn something new."

Just then my cell phone rang. It was my sister, who lived a block over and had helped me find the house I'd just moved into.

"Hey, John, what say you and Otis and I take a walk around the neighborhood and get some exercise. I can introduce you to some of the folks on your street that you haven't met yet."

"Sure thing, Nadia. It'll probably take me a few minutes to uncover Otis' leash from the partially unpacked boxes in the front room."

"Sure. I'll be over in ten. And see if you can find a plastic bag to bring along. The neighbors here are pretty anal about keeping their yards free of dog poop."

Otis is my beautiful seventy pound Dalmatian that I've had since he was a pup. I was still looking for his leash when the doorbell rang.

"Hey, Nadia. Come on in and help me dig through this stuff! I'll be glad when Serena gets here and can help me finish unpacking and organizing."

"Yeah, kind of inconvenient for you that your wife is at a three week seminar in Miami while you are here in San Antonio trying to get moved in! The male of the species is just not cut out for this type of work. Especially you, bro!" Nadia smiled as she gave me a sisterly punch on the shoulder.

"There it is!" I yelled triumphantly as I spotted Otis' leash in the bottom of a box labeled kitchen utensils.

"Ha," laughed Nadia as she spied the box label. You need even more help than I thought!"

"I'll have you know, Sis, the leash was in the kitchen pantry in our old house. So it's natural I would put it in a box of kitchen stuff."

"Whatever! Did you find a plastic bag for poop? I know Otis can be pretty prolific!"

"Right here in my back pocket."

Soon Nadia, Otis, and I had started on a nice walk around the neighborhood. Since Nadia was a realtor, she knew the name of just about everyone we encountered. There was Domingo

Garcia, who worked for the post office. Next to him lived Joe Walker, a detective with the San Antonio PD.

"Hi, Katherine! This is my brother, John, who just moved in. John, this is Katherine, a middle school teacher who is the chairperson of our landscape committee."

"Hello, Katherine," I said as I shook her hand and asked, "How did you get roped into the landscape job?"

"I like plants and I'm very interested in keeping the neighborhood looking attractive. Besides, no one else wanted the job," she smiled.

"I noticed that my neighbor, Mrs. Sanchez, likes to work with plants, too."

Katherine gave me an icy stare as she stated, "Mrs. Sanchez mostly likes to entice neighborhood men with her choice of outdoor attire. Well, I've got to be going to a meeting."

A couple of doors down I noticed a dour looking older gentleman sitting on his front porch with a six pack of Coors. Just then a blonde bombshell who looked thirty years younger sauntered out the front door.

"That's Bill Bronson, a retiree from New Jersey, who moved here a couple years ago with his trophy wife, Eva. He mostly keeps to himself, although Eva seems fairly outgoing."

As soon as we got in front of the Bronson's house, Otis decided to empty his colon in their front yard. No sooner had he started than Mr. Bronson jumped up with beer bottle in hand. "Get that damn dog off my property. And clean up his crap before you leave!"

I reached for the poop bag in my back pocket but it had fallen out somewhere along the way! I turned around helplessly and looked at Nadia.

I tried to explain to the old man as he gestured and cursed me from the porch. "My plastic bag must have fallen out, sir. But I will clean up this mess."

"You damn well, better, mister! I can see that you are new to this neighborhood, so you don't know me. I have one rule: you keep your damn dog and their crap out of my yard and I won't go crap in your yard!"

I left Nadia there with Otis and hurried back home to get another plastic bag. I was back a few minutes later and scooped up the poop under Mr. Bronson's watchful eye. Then Nadia and Otis and I walked around the block before I went back to my unpacking.

That evening when I took Otis for a walk, I was careful to stuff several plastic bags in my pockets, just in case. As we walked by the Bronson's yard, I was surprised to see a couple of large piles of dog poop near his front porch. "Wonder who did that, Otis? Glad it wasn't you!"

That night I was watching the 10 o'clock news when I heard a crash in the front of the house. Someone had thrown a whiskey bottle through my front window! It had apparently been filled with dog poop, as there was a stinky brown stain on the wall where the bottle had broken. I stood there shaking as I tried to gather my wits about me. By the time I'd dialed Nadia's number on my cell phone, I was livid.

"What kind of neighborhood is this, Nadia?" I exclaimed and told her what happened. A few minutes later, she was at my door with Joe Walker, the neighborhood SAPD detective.

"Joe, the only person who I can think of who would do this is that cranky old Mr. Bronson."

"Well, it looks like there might be some good fingerprints on the neck of the broken bottle, John. I'll take it to the lab and if we can get a match in our databases, we'll know who threw it. But unless your neighbor has a record, it won't help us."

Monday after work, I was shocked to see two US Government vehicles parked in front of Bronson's house. I was even more surprised to see two FBI agents lead him out of the house in handcuffs.

"Is throwing a bottle of dog poop a federal crime?" I asked Joe later.

"No, but escaping from Leavenworth is. The prints on the bottle matched Joseph Muzzarini's, the notorious mob kingpin. He escaped five years ago and was hiding in plain sight here as Bill Bronson!"

All Saints Day

Looking toward the sky as he ambled into St. Luke's cemetery, the eighty-two year old man muttered, "It figures that All Saints Day would be cold and gray." Cold and gray, the way he felt.

Joe Thomas had been coming to this cemetery on All Saints Day every year since he was nine years old, except for the two years he fought in the Korean War. He thought about the first time he went with his parents and his siblings to visit the graves of their relatives and ancestors.

"Kids, these are the graves of our loved ones who've gone on before us," Joe's dad had explained. "We come here to give prayers of thanks for what their lives have meant and to pray for their blessings in the afterlife."

Joe thought back to that first visit to the cemetery when he had seen the tombstones of his great grandparents and one of his dad's brothers, as well as some cousins of his mother. There were about ten relatives buried there at the time.

"Now there are so many graves here of people I knew and loved, I can scarcely count." Joe muttered.

"I'm sorry sir. I didn't catch what you said. Were you talking to me?"

Joe turned to see a man in overalls with a rake. "No, I was just thinking out loud. Are you the new caretaker? Somebody told me that old Ralph had died."

"Sure enough. Ralph is buried over by that big oak tree. One of the perks of the job, you know, is a free burial plot. So I took the job over back in June. I'm Clint. Clint Greene."

"Joe Thomas. Pleased to make your acquaintance, Clint. I had an uncle named Clint, but he's buried here along with every one of my relatives and nearly all my friends."

"What you said, Mr. Thomas, reminds me of what my gramps used to say. He said the good news was that he'd lived a very long life, but the bad news was that he had outlived all his family and friends. He died a lonely man."

"Yes, yes. My father and mother and sisters are buried here. My wife of 54 years passed away a couple of years ago and our only son was killed while serving his country in Operation Desert Storm. I used to have a lot of friends, but most of them have passed on or have moved out of town to be close to their great grand kids."

"So all your immediate family are buried here?"

"Pretty much. All except my younger brother, John, who is ten years my junior. The cemetery owner should probably have given our family some kind of volume discount!"

Clint chuckled. "So what about your younger brother. Is he still alive?"

"That's the $64,000 question. The last time I saw John was at my mother's funeral, thirty years ago. He had joined the CIA after retiring from the Army and was getting ready to go overseas as a top secret undercover agent. I asked him where he was going and what he'd be doing and he said he'd have to kill me if he told me. He laughed as he said it, but when I looked into his eyes, I could tell he meant it."

"So no word after that?"

"Once in a while I'd get a Christmas card mailed from a postal address in Langley, Virginia. I knew that wasn't the original place they were mailed from, however. Then about ten years ago I moved to the other side of town. Haven't heard from him since. Maybe he didn't know how to find me, or maybe he lies dead on foreign soil somewhere. Surely he's retired from the agency by now, if he's still alive. Who knows?" Joe said with a catch in his voice. "I pray for him every All Souls Day, too; I pray for them all." He motioned toward the graves.

"That must be tough. So what line of work were you in?"

"I was a newspaper journalist until I retired and then I took up writing detective stories. I've gotten a few books published; working on my fifth one now. If you think you'd be interested in reading any of them, I can give you a business card that has my email address, phone number, and a link to my website."

"Sure, I'd be interested. I read a lot in the evenings to help forget about gravestones and funerals. Thanks for your card. I'll let you be alone with your thoughts, Mr. Thomas. it was good to meet you."

Joe spent the next couple of hours in prayer and reflection as he silently stopped by the graves of his relatives and friends. By then it was after noon and he stopped at his favorite restaurant for lunch and a chat with Victoria, the redheaded waitress who usually waited on him. He appreciated her sass, and that she always smiled when she saw him.

"So how is All Saints Day treating you, Joe?"

"Harder than usual. I know so many people in that cemetery now. When I was a boy it was filled with names. Now it is filled with all the faces I have known."

"Don't forget to pray for yourself, Joe. My dad prayed and gave thanks every day that he was still alive. Thanks for being able to see another day dawn. He used to say that every sunrise is a blessing from God."

"You're right as usual, Victoria. You should have been a shrink or a priest! I will pray for myself when I get home."

When Joe pulled up in front of his rental house, there was strange car parked at the curb. As he walked up to the entrance he saw a man sitting on the front porch with a book in his lap. As he got close he could see it was the first novel he'd written, titled "The Lost One."

"Can I help you?" quizzed Joe.

"Hello, Joe. It's been awhile." replied the stranger as he looked up.

Joe knew the voice, but not the face. "I'm sorry, I don't recognize your face."

"Do you remember this?" The man pulled up his sleeve and showed a scar on his forearm. "Do you remember when I got it falling out of our play fort onto a broken beer bottle?"

Recognition dawned. "John, is that really you? How did you get here?"

"Well, I retired last week from the Agency. After getting a few things in order, I came back here to Des Moines to see if I could find you. At the airport I bought your novel and wondered if you'd written it about me. I came to the cemetery this afternoon as I remembered your yearly All Saints Day ritual, hoping to catch you there. Thanks to the caretaker, I got your new phone number and email address. I'm CIA, we can find anyone."

"So good...so good to see you, my brother. We've got a lot to catch up on."

John smiled and said, "If I told you everything I'd have to kill you. But maybe I can give you some ideas for your next book."

A Mystery of Olympic Proportions

"Listen to this, Gene!" exclaimed Trudy as she perused the morning paper. "Mystery of Olympic Proportions: Swimmer's awards from the Games in 1996 and 2000 vanish from bag in car."

"How did that happen?" Gene questioned his wife of 30 years as he savored another sip of morning coffee.

"Looks like the car was unlocked, or rather, the lock on one side wouldn't work."

"And he's surprised that they're gone? Doesn't sound like a mystery to me why they're missing."

"Don't be so cute, hon. The mystery is who took them and how to recover them," she chided as she put down the newspaper and took her coffee cup to the sink.

"I doubt he'll get much help from the local police. Probably needs to call a modern-day Sherlock Holmes."

Trudy knew that Gene had been a Sherlock Holmes fan since he was in elementary school, back in Phoenix, Arizona. That was about the time that he'd formed his own detective club.

"Too bad your old detective club isn't solving cases like that. What was the name again that you had for the club?"

"Oh, yeah! We called it Gene's Private Eyes. Boy," he reminisced, "that was a lot of fun! And we actually solved some real mysteries."

"Did you ever solve a mystery of Olympic proportions?" chuckled Trudy as she started out the front door to walk the dog.

"Matter of fact we did. Sort of." As the door banged shut, Gene was transported in his thoughts back to 1965 when he was a fifth grader.

* * * * * * *

"Gene, come in and get ready for supper. Tell your friends it's time for them to go home, too," Gene's mother yelled out the back door as she dried her hands on her apron. When she didn't get any response, she opened the door again and gave the second call for supper. This time her voice had that tone that meant this was the final call and there'd be hell to pay if it wasn't answered.

The screen door banged behind Gene as he came in and protested: "Mom, we were just getting started on making up the rules for my new detective club."

"Detective club?" queried his mother as she chuckled. Gene was an organizer and had started up several clubs the last couple of years. First there was the Weather Club, then the Walkie-Talkie Club, then the Stamp Collector Club.

"Yeah, Mom," said Gene as he washed his hands and sat down at the dinner table with his little brother. "We're going to have a secret club that will solve real-life mysteries. We're going to use Sherlock Holmes' techniques to solve cases that even the cops can't. We'll have ID's that say Gene's Private Eyes." Gene's enthusiasm showed as he talked on and on about the new club. Finally his dad came in from work, after having been caught in traffic on I-17 as he drove back from the Sun Valley Power Plant.

The conversation turned to Dad's day at the plant and Mom's at the pre-school where she volunteered three days a week.

The mettle of the new club was soon tested by a real live case. Tommy Smith's mother had her Olympic Vacuum Cleaner stolen off their front porch one morning when she went into the house to answer the phone. Mrs. Smith, a cleaning fanatic, vacuumed her front porch as often as she did the inside of the house, which usually was every other day. The vacuum cleaner was a recent purchase from Sears and it would strain the monthly budget to replace it. Tommy called a special meeting of the club to consider the case. "We've got to do something to help my Mom. She's going frantic," explained Tommy. "And the policeman that came by just laughed when Mom told him what happened. He said he had to spend his time on a lot bigger cases, like the theft of Mrs. Rodriquez's car out of her driveway last month."

"Hmm," grunted Gene as he put on the Sherlock Holmes hat he'd convinced his mother to make for him. She was an accomplished seamstress in addition to having numerous other talents. "Sounds like a worthy subject for the club's first case."

After an interview with Tommy's mother, the club members didn't learn much that would help in tracking down the culprit. All Tommy's mom saw was a beat up white van rounding the corner at the intersection up the street. She wasn't sure that the van had stopped at their house, but it had apparently driven past just before she came back outside. Gene did find some large footprints across the corner of their front yard near the driveway. Thankfully the yard had just been watered, to help keep the Bermuda grass alive in the hot Phoenix summer.

After making plaster casts of the best foot prints, the club did discover that the shoe size was a 13 and the wearer had walked with a limp, favoring his left leg. They took this information to Gene's Uncle Ben, a detective on the Phoenix police force.

"Well, well, boys, looks like some good detective work!" smiled Uncle Ben as he puffed on his pipe. Gene liked Uncle Ben and enjoyed the smell of the cherry tobacco that his uncle normally used. "I happened to find a burglar in Emerson's appliance store last night who walked with a limp and had big feet. Good thing that the burglar had a limp, as he was slow in getting out of the store after the alarm went off. What really got him though, was that the store was just around the corner from the station house! I'll take these plaster casts and see if his shoes match."

The check of the shoes confirmed that the suspect had made the prints in Mrs. Smith's front yard. After obtaining a search warrant for the suspect's house, they found the missing Olympic Vacuum Cleaner, two stolen lawn mowers, and four stolen TV sets in his garage. "I wonder if the suspect was going to start up his own appliance store?" Uncle Ben asked with a wink when he presented the stolen vacuum cleaner to its rightful owner.

This was the first in a line of several successes for Gene's Private Eyes, which included the return of Ma Green's cat that spent the night in a neighbor's tree, and the apprehension of the vandals who broke the windows of the principal's office at the elementary school. The club was even written up in an article in the Saturday Community Interest page of the Phoenix Gazette. But, by the end of the summer, the members had lost interest in detective work, and instead formed a model airplane club.

* * * * * * *

The squeak of the front door opening jolted Gene out of his reverie and back into the present.

"So, Gene, do you think you could help this Olympian solve the mystery of his stolen medal?" asked Trudy as she returned with the dog.

"Maybe if I was a wide-eyed fifth grader again."

It was the first Saturday of the new year and the clanging of extension ladders woke Jake Clapper from his afternoon nap. "Must be the neighbors taking down their Christmas lights. Glad I don't have any to take down this year, " he remarked to his cat, Boots.

Jake had lost Olga, his wife of 35 years, at Thanksgiving. But her cat, Boots, had outlived her and was both a comfort and a distraction to him. "Glad you weren't in the car when she skidded off the bridge, Boots," Jake said as he fished a can of Boots' favorite cat food out of the pantry. Then he opened the scrapbook that he and Olga had updated every January. The last item was a newspaper clipping from the day after Thanksgiving, that still chilled him to read:

"STATE DEPARTMENT EMPLOYEE'S BODY FOUND IN THE POTOMAC, THE DAY AFTER HER CAR SKIDDED OFF THE THEODORE ROOSEVELT BRIDGE INTO THE ICY WATER. Mrs. Olga Clapper was a senior staffer at the department and her co-workers declared shock at the news."

The ringing doorbell roused Jake from the scrapbook and he glanced through the peephole. "Hey, Boots, it's your friend, Ms. Sanchez."

"Hello, Jake. May I come in? I have some catnip for Boots."

"Certainly, Maria. My, don't you look fetching in your red jumpsuit!" Maria Sanchez loved red, and was known and admired by the males in the neighborhood when she worked in her front yard in her little red bikini. However, now was not bikini weather in northern Virginia.

After spending some time cuddling Boots, Maria reminded Jake of the neighborhood party that evening at the Smith's down the street. "Hope you will get out of the house and socialize with your friends, Jake. I know you're still grieving your loss, but it's not healthy to stay in your house and become a hermit."

"You know what, Maria, you're right. I'll venture over there about 7."

Promptly at 7 p.m. Jake, dressed in a tweed jacket and turtleneck sweater, and carrying a bottle of wine, rang the Smith's doorbell. "Come on in, Jake. So glad to see you. I think you know most everyone here, except our newest neighbor, Sofia. Thanks for the wine. Let me take it and I'll introduce you to her, as she has expressed an interest in meeting you."

Jake's eyes opened wider as Jane Smith led him over to an extremely attractive blonde, and said, "Sofia, here's the neighbor you asked about, Mr. Jake Clapper, or should I say, Major Clapper."

"Hello Major. I'm Sofia Wilson, and just moved into the neighborhood."

"Ms. Wilson. Glad to make the acquaintance, but I don't go by Major anymore, since I retired from the Air Force years ago."

"Call me Sofia, Mr. Clapper. I heard about your distinguished military career, and understand you still work for the DOD in a civilian capacity."

"It's no secret I do work in the Pentagon, though I've been on personal leave since my wife's untimely death. Pardon me for asking, but what line of work are you in?"

"I was a professor of history at Georgetown, but got tired of university politics. So I switched careers and now work as a professional trainer."

"Wow, that is a career switch. But noticing how, ahem, fit and trim you look, I imagine you are a natural as a trainer."

Their conversation was interrupted as Jane Smith called everyone to attention by tapping on a glass with her spoon. "Thanks to you all for coming! I know it's a few days past New Year's Day, but this is the earliest we could get everyone together. For starters, why don't each of us share our New Year's Resolutions?"

After most of the neighbors had shared their resolutions, Sofia whispered to Jake, "frankly this is boring me. Most of these resolutions won't be kept more than a month or two."

"Or less," chuckled Jake. "I stopped making resolutions years ago when I realized I really didn't intend to keep them. The only resolution I did keep was not to get rid of the cat Olga brought home a few years ago. And I'm glad I didn't as Boots keeps me company now."

"Really? I love cats. What kind is he?"

"A Russian blue hair."

"Would you mind introducing me to Boots? I'd love to see him?"

"Well, sure. What's keeping us? I'll tell the Smiths good night."

Sofia took Jake's arm as they walked back to his house. The scent of her perfume made his pulse quicken as he unlocked the door where they were greeted by Boot's meows.

"Oh, he's so pretty, Major!"

Soon Jake and his new neighbor were trading cat stories and laughing. After awhile, though, Sofia brought an abrupt end to the pleasant conversation. "Major Clapper, I need to tell you about the real cause of your wife's death."

"What? Why would you know anything about my wife or her accident?"

"Your wife was a sleeper agent for mother Russia, sent here many years ago as a college student. Her services were never called upon until last fall, when she was given an assignment of utmost importance for her homeland. Instead of accepting the job, she contacted the FBI with the intent of exposing her handler. She was actually on her way to meet with an FBI agent when we arranged for her accident as she crossed the bridge."

Jake recoiled as though he'd been shot. "My wife a sleeper agent? Is that a terrible attempt at humor? Don't be ridiculous! And who are you really?"

With a smile on her face, Sofia drew a Makarov pistol from her handbag and leveled it at Jake. "I'm an agent for the SVR and I'm deadly serious."

"Okay, okay. But why tell me all this?"

"Because we know that you have access to the plans for the US military's secret space shuttle known as X-37B. Olga's assignment was to get the plans from you and give them to her Russian handler. She refused. So we want you to provide those plans."

"Betray my country? And cooperate with the people who you say had Olga killed. Why in the hell would I do that?"

Sofia's reply was interrupted by the someone incessantly ringing the front doorbell.

"I need to get that."

"Okay. I'm keeping my pistol hidden but ready, should you try anything brave."

Opening the door, Jake saw Maria Sanchez with a serious look on her face. "Jake, please let me in."

Glancing back at Sofia, who nodded okay, Jake opened the door. "What can I do for you, Maria?"

"You can get behind me, Jake," she said in a husky whisper as she drew a Glock out of the waistband of her jumpsuit.

"Sofia Wilson, or whatever your name is. You are under arrest. I know about the handgun under your sweater. I don't advise you using it, because several of my fellow FBI agents are just outside with their shotguns."

An hour later, Jake sat across from Maria. "I can't believe you are with the FBI! But how did you know what was happening here?"

"Boots kept me informed," she smiled and removed a bug that she'd planted in the cat's collar after Olga's death.

A Rooster in the City

I never thought I'd hear a rooster in the city, much less Greenwich Village. My partner, Detective Angie Delgado, and I were answering a public nuisance call and heard the piercing crow of a rooster on the balcony above the sidewalk.

"Joe, I thought roosters were supposed to crow at sunrise. It's 4 o'clock in the friggin afternoon!" Angie remarked quizzically as she rang the doorbell.

"That's because you didn't grow up on a farm! We had a rooster when I was a kid who would crow every hour, from dawn to dusk. I still remember him strutting around the yard and crowing in front of the hens."

In New York City, you can have as many hens as you want as pets, but roosters are outlawed. Normally a complaint about a rooster would be handled by a street cop or someone from Animal Control, but this case was certainly different.

"Hello? What can I do for you?" asked a diminutive brunette as she opened the door a few inches. The pungent smell of incense drifted out the opening.

Angie took the lead. "Hello, I'm Angie Delgado with NYPD and this is my partner, Joe Hanrahan. We've had several recent complaints from your neighbors about a rooster crowing at all hours of the day and night."

Visibly relieved, the young lady opened the door a bit further. "Oh, that would be Randy, my sister's pet. I know he's a bit noisy, but my sister will be taking him back home tomorrow to Michigan. She's been here on vacation the last week and brought Randy with her."

"Maybe you're unaware that it's illegal to have a rooster in The City, Miss, Miss…" Angie questioned.

"Smith. Janice Smith. You must be kidding about roosters? I know several people here in The Village who have chickens."

"Hens are okay, as long as there's not a cleanliness problem. But roosters are a different matter."

"Gee, officers. I didn't know. Is there some sort of fine?"

"Since the rooster is leaving tomorrow, we may be able to overlook the infraction, Miss Smith," I took over from Angie. "But what we really need from you is some information."

"Information?"

"Yes. Have you noticed any suspicious activity on your street lately? Strangers? People coming and going at odd hours?"

"Most of us keep to ourselves."

"Nothing unusual going on at all, except for your sister's rooster?" pressed Angie.

Miss Smith caught her drift and quickly volunteered some information about a woman who'd moved into an apartment across the street maybe a month ago.

"I met her once and she told me her name is Jayne somebody. Used to be a dancer in a high class gentlemen's club, but said now she's more of an artist. Louie, the old guy who lives next door to her has complained to me about all the men who frequent her apartment late at night. That's really all I know."

Back at HQ, Angie and I briefed our boss, Lieutenant Jackson, about the conversation with Miss Smith.

"Hmm, this could be the break we're looking for. I know you're both wondering why I got you involved in what should be a matter for Animal Control," Jackson's gruff voice intoned.

"You're right about that, Lieutenant."

"Here's the scoop. The media doesn't know about it yet, but the Mayor has been missing for two days."

Seeing the surprise on our faces, Jackson continued, "He called his wife about 9 o'clock Friday night and told her he'd be working late and not to wait up for him. When he hadn't shown up by 10 the next morning, she called the police commissioner and asked him to launch an investigation. Here it is late Sunday, and still there's no word of his whereabouts."

"Is it his habit to work late at night? And has he been AWOL before?" Angie probed.

"Apparently he's been working late more usual the last few weeks. But this is the first time he's not come home at all."

"So what does this have to do with the public nuisance case you sent us out on?" I asked.

"The mayor's wife mentioned she heard a rooster crow in the background when he called her Friday night. She didn't think much about it until she talked to the commissioner. We've been searching our database and Animal Control's for recent reports of rooster complaints. That led to your assignment this afternoon. Sorry I had to keep you in the dark until it looked like it might be a valid lead. Now I need you to go back and check out Jayne, the former exotic dancer, as well as her neighbors. Meanwhile, we'll run a background check on Miss Janice Smith and her sister, to make sure they're clean."

"Looks like we'll be working late this evening," I complained to Angie as we left the building.

"Yeah, but this is a really big case. If we can help crack it, maybe we'll get the promotions we both deserve," Angie volunteered, ever the optimist.

Jayne didn't answer her door and the shutters on her windows were tightly closed. So we went next door to talk to Louie, who answered right away. The old man was more than willing to talk about his new neighbor, Jayne Molina.

"Honestly, Detective Hanrahan, she dresses like a high class call girl. I think she's turning tricks in her apartment, with all the guys coming and going in the middle of the night. I'm a light sleeper and all that activity going on next door interferes with my sleep!"

"When's the last time you saw her?

"Friday evening. I saw her walk up the sidewalk when I was watching the 6 o'clock news. Haven't seen her since."

"Did you see anyone else going into or out of her apartment after that?"

"Yeah. Probably an hour or so after she got in, a cab pulls up, and a guy in a business suit rang her doorbell."

"Can you describe him?"

"Sure; I used to be a security guard before I retired, so I watch people. White guy. Prematurely gray hair. Medium height and build. I've seen him go into her apartment before."

"Does he look anything like the man in this photo?" Angie asked, holding out a photo of the Mayor.

"That's either him or his twin brother. Who is he? No, wait, I think I know. Mother of God, that's the mayor isn't it!"

He's a sharp old cookie, I thought. "Louie, we need to keep this quiet until we verify your suspicions. Okay?"

It was 10 p.m. before we had a warrant to search Jayne Molina's apartment. I picked the lock and Angie and I walked in with our side arms drawn. The apartment was strangely quiet and at first we thought no one was home. Then we came into the bedroom.

"What the hell?" exclaimed Angie as she saw two people on the massive bed, totally nude except for the chain that bound both of them together around the neck. Other whips and chains lay around them. The busty former dancer lay on top of the man, and both were very still.

"Looks like autoerotic asphyxiation gone horribly bad," I said as I leaned over to take their pulses. "Call 911, Angie! She still has a faint pulse."

As Angie dialed 911, I felt for a pulse on the man underneath Ms. Molina, and I looked into his face. It was the Mayor, all right, and he was dead, very dead.

A Taxing Day

"Today is the last day for filing your Federal tax return. For all you who put it off to the last minute, the Airport Post Office will be open until the stroke of midnight," blared the TV reporter on the noon news. Marsha reached for the mute button as a commercial for EZ Tax People started.

"Aren't you glad, Dick, that we e-filed with TurboTax last week? No standing in that long line like last year!"

Dick's reply was interrupted by the ringing of the front door bell. Marsha opened the door as soon as she saw who it was.

"Dick, it's your brother, Sam. And he's got a stack of papers in his hand!"

"Hey guys, sorry to barge in on you like this, but my printer crapped out on me this morning just when I was about to print out my 1040. Darn HP printer!"

"Sure bro, you can use my computer and printer; just leave a dollar for each page you print. Wonder why your printer quit; could it be because you've had it forever?" teased Dick.

"Only ten years! It should last longer than that. I saved my file on this thumb drive, so it shouldn't take me long to fire up your copy of TurboTax and print it out. "

An hour later, Dick was showing his now-happy brother to the door with his printouts. "Wow, Dick, who is that neighbor of yours sunning on her front porch in her red bikini? If I didn't know any better, I'd say she's Sofia Vergara's twin sister!"

"Get your eyes back in your head, Sam. That's our new neighbor, Maria Santiago, and she has at least ten boyfriends, most bigger than you."

"Only been divorced a month and he's already back in the hunt?" remarked Marsha as they watched Sam drive off.

"Oh, oh, Marsha. Look down the street, it's crazy Bill with clipboard in hand, stopping at every house as he heads this way. You know what that means?"

"Yes," she sighed, "He's got another crazy petition about something or other that he wants us to sign. Poor old man, doesn't have any pets or hobbies, guess that's why he's always starting a petition drive of some sort. Might as well stay here on the front porch since it looks like he already spotted us."

The white-haired gentleman smiled and waved as he hurried up their front sidewalk. "Afternoon, neighbors! I've got a petition here, Mr. and Mrs. Wilson, that will save us all a lot of money!"

"Is that so, Bill? What do you have?" Dick eyed the clipboard with obvious skepticism.

"This is a petition to abolish the Internal Revenue Service. I've already collected two dozen signatures."

"Is that a fact?" questioned Dick, while wondering how 24 people in the neighborhood could be as crazy as Bill. "You know that will never fly. If the government didn't have a way to collect taxes, it would screech to a halt."

"Exactly. We don't need anyone governing our lives anyway. And as a protest until I get enough signatures, I don't plan to pay any taxes."

"Bill, you know that if you don't pay taxes, the Feds will send you to prison!"

"Keeping people in prison costs the government a lot of money! I plan to remind them of that and propose a deal: I won't pay my taxes if they won't put me in prison. Then we'll call it even! I heard that on a late night TV show."

"Bill, you know that was a joke don't you? I don't like paying taxes any more than the next guy, but I do. And so should you!"

"Okay, but will you sign my petition?"

"Sure; guess it won't hurt." As Dick took the clipboard and signed on the next blank line, he saw that Marsha's lips were mouthing are you crazy, too?

They were about to go in the house when Ms. Santiago, still in her bikini, came out of the house with a step stool, set it next to her garbage bin that was on the street awaiting pickup, and proceeded to start digging through the contents.

Marsha started laughing as she saw Crazy Bill's eyes focusing on the view across the street. "Hey, Bill, maybe you should start a petition to prohibit scantily clan women from digging through their garbage in public."

Red-faced, Crazy Bill muttered something and continued on down the street.

"Ms. Santiago, what are you looking for? Do you need some help?" Marsha yelled.

"My W-2. I threw it away by mistake with a bunch of old papers. Ah, here it is!" she smiled triumphantly as she pulled a wrinkled document out of the bin.

Wanting to be a good neighbor, Dick sauntered across the street with Marsha on his heels. "Sounds like you haven't filed your taxes, Ms. Santiago. Do you need any help with your return?

"Yes, I might! I had my taxes all ready to print out but couldn't find my W-2 from the club where I work. But, when I do print it out, I could use a ride to the post office., since Lorenzo borrowed my car when his broke down."

"Lorenzo?" asked Marsha.

"Yes. He's my main boyfriend. You know, the tall handsome one with the black ponytail."

"Sure, I can give you a ride to the post office." Dick winced as Marsha poked him.

"Okay, thanks, neighbor. I'll call you when I get ready to go."

An hour later, Maria Santiago, now in a stunning blue dress and spike heels, knocked on their front door. "I have a big problem, Mr. Dick and Mrs. Marsha. The computer ate my tax return!"

"What happened?"

"When I opened the tax program and tried to print out my 1040, a window popped up that said Error: Unable to read file. Then my hard drive started making screeching noises and I pulled the plug on the computer. What shall I do?"

Dick and Marsha eyed each other and then volunteered to let Maria use their computer. Soon she was deep into TurboTax, inputting all the data needed to generate her return.

Dick helped her with some tax questions. but it was nearly dark by the time she had completed and printed out her 1040 and accompanying forms.

"Thank you so much, Mr. & Mrs. Wilson. I want to thank you with dinner. I am making some of my famous fajitas tonight and want you two to eat them with me!"

"Sure, but what about mailing your return?"

"No problem. You can drive me there after dinner. I'll whip up my fajitas and call you in a few."

It was after 9 p.m. before the three finished the dinner. Soon after, Dick drove Ms. Santiago down to the Airport Post Office. As they got out of the car, they joined the long line that had formed a block down the street from the entrance.

"Ladies and gentlemen, please be patient! We will make certain everyone has their return hand postmarked before midnight!" instructed the tired postal employee standing outside.

Dick shook his head as he realized he was standing right where he was last tax day.

A Veteran Reflects

At first glance, I thought he was a character from one of the old Western movies I'd enjoyed as a kid. Maybe it was the craggy face that looked like time had sculpted it with wind and sun, or maybe it was way he walked, straight-backed and erect, despite a pronounced limp. Visions of a sixty plus Clint Eastwood came to mind as the older gentleman approached the park bench where I enjoyed the sun on a crisp November afternoon the day before Veteran's Day.

"Do you mind if I share the bench with you for a spell?" he asked in a friendly but assertive tone. I nodded okay and noticed he winced as he slowly eased his tall frame onto the bench.

"Thanks for moving over. Beautiful weather, isn't it? I've been out for my usual walk and still have a ways to go, but this hip has been acting up today. Old war wound."

"Oh, which war?"

"Vietnam. I took a piece of shrapnel from a Viet Cong mortar during the Tet Offensive. But I was luckier than the guy next to me, who lost his life."

"Yeah, they say war is hell. I've never been in one, but I had buddies who were and that saying pretty much reflected their assessment," I chimed in.

"The Tet Offensive was hell, hell on earth, with the North Vietnamese military being the demons behind it. What bothered me the most was how many innocent civilians were killed during that campaign. It changed my life, young man."

"Thanks for your service." I ventured, not knowing what to say next.

"No offense, but that's the politically correct way of saying 'I'm glad it wasn't me that risked life and limb and sanity to make our country more secure.'"

I gulped and admitted his assessment was not far from the mark. "But I do at some level appreciate the sacrifices that people like you make to maintain our freedom. And since tomorrow is Veteran's Day, I want to thank you personally."

"You're welcome, young man. But think back to the wars our country has been in since World War II. Which one of those wars really helped secure the freedom you and I enjoy today? It sure as hell wasn't the war I fought in. Over 58,000 US servicemen died in Vietnam and we finally pulled out and let the North Vietnamese take over the country."

"I wasn't born until after it was over. But I see your point. Like many Americans I've come to believe our invasion of Iraq and the toppling of Saddam Hussein was a mistake and certainly hasn't made the country any safer."

"The problem with most wars, young man, is that powerful old men and women, most of whom have never been in combat, needlessly send young men and women into battle to fight and die or be maimed physically or mentally."

After giving me time to reflect on that, he continued. "But I'm not saying that all wars are needless. Every Veteran's Day I stop and give thanks for my Dad and all those in his generation who fought in World War II to keep the world from being overrun by madmen."

"Yeah, my grandfather lost a leg when his unit stormed Omaha Beach on D-Day. He was a true hero and I put flowers on his grave every Veteran's Day."

"Good for you. Everyone I know of who went through war was changed by the experience. Some more than others. It sure changed my life!"

"I'm sure it did, sir. Would it bother you to tell me more about that?"

"Not at all. After I got back from Vietnam and got discharged from a Veteran's hospital, I lost my way and went from bad to worse. I was filled with guilt over the horrors of war I'd seen and been unable to remedy. Plus I was consumed by self-pity about my bad hip. Forty years ago, I showed up at Saint Theresa's Homeless Shelter, a broken down drug user, just looking for a warm bed. I'm so thankful for the love and care I received there that turned me around!"

"After being at Saint Theresa's awhile, I stopped having nightmares about the battles I was in. I remembered an old folk song that Simon and Garfunkel sang, "Last Night I Dreamed the

Strangest Dream," and the words of that song became my dream too."

"Sounds vaguely familiar. How does it go?"

"You can google it for the exact words, but it's about a dream the writer had about the powers that be signing a paper that said they'd never fight again. They distributed a million copies and joined hands and gave grateful prayers. Then all the people in the streets were dancing and their uniforms and weapons of war lay scattered on the ground. You see, his dream was that all the world had agreed to put an end to war."

"Sounds like a powerful song."

"Yes. It was an inspiration to the anti-war movement of the sixties. And it became an inspiration to me! After getting my head on straight at Saint Theresa's, I decided the best way to promote peace rather than war was to join the Peace Corps. I served in Afghanistan until the Corps pulled out in 1979. Then I served in Cameroon, Columbia, and Mongolia until I retired in 2005. Saw a lot of good being done in some very poor countries despite the evil all around."

"That must have given you a great sense of satisfaction."

"True, it did. But even more it helped me live with the guilt of what I did and didn't do when I fought in Vietnam. Well, I best be going now. I'm supposed to be at Saint Theresa's by 5."

"Thanks for telling me your story. You're going to Saint Theresa's?"

"You heard me right. I volunteer there two or three days a week. This evening I'm going to help them get ready for their big Veteran's Day meal. You may not realize it, but a lot of the homeless here are veterans. In fact, there are over 50,000 homeless veterans in the US right now."

"I had no idea."

"Many people don't. It's a crying shame."

I nodded in agreement and watched him walk off with a limp.

Barbershop Mystery

Detective John Sanchez walked into Sam's Barbershop about 8:30 a.m. for his bi-weekly haircut. A regular customer of Sam's, he'd been coming in before his shift with the LAPD for years. Only this morning things seemed different.

"Sam? Sam, it's John Sanchez. Are you in back?" The only thing John heard in response was the low sound of golden oldies from Sam's radio toward the back of the shop. This was a day off for Sam's new assistant, Monique, so Sam should have been out front.

Thirty years on the police force had made John suspicious, so when his knock on the door to the back room wasn't answered, he turned the knob and walked in. He stepped back in surprise as he saw Sam crumpled up on the floor, with blood slowly oozing out of the back of his head. No one else was in the room.

John bent over his barber friend and felt a faint pulse. Calling the dispatcher, he barked into his cell phone, "Get an ambulance ASAP over here to Sam's Barbershop, 2911 South Main! Looks like someone mugged him and I can only get a very faint pulse!"

Within five minutes the paramedics arrived, started working on Sam, and quickly loaded him into the ambulance. As the ambulance sped away, one of John's associates, Detective Ann Hughes, drove up.

"So what do you make of this, John? Someone get upset about a bad haircut?"

"Not funny, Ann. Sam's hurt really bad, and I hope he makes it! Looks to me like it was a robbery, as the door on his small safe is open and there's nothing in it."

"Do you think there could have been a lot of cash in it? This is a small two-person shop and I doubt it makes a lot of dough!"

"Probably not, especially since Sam usually deposits his daily cash each afternoon after he closes up shop. And some of his customers pay with credit cards now. I wonder what else was in the safe and who would have known?"

"Doesn't look like the safe has been jimmied, John. Sam must have opened it for the perp. Could it have been his ex-wife? I hear they had a nasty divorce recently. Maybe she came back for something she thought she deserved."

After the street cops arrived and cordoned off the shop, Ann and John went to LAPD headquarters and went over every thing they knew about Sam and his business.

After lunch the hospital informed them that Sam was awake and should pull through. John sped over to talk with him.

"Sam, good to see you, friend! What happened?"

Sam was still groggy and his voice was low and hoarse. "Somebody in a mask walked in right after I opened the shop and made me open the safe. Next thing I know, I'm in this hospital bed."

"Male or female?"

"Male. Average height and build, I'd guess. He claimed to have a gun in his pocket and I was afraid to argue."

"And what exactly was in the safe?"

"Sorry, I can't tell you…" the barber's voice trailed off and he fell asleep.

Puzzled, John recounted the conversation to Ann.

"John, what do you know about his assistant, Monique?"

"Well, she's a good barber and quite attractive. Speaks with a bit of an accent. I think she's been working in the shop a couple of months. Her last name is Franz. Let's see what the computer can tell us about her."

The database search showed her as a citizen of South Africa, here on a work visa. That aroused their suspicions and they called the number listed for her. After a number of rings, she answered. They could hear the sound of waves in the background.

"Hello, hello?" she said. "Can you speak up? It sounds like a bad connection and it's pretty windy down here at Manhattan Beach."

"Monique, this is John Sanchez. Do you know where Sam Jones is?"

"No. Isn't he at the shop?"

"No. He's in the hospital. Somebody mugged him after he opened the shop and cleaned out the safe in the back room!"

John could hear the surprise in her voice. "What? Is he going to be all right?"

"Yes, he's going to make it. Do you have any idea what could have been in the safe?"

"I have a pretty good idea, Detective. And I think I'd better come up and talk to you about my suspicions. It'll take me about an hour to go home, get dressed, and be at your office."

After she hung up the phone, John and Ann discussed her surprising offer. "Usually we have to ask parties of interest to come in and talk to us. Monique is volunteering to come!" Ann remarked.

Promptly an hour later, the sweet savor of Monique's perfume preceded her entrance. Soon John and Ann saw her walking toward their office, wearing an attractive business casual outfit. John admired the young German-African woman's lightly tanned olive skin and firm athletic body.

"Monique, I think you've met my associate, Ann Hughes, when she once came to pick me up at the barber shop."

"Yes. Good to see you both. You probably know that I'm here on a work visa from South Africa. What you may not know is that I'm a special investigator for the De Beers Company." Monique showed them her De Beers ID as she spoke.

"The world's largest diamond company?" Ann queried.

"Yes. My company sent me here four months ago to investigate a ring of criminals that we believe are smuggling blood diamonds to the US from South Africa. We had reports that the diamonds are being flown into LAX and then distributed to a local network."

"So what does Sam and his barbershop have to do with this?" John asked with raised eyebrows.

"We traced the illegal diamond traffic to the neighborhood Sam's shop was in. Since Sam's shop has a lot of customers and I had some experience as a barber working my way through college, I answered Sam's help wanted sign two months ago so I could observe his clientele."

"And what did you learn?" questioned Ann.

"About once a week a suspicious looking character would come in and go straight into the back room with Sam just before closing. After a few minutes, they would both come out and the man would leave. It was a different person each time, someone I didn't recognize. But the one who came in late yesterday looked a lot like a certain criminal wanted in my country for diamond smuggling, among other things."

"Why didn't you report this to us?" demanded John.

"Because I couldn't prove any suspicious activity. Not yet. I did call my superiors in South Africa and alerted them of this man's whereabouts."

John was stunned that his old friend could be involved in diamond smuggling and after talking some more with Monique, went back to the hospital.

Sam wept as he confessed to John. "My ex-wife took me to the cleaners. It was the only way I could get enough cash to pay the mortgage on the shop. I think the guy who came in yesterday is the same one who mugged me, as I recognized his voice. I don't know his name, but I do know who he works for…"

And that's how John and Ann both got promotions for breaking up the largest diamond smuggling ring in LAPD history.

Baskin Robbins Encounter on a Hot Summer Day

"It's a dry heat!" smiled the old codger in shorts and a tee shirt that read "Official Arizona Sweatshirt" with a cartoon of a chili pepper sweltering in the scorching sun. He held the door open as I hurried into the air conditioned comfort of Baskin Robbins to escape the late afternoon 113 degree heat. The place looked more crowded than usual as I blinked my eyes to help them adjust to the lighting after being outside in the brilliant Phoenix sunshine. The aroma of waffle cones helped revive me from the oppressive heat outside.

When my vision cleared, I saw about fifteen people who all seemed to be in the same party. Two were well-dressed women and the rest were males in casual attire: shorts, sandals, and short sleeve shirts. One of the men was clearly the leader of the group. My eyes were drawn to him for some unknown reason and I unconsciously eavesdropped on the conversation the leader was engaged in.

"So, Pete, I noticed that you've again picked the flavor of the month. How does this one taste?" the leader asked in a genial manner.

"This month's new flavor is really quite good, Lord. Much better than last month's. But how about you, what flavor of chocolate are you tasting this time?"

"Chocolate fudge" smiled the leader, obviously enjoying the ice cream, but apparently even more enjoying the company of his friends.

I wondered why in the world the man called Pete had addressed the leader as Lord. Perhaps it was a nickname or some type of code. Or could this guy be the leader of some crazy cult? But as I continued to look at the leader, the man's face looked strangely familiar, like someone I had known all my life.

"Can I help you, sir?" suddenly interjected the perky teenage girl behind the counter and I turned to place my order. Just then one of the evening shift employees I've seen before came through the front door, hurriedly making her way through the crowd, looking rather harried and distraught.

"Julie, what's the matter?" quizzed Miss Perky, as the distressed-looking employee got her apron out of the back room and prepared to begin her shift.

"My car had a flat a couple of blocks from here. My spare was flat too, so I just drove the rest of the way here on the rim. I'm afraid the tire is ruined and I can't really afford another just yet. On top of that, I have a splitting headache from the heat."

The man called Lord turned toward Julie and offered to send a couple men from his party – he called them apprentices – to see if they could salvage the tire. I watched him then look her straight in the eye with a very kind but penetrating look as he quietly said, "I instruct this headache to be gone."

I looked at Julie and saw the pain and stress in her face suddenly melt away. "Why, thank you, sir. I really do think I feel better. My headache seems to be gone." She was interrupted by the men who'd been out to look at her tire.

"Lord, we went out to examine the tire. Pete and I were going to remove it and take it over to the service station, but when we touched it, something happened. Suddenly the tire re-inflated and its appearance changed. It looks like a brand new tire."

When Julie heard this, she excused herself for a minute and went out to see. She came back in with a bewildered but happy look on her face. "Mister, I don't know who you are and how you did that, but thank you very much."

The man she'd addressed turned to her with the most compassionate look I have ever seen. "Julie," he began. "I know you're a single mom who's working hard to support yourself and your little girl. I also know that the God you've called on in your frustration and pain loves you very much. Know this day that the Kingdom of God has come to you."

I was fascinated by what had just transpired in front of me. Suddenly it dawned on me why the man they called Lord looked so familiar. And I realized who was in his party. Maybe this was actually the one I'd heard about when I went to church as a kid: Jesus, the Christ. Then the people in his party must be his followers, his disciples.

Just then Ms. Robinson came through the door. She was the manager of the local Planned Parenthood clinic and a strong pro-choice advocate in the community. "I've had a very tough day, Julie. Please give me a double size banana split."

Ms. Robinson had barely placed her order when a prominent minister came through the door with his wife. When he saw Ms. Robinson, he moved to the far end of the counter and motioned for his wife to join him. When they got their ice cream they hurried off to a corner of the establishment and talked about Ms. Robinson's sordid reputation within the church community.

The only seat left in the house when Ms. Robinson got her order was at the table next to where the man called Lord was seated. He turned toward her and instantly engaged her in conversation. As he did so, the minister loudly remarked something to his wife about the kind of man who would visit with Ms. Robinson.

When Ms. Robinson finished her ice cream, she didn't leave, but instead seemed caught up in conversation with this man who at once seemed so loving and accepting and also so pure and holy. As I looked over at this encounter, I noticed a tear run down Ms. Robinson's cheek. Then she started pouring out her life's story to this man she'd never seen before.

After about thirty minutes of conversation, I saw the man called Lord gently touch Ms. Robinson on the shoulder and I cocked my ear to hear him say, "I don't condemn you. God loves you and wants you to learn to love him and your neighbor as you now are able to love yourself."

With that, the man known as Lord motioned to his party and they put their trash in the trash container, wiped off their tables, and walked out the door. I saw them get on some motorbikes parked outside and ride off into the setting sun.

I blinked my eyes again and noticed that the place was now empty. "The Phoenix heat must be getting to me! Did I imagine all this?" I muttered to myself. "Or did it really happen?"

Catastrophe!

The storm driven waves were already lashing the seawall by the time that Jeremy and the camera man reached the Galveston seawall. Dark clouds formed by the outer bands of Hurricane Wanda gathered on the horizon, portents of trouble brewing.

"Let's set the camera up here, pointing straight out to sea, Manuel," instructed Jeremy, as he started thinking about the words he'd use on the 5 o'clock newscast.

"Sure thing, Jeremy. Do you think that Galveston will see another catastrophe, like it did with Hurricane Ike?"

"If the Hurricane Tracking Center is correct, I suspect it will." He wondered how bad the damage would need to be in order to call it a catastrophe. Then he thought of a conversation he'd had the prior week with his ten-year old, Ben.

"Dad, what does c-a-t-a-s-t-r-o-p-h-e spell?"

"Catastrophe, son."

"What does it mean?"

"Well, remember when our two cats cornered the mouse in the garage the other day?"

"Yeah?"

"That was a cat-astrophe for the mouse, Ben!" Jeremy declared with a chuckle.

"Jeremy, be serious!" interjected Jeremy's wife, Heidi. "A catastrophe is a big disaster that causes a lot of damage and suffering."

Somehow that didn't seem as funny now, as Jeremy viewed the oncoming storm and saw the first drops of rain stain the pavement.

"Okay, let's shoot this segment and then we'll move over to the Hotel Galvez."

By the time they finished shooting the news segment and had loaded their equipment up in the KWHO van, the rain had started to come down in earnest and an occasional wave splashed over the top of the seawall.

As they checked into the Hotel Galvez, the desk clerk noted, "You are the first people who have checked in this afternoon. Most people are checking out!"

"I know," Jeremy grimaced. "All the smart people are heeding the voluntary evacuation. But my boss wants us to ride out the storm here and report in as we can."

"Well, this hotel is a good place to do it. It's been here over one hundred years and withstood the 1915 Hurricane as well as Ike in 2008. And we have emergency generators that will kick in when we lose electricity."

After Jeremy and Manuel had settled into their hotel rooms, Jeremy checked the latest news from the National

Hurricane Center and learned that the hurricane had been downgraded to a Category 1.

"That's good news!" Manuel exclaimed. "That means it shouldn't do as much damage as Hurricane Ike, that came in as a strong Category 2 storm."

"Yep. Plus the city and it's residents are better prepared this time around!"

Back in the lobby downstairs with their equipment, Jeremy and Manuel watched the palm trees outside whipped by the wind as it gathered strength. Suddenly they heard a loud snap as one of the trees broke off just above the ground.

Just then Jeremy felt something brush against the back of his jeans and turned around to see a beautiful collie. 'What do we have here?" he quizzed the desk clerk.

"Oh, that's George, our hotel mascot. Having a dog around makes most of our guests feel more like they're at home. Plus some people feel more secure with him around. And he's very smart. One time an elderly lady couldn't get up on her own after she fell in the hallway and George alerted us with his bark!"

Jeremy started to ask if the lady had fallen because she'd tripped on the dog, but decided not to be a smart aleck.

"So this is a pet-friendly hotel?" asked Manuel.

"Yes, we allow cats, small dogs, and birds. With an additional deposit of course."

As night began to fall, the howl of the wind through the front door and the pelting of heavy rain on the glass announced the arrival of the main force of Hurricane Wanda. Jeremy and Manuel donned their rain gear and pushed their way out into the storm, bending forward to keep from being slammed back by the force of the gale. For some reason, George tagged along with them, though his coat became thoroughly wet in a couple of minutes.

Jeremy and Manuel sloshed through ankle-deep water in the hotel driveway and made their way to the now-flooded Seawall Boulevard, which was flowing like a river.

"Hey, look, Jeremy. There's a stalled car over there next to the seawall. And it looks like someone is trying to get out of it."

Wading through water about a foot and a half deep, the TV men and George struggled over to the vehicle just as an elderly woman endeavored to get out of her car. They saw she was holding a squirming bundle under one arm and a wind-whipped umbrella. Suddenly the squirming bundle got free and fell into the water with loud howl.

"Somebody save my cat!" screamed the woman, as she watched the little animal get swept up in the current.

Before Jeremy or Manuel could think what to do, George leaped into action. Quickly he swam after the cat, grabbed it in his mouth, and clambered onto the nearby sidewalk that was only a couple of inches under water. He held the cat there until Jeremy strode up and relieved the dog of his burden. Soon Manuel arrived with the elderly woman. Jeremy placed the rain-soaked and sputtering cat in her arms.

"Thank God, you're safe, Kitty!" exclaimed the now-bedraggled lady, seemingly impervious to the storm around them.

Jeremy and Manuel, followed by the faithful canine, helped the lady and her cat get into the hotel lobby.

"I'm Mrs. Whitcomb, and I was foolish enough to think I could make it down Seawall Boulevard to my house. Here," she said as she opened her purse, "let me give you boys some cash for rescuing Kitty. She's my only companion, since Mr. Whitcomb died."

"No, Mrs. Whitcomb, we appreciate the thought, but can't take your money. Besides, George is the one who really saved your cat." Manuel explained.

"Yes," smiled Jeremy. "George averted a real catastrophe!"

Christmastime Again

It was Saturday afternoon in early December and the sound of extension ladders echoed through our neighborhood. That familiar sinking feeling hit me as soon as I recognized the sound. Moments later my wife, Marsha, interrupted my afternoon reverie on the back patio with her lovely but piercing voice.

"John, why haven't you gotten the Christmas decorations out of the attic yet? All the neighbors are getting their outdoor Christmas decorations up today and we're going to look like Mr. and Mrs. Scrooge."

Mumbling a question about what's so bad about being Scrooges, I put down my drink, pulled my timeworn body out of the lawn chair and started mentally preparing myself for the task ahead. It wasn't that I didn't enjoy Christmas, with all of the festive decorations and lights. It was hauling everything down from the attic, setting up the tree, and putting up all the outdoor lights that I hated. Plus there was the safety angle. There have been very few Christmases where there hasn't been some sort of injury to myself or to our house.

As I climbed the pull-down ladder into the attic, I recalled the Christmas when I stepped through the ceiling while reaching for the Christmas star that had fallen out of ornament box #37 (or was it #36?). Besides the sheetrock repair, there was the embarrassment of yelling so loudly that the neighbors came to gape at me painfully sitting astraddle the 2x10 ceiling joist. At least my wife and I didn't have to worry about needing to use birth control after that.

This time I was successful in retrieving all 40 Christmas boxes from the attic without inflicting any damage. "So far so good," I told our cat as she peered out of her green eyes with an inscrutable look. I smiled as I pulled the box with our artificial self-lit tree out of the corner of the garage and congratulated myself into talking Marsha out of using real Christmas trees two years ago. No more worries about the tree toppling over due to a crooked trunk! I still shudder as I recall the crash a few years ago when the fully-decorated tree hit the floor and nearly took out our Chihuahua. And no more hassles with hanging hundreds of Christmas lights evenly around the tree and readjusting them until Marsha felt they looked just right.

After setting up the artificial tree in the front dining room window where all the neighbors could dutifully note how beautiful it was, I turned over the ornament unpacking and hanging to Marsha, who's more than happy to put her Christmas interior decorating expertise into practice. After all, she's the one who took a course in it last year at the community college!

Now it was time to focus my skills and attention on installing our outdoor Christmas lights. Remembering the time I suffered a body tingling and mind-numbing shock from faulty wiring, I carefully tested each of the 30 strings of multi-colored or white lights. Finding two strands that needed replacing, I took my trusty pickup down to Home Depot and bought new ones. I thought it horrible how much the price had increased since I'd bought the old strands, until I noticed the 1985 date on the old tags. Oh how time does fly!

I was soon adding to the sounds of extension ladders being extended as I launched myself into my main task. Thankfully the ladder was long enough to reach the roof of our 1-1/2 story house. (I've been forbidden to actually get on the roof since the time I narrowly missed the gas meter when I fell off the steeply-sloped roof of our prior house. I'd been sweeping off the pine needles with a push broom when I realized that I was sliding toward the roof's edge and couldn't stop. Talking about seeing your whole life flash in front of your eyes! Amazingly, I suffered no broken bones.)

I consulted with Marsha for last-minute instructions before taking the first strand with me up the ladder. Hanging the strand temporarily over one of the legs, I pulled some plastic light clips out of my shirt pocket and pushed them underneath the shingles at the roof's edge. Then I began stretching the light strand between each clip, careful to not let any of the lights sag. In my mind I could hear Martha's reminder, "Keep all those lights in a straight line honey. We don't want to have our decorations looking like the sloppy job the Garza's did across the street."

Within the space of a mere four hours, I finished stringing the last strand of lights on the front of the house and stepped back to admire my work. "It looks like a professional job," I boasted to our cat as I looked at the festively lit house silhouetted against the sunset sky. The cat looked at me like she wasn't so sure. Then Marsha came out for a final inspection.

"That looks great honey," she began, but then noticed a fatal decorating error. "Except that the icicle lights on the left side start about six inches from the corner of the roof. That won't do, of course."

Reluctantly I moved the ladder into the flower bed by the left corner of the house and explained that I'd wanted to keep the ladder out of the flower bed to protect her flowers. Soon I was trying to pull any remaining slack out of the icicle light strand in order to gain the prescribed six inches. That's when I got my broken arm. The ladder shifted in the soft soil of the flower bed as I stretched to install a plastic clip at the very corner of the roof. As the ladder fell, I instinctively grabbed the gutter with both hands. I hung between earth and sky for what seemed like a lifetime as Marsha ran across the street to the Garza's for help. The last thing I remembered before waking up in the hospital was the feeling of sheer terror as I felt the gutter come loose from the roof.

I'm looking forward to Christmas next year. Marsha has decided it will be cheaper to hire a professional to hang the lights.

Fired!

As my apartment caught fire, I had only sixty seconds to grab one thing. I pulled it out of the desk drawer, opened my purse, and dropped it in. Then I ran like hell out the door, into the dark street and down a couple of blocks as fast as I could sprint on my high heels.

Stopping near a street lamp to catch my breath, I spied a taxi. Hailing it, I said in Russian, "Take me to the Maritime Terminal." In the back of the musty-smelling cab, I reflected on the last hour's events. I'd been relaxing after a long day at the school where I taught English to Russian elementary-aged children, including Vladimir Putin's granddaughter. More about that later. I heard a frantic knock on the door and was surprised to see my handler, who had never before been to my apartment. It was against protocol.

"Christine," I cried as she staggered through the doorway, white as a ghost. "What's wrong? Why have you come here?"

Slumping down to the floor, she gasped, "Stacy, our cover has been blown. My Russian contact, Boris, has been turned by the FSB. You must initiate Protocol 99 and save yourself! It's too late for me."

"What do you mean? What's happened to you?"

Wiping big beads of sweat off her forehead, Christine explained, "Boris arranged for us to meet at the Soyuz Cafe. After getting us coffee, his face suddenly turned cruel and he held up my laptop. How did you get that? I queried."

"I picked the lock to your apartment door and helped myself. Does that surprise you?" Boris snarled. "I have another surprise for you. The coffee you just drank has been poisoned and you have less than two hours to live. As soon as we break the encryption on your laptop files, we'll round up your accomplices. Goodbye!"

"Within minutes after Boris left, I could feel the effects of the poison. I suspected that my   mobile phone has been bugged, so the only way to warn you was to come here. I'll be dead in a few minutes and if you don't leave soon after, they'll kill you."

Gulping down the stomach acid that was burning my throat, I put a pillow under Christine's head and tried to make her as comfortable as possible. "How do I make contact with Langley when you're gone?"

I could barely hear her as she whispered. "Go to the basement of the Maritime Terminal. Here's the key to locker 897; it contains the name of my Langley contacts and how to get hold of them. Hurry..."

Feeling her pulse, I confirmed that the poison had done it's work. Tears streamed down my face; tears for her and tears for me. But I had no time to lose. Protocol 99 was known as the Scorched Earth Solution. All records and personal effects had to be burned, you had to change your identity, and if possible, fake your own death.

I ripped open the couch cushion that held my escape packet: a fake ID, fake US Passport, and enough money to get me back to the States. Grimacing, I pulled the ID out of Christine's back pocket, cut it up and flushed it down the toilet, and replaced it with my own. Thankfully she was about the same size and build as me. After emptying out my purse, I replaced the contents with my fake ID and passport, the cash, and some lipstick. Then I went to the bathroom mirror and took a scissors to my shoulder-length black hair and worked a bottle of hydrogen peroxide into it. Instead of being Stacy Smith, a Sandra Bullock look-alike and English teacher, I would now be Tonya Wilson, a party girl here on holiday and sporting short blondish hair, like the photos in my fake ID and passport. Slipping on a cocktail dress and high heels, I was now dressed for the part.

Next I went out back and grabbed the gasoline can I kept full for my motorbike. Soon everything in my flat was drenched in gasoline - including my laptop, my Sig Sauer handgun, my personal papers, and Christine. I gave one last look at Christine and at my home for the last two years here in Sochi, Russia, and threw a lighter onto the couch. Things flamed up quicker than I'd expected and I barely had time to get my most important possession out of the desk drawer.

The sound of emergency vehicles speeding toward my apartment made me consider what might be ahead of me as I sat in the back of the lumbering taxi. Why didn't these Russian drivers drive like the cabbies back in New York? Finally we reached the Maritime Terminal, I paid the fare and added a nice tip and suddenly was all alone with a view of the Black Sea to my left and the terminal building to my right.

Trying not to look suspicious as I walked into the building and descended the stairs to the lockers, it felt like my heart was beating so fast it would fly out of my chest. It took me awhile to find locker 897 but the key easily turned in the lock and I found the instructions for contacting George Welch in Langley, as well as a satellite phone with a partially charged battery. It was the next morning on the East Coast, so George was on duty when I reached him on the satellite phone.

"Stacy, you say Christine is dead and that Boris has been turned by the Federal Security Service? That means both you and two other agents that reported to her are in extreme danger. Especially you, with the information you have been able to discover about Putin. Here's what you need to do. Take the next ferry across the Black Sea to Istanbul. When you disembark you'll be met by Jerry Reed, a red-haired man who will ask you what day it is. Reply with the word YESTERDAY. Got that? Jerry will have plane tickets for Tonya Wilson. You'll be flying non-stop to JFK in New York. Good luck!"

Security to board the ferry was not as tight as flying out of Sochi. The FSB agent did rifle through my purse and carefully compare the photo on my passport to me. I tried to smile and after giving a lurid look at the cleavage showing above my dress, he stamped the passport and motioned me to proceed.

Trying to sleep on the twelve hour ride across the Black Sea was useless. I looked back at the lights of Sochi with mixed emotions. If you had to be a CIA spy in Russia, here on the Russian Riviera was not a bad place to be.

True to George Welch's word, Jerry Reed met me as I got off the ferry. Handing me my plane tickets, he said, "Miss Wilson, your Turkish Air flight leaves in two hours. I'll drop you off by the ticket counter. When you arrive at JFK, George will be there to meet you. He'll be holding up a sign with your name. Be careful not to do or say anything before you board the flight that might arouse suspicion. The FSB in Sochi id'd your handler's body and are on the lookout for you. I know they have a couple of agents here in Istanbul."

Thank God, I was able to board the flight without difficulty. As we took off, I thought about the information I'd been able to learn about Putin's idiosyncrasies and some secret meetings he'd had recently with leaders from Iran and China. Since his daughter and grand-daughter lived in Sochi, he took several vacations there a year to visit them.

Finally I drifted off into a fitful sleep and only awoke twice for food and bathroom breaks before the flight landed.

Deplaning, I spotted George Welch and he walked me to the car he had waiting for us.

"Were you able to bring it with you?" he anxiously inquired.

"Yes," I smiled and pulled the face powder compact out of my purse. Snapping out the mirror, I removed the memory stick hidden behind it. "Here it is: all my detailed notes about Vladimir Putin gathered over the last two years."

Flood Quandary!

Rosa Cisneros held her summer session's attention as she continued the severe weather discussion that she'd begun on Tuesday. After all, she'd twice been recognized as the students' favorite professor in the Department of Atmospheric Physics at Pima University. At age 33 she was young enough to remember what being a young college student was like, old enough to be nationally recognized in her field, and attractive enough that she turned the heads of many male students.

"Since today's class is on Flash Floods, I'm going to start by showing you an article from last week's Tucson Daily News," she began, as she projected the on-line version on the huge screen above her. This is about a couple here in southern Arizona that was lucky to escape with their lives when their Ford Explorer was caught up in a flash flood. It was caused by a thunderstorm up in the Catalina Mountains, many miles away. The article goes on to explain that flash floods occur in arid regions due to heavy rains, and that an arroyo or dry river bed can become a raging torrent within a very few minutes."

"Doctor C, aren't flash floods pretty uncommon?" blurted out a crew cut student in a T-shirt and faded cutoffs.

"Actually, Tom, flash floods have claimed more lives in the last several decades than tornados have. And the area around Tucson has seen its share, especially during the summer monsoon season like we're experiencing now." (Rosa had made it a point to learn each student's name, a fact that helped endear her to her pupils.)

"But Doc Rosa, tornados seem to get a lot more press than flash floods do. Why is that?" asked Yolanda Rojas in the back.

"I'm not sure why that is, Yolanda. There seems to be a lot of public apathy about flash floods, much to people's harm. For example, one of my close friends in high school, Louis Glassman, drowned in a flash flood when his jeep was washed away as he crossed the Pantano Wash." Even now, the loss of this friend caused her to choke up when she related it. She regained her composure and finished the lecture with another warning to be careful of flash floods during the current rainy season.

On the way from class to her home up in the foothills, Rosa had to cross through a dip in the roadway that she had occasionally seen flooded after heavy rains. This time the asphalt in the arroyo was still dry, but the ominous-looking thunderstorm that was gathering at the peak of the mountain above made her think twice about entering it. She breathed a long sigh of relief when she got to the other side.

Shortly after Rosa got home, the winds picked up and brought the dust storm that often precedes Arizona's monsoon rains. Soon after, the skies lit up with multiple flashes of lightning and ear-deafening rumbles of thunder rolled down the mountain. Minutes later the sky opened up and dumped an inch of rain in less than 20 minutes. After it was over, Rosa stepped outside and took a deep breath of the newly cleansed atmosphere. She loved the smell of the desert just after a rain.

Just then Rosa's cell phone rang. It was the day camp where she'd dropped off her ten year old niece, Adriana, that morning. Rosa's brother, a single dad, was out of town on business and Adriana had been staying with her "favorite" – and only – aunt. It was the day camp nurse, saying that something had happened to the bottle of insulin that Adriana had put in her backpack this morning. Rosa had made sure Adriana had it with her, as she needed twice daily injections to control the childhood diabetes she'd been diagnosed with two years earlier.

"It couldn't have just disappeared, could it? Did it fall out of the backpack outside, or did someone take it as a joke?" Rosa asked the nurse, who had no answers. "Okay, I know it's critical she get her afternoon dose, so I'll bring another bottle from home. I should be there in 30 minutes."

Rosa hurriedly grabbed the spare insulin bottle and jumped into her CRV. She gunned the engine in the little silver SUV and hurried up the road to the day camp. As she rounded the bend, she came to the edge of the normally dry bed of the Rillito River. Only now there was already a long section of the road that was covered with about six inches of rapidly moving runoff. Rosa knew this was the advance edge of a menacing flash flood!

Rosa quickly dialed the number of the day camp and breathlessly told the person who answered, "This is Rosa

Cisneros. I'm trying to get the insulin to my niece, but the road is already under water at the Rillito crossing. I'm going to try to make it across, but if I don't arrive at the camp within ten minutes, you'd better send out a search and rescue team."

Dr. Cisneros started the little CRV through the advancing flood waters. "At least it has four-wheel drive," she thought out loud. At one point she could feel the current starting to catch the vehicle, as the water was now up to the bottom of the doors. But she said a little prayer, gave the SUV more gas and suddenly felt the wheels gain traction. Soon she was across the flood on the other side of the crossing. She breathed a *Thank-you, God*, and drove into the day camp entrance. Adriana came running out, so glad to see her aunt and unaware of the risk Rosa had taken to get the insulin to her.

Galveston Halloween

It started as a quiet night in a small restaurant on Seawall Boulevard

"Mr. Jacks, is there anything else you'd like, or shall I bring you the bill?" asked the forty-something redhead.

"Probably one more drink and then I'll call it a night. Where is everybody, by the way? This place looks almost deserted. Is there some big Halloween party on The Strand that I'm missing?"

"There may be some parties, sir, but I suspect most of the locals are staying away from this section of the beach, due to the Great Storm Halloween Legend and all."

"Legend? That piques my interest, Jeri. My fiancé and I are both history buffs. I came down here tonight, after some business meetings in Houston, to scout out the city for our upcoming honeymoon. We're getting married this Christmas."

"Good choice. A lot of folks take their honeymoons here. And if you're interested in history, Galveston has an interesting one."

"Jeri, tell me about this legend you mentioned."

She cast one eye toward the manager and the few other patrons before deciding she could spare a few minutes. The tired waitress began. "You know about the Great Storm of 1900 that destroyed the city? Well, on each of the Halloweens starting with the one in 2000, exactly 100 years since The Great Storm hit

Galveston, people have mysteriously disappeared along this section of the Seawall. Some of them were later found dead, and some never resurfaced. It even happened in 2008 when we were still trying to clean up after Hurricane Ike. I didn't put a lot of stock in the stories that were circulating until last Halloween, when one of my co-workers disappeared. Her body washed up on Stewart Beach three days later."

"What happened to her?"

"We both got into our cars after our shift ended. Bonnie's car was found abandoned along the seawall the next morning. The only explanation anyone has is that it was those spirits."

"Spirits?"

"Several have reported seeing ghostly figures walking across the seawall onto the beach and into the water just before daybreak the morning after Halloween. Some claim that they are the spirits of those whose bodies were lost to the sea in The Great Storm. After 100 years they're back looking for another body to inhabit during Halloween. When daybreak comes, they have to return to the sea for another year."

"Interesting story, but surely you don't believe in superstitions like that. I'm sure there are better, more rational explanations for these disappearances," I said as I picked up the bill and left Jeri a nice tip.

Back in my nearby hotel room, I turned in for the night and was almost asleep when I heard a knock on the door. Then I

heard a voice that sounded like my fiancé's. "Helen?" I called as I
unbolted the door and opened it. Before me stood one of the most
beautiful women I have ever seen, with a voluptuous figure and
perfect ivory skin and provocatively dressed - like a high-class call
girl. She gazed into my eyes and flatly stated, "I'm here, Jon."

"Look, there must be some mistake," I protested, my pulse
starting to race. "I don't know who you are or how you know my
name, but I'm not interested in your services. I'm engaged to a
wonderful woman." But she brushed right by me, walked into the
room like she'd been there before, ducked into the bathroom and
locked the door. I purposely left the hallway door open and
hurriedly knocked on the bathroom door. I even threatened to call
hotel security if she didn't leave immediately.

"Jon, I'm afraid that calling them won't do you any good."
With that she flung open the bathroom door with such force it
generated a wind that suddenly slammed shut the outside door to
the hall. A strange feeling of impending doom swept over me as I
turned toward the sound. Then behind me, I heard her say, "Jon, I
want your body." Whirling around, I was shocked to see she was
now wearing a vintage 1900 showgirl outfit. But what sent chills
down my spine was the woman's appearance. Her ivory skin now
looked like that of a corpse: cold, lifeless, colorless. Her eyes were
sunken back in her head and she had her bony arms outstretched
as if to embrace me. No, suddenly I realized she intended to choke
the life out of me! The smell of her perfume no longer hid the

stench of death and her bony hands reached for my throat as I frantically struggled to open the hallway door. I gasped for breath as everything went blank.

****

"Mr. Jacks. Mr. Jacks! Are you all right? Please answer us!" I struggled to regain consciousness as my eyes tried to focus on the two people standing over me. One looked like the waitress, Jeri, and the other wore a policeman's uniform.

"I, I don't know!" I stammered. "The last I remember I was being choked by a skeleton in a showgirl outfit. What happened?"

Officer Gonzales introduced himself and explained. "We've been trying to catch a husband and wife team who have been mugging tourists and stealing their wallets, watches, and jewelry. They seem to be hanging around restaurants and bars on The Strand and spiking the drinks of these tourists with something like ketamine, one of those date rape drugs. It causes hallucinations and unconsciousness."

"So that's what happened to me?"

"Apparently so. We'd asked Jeri and the other servers to be on the lookout for a suspicious couple that may be spiking the drinks of customers. Tonight she noticed an attractive woman brush your table as she walked by, just before you took your last drink. Then that woman followed you out of the cafe where she met a rough looking male. Suspecting them, Jeri looked out the window and saw them walking a few yards behind you as you made your way to your hotel. That's when she dialed 911."

Jeri picked up the story from there to explain "Officer Gonzalez found the couple leaving the hallway right outside your room with your wallet and watch. You were lying in the doorway, obviously unconscious. After arresting them and calling for an ambulance, he called me and I came here to the hospital to check on you. He joined me after the robbers had been booked."

She continued, "We think they may have been responsible for the mysterious disappearance of my coworker last year."

"Really?" I asked.

"Yes. You can rest assured that evil spirits from the Great Storm weren't involved, Mr. Jacks. Evil people did it." Officer Gonzalez stated emphatically.

"Wow! Well, I can't thank both of you enough! This has been a Halloween I won't forget!"

He Did Not Show up for Work

"He didn't show up for work today, Jim."

I looked up from my work on the lead story for tonight's "Tucson Daily Times" to address the Managing Editor. "I know, Joaquin, and that worries me."

"Oh, how so?"

"You know he's been working undercover on that story about Mexican drug lords moving into Southern Arizona. A dangerous assignment for a young reporter."

"Yes, but he can handle it. Are you sure he's not just hung over from a wild party this weekend? I've heard he's pretty popular with the ladies."

"Whatever. I'll track him down and see why he's AWOL," I sighed as I picked up the phone. I got no answer on his cell phone or his home phone, so I called his girl friend, Carmen.

"Yes, Mr. Michaels, this is Carmen." The sound of her sultry voice brought to mind an image of this dark-haired beauty. I thought how different she was from the blond blue-eyed kid from New York that I'd hired to be the paper's investigative reporter. It's true that opposites attract.

"No, Mr. Michaels, Eddie didn't come home last night. I haven't seen him since yesterday morning. I don't know where he is, but this isn't the first time he's been out all night. He tells me that being a reporter for your newspaper can be a 24/7 job."

I asked her to let me know when she heard from him and hung up the phone. I was pretty sure she knew more than she was telling me. I didn't have long to think about it because the front desk buzzed me on the intercom.

"Jim, there are two FBI agents here who want to see you. I'm sending them up."

"What the hell?" I exclaimed to my computer screen.

Soon the agents were sitting across my desk and produced some photos for me to examine. The one who looked like a pro-football player started asking me questions.

"Mr. Michaels, do you recognize the young man in these photos?"

"Well, yes. It looks like our reporter, Eddie Lavalle."

"Two of the men in the photos with your reporter are honchos in the local drug mafia and the rest are representatives of a Mexican drug cartel. We'd like to know why Mr. Lavelle is meeting with these notorious criminals."

"Certainly. He's on an undercover assignment to discover the truth about rumors that the Mexican drug lords are starting to operate here in Southern Arizona. He's been working on it for three weeks."

"Well, call him off the assignment. We can't have a civilian interfering with our investigation. Plus we're concerned that he may be getting too cozy with the bad guys. The drug lords have lots of cash to throw around and I know that your reporter just bought a brand new mustang convertible last week. Can he afford that on a junior reporter's pay?"

Incensed by the insinuation that Eddie was taking money from the drug lords, I spoke through clenched teeth. "I happen to know that Eddie didn't pay cash for that vehicle. The dealer called our offices to verify his salary when they were checking his credit."

"Maybe so, maybe not, Mr. Michaels. But we're warning you to take him off this investigation unless you want the government to take the newspaper to court."

After the agents had gone, I sat for a few minutes trying to decide what course of action to take. I decided to call my old friend, Lee, a supervisor in the local FBI office that I'd known since college.

"Hey, Lee, this is Jim at the newspaper. Can you tell me why two of your agents are ordering me to pull my investigative reporter off a story he's working on?"

"Who would those agents be, Jim? They haven't discussed this with me."

"Their ID's said Manuel Garcia and William Evans."

"Jim, I don't have any agents working out of this office with those names. I'm checking the Bureau database as we speak and it doesn't show any agents anywhere named Manuel Garcia or William Evans. Those guys don't work for the Bureau."

"If they're not Feds, then who are they, and why were they here asking about Eddie Lavelle's undercover work regarding the Mexican drug lords moving into Southern Arizona?"

"Good question Jim. If I had to guess, I'd say they work for one of the opposing drug cartels and wanted to confirm what Eddie's business was with the opposition. If that's the case, now that they've confirmed his connection, they may have a hit out on him."

"Good grief, Lee! He's just an innocent young kid, trying to make a name for himself as a reporter. Can't you do something to protect him?"

"Well, I could assign one of our agents as a security detail until we're sure Eddie is safe. What are his whereabouts now?"

"Good question! I wish I knew. He hasn't shown up at work yet, he doesn't answer his phones, and his girlfriend, Carmen Rivera, doesn't know where he is."

"Did you say Carmen Rivera, and is she about 25 and a real knockout?

"That would be the one."

"Well, if he's mixed up with her, he is in trouble. She's the granddaughter of one of the Mexican drug lords and we have reason to suspect that she's been facilitating their encroachment into the local drug mafia's territory."

Suddenly I had images of Eddie lying in a back alley in South Tucson with his throat cut. Or screaming in pain as he watched them cut off his fingers one by one. After asking Lee to contact the local police and put out an APB for him, I walked up to Joaquin Soto's office and explained my concern to him.

"Holy cow, Jim. I knew it wasn't wise to put such a young reporter on a case like this. But you convinced me he could handle it."

I was stunned by my Managing Editor's twisting of the facts, since he'd been the one who had talked me into letting Eddie work this one. Obviously if Eddie turned up dead or maimed, I would be the scapegoat. But more than my concerns for myself were my fears for this young reporter - whom we may have sent to his death.

"Hello, Mr. Michaels, and Mr. Soto. Sorry I'm so late."

We both turned to see Eddie walking into the doorway. He looked tired and his clothes were bedraggled, but he was very much alive.

"Last night my car skidded off the wet road into the ditch and landed on its side when I was coming home from a meeting in Nogales with one of my sources. Somehow I lost my cell phone in the process and had to hike ten miles to Green Valley. Nothing was open that time of night! So by the time I got a tow truck to pick up my car and take it to a garage, it was already 9 a.m. I had a cup of coffee and a donut at the garage and then paid the mechanic's wife to give me a ride to Tucson. Hope you don't mind my clothes, but I had her take me straight to the office since it's almost noon."

Putting a hand on his shoulder, I exclaimed, "Hey we're just glad to see you're okay, kid."

"If you gentlemen will excuse me a minute, I need to call Carmen to tell her I'm okay. She's probably worried sick about me."

"Eddie, we need to talk before you make that call to Carmen."

Home for Thanksgiving

The gentle fall breezes were giving way to the cold winds from the north as Jack started the long trek home for Thanksgiving. He'd missed sharing this holiday with his family for years. Last year he'd spent it in a homeless shelter, not even sure who he was or how he got there. The kind social worker had helped him recover his identity after she'd matched his fingerprints with a database of missing veterans.

"Your name is Jack. Jack Schmidt. And you were born in Phoenix, Arizona in 1960." These words from the social worker had started him on the long journey out of the amnesia that fogged his mind. Slowly childhood memories had surfaced as she showed him pictures of his parents and brother and of the neighborhood where he'd grown up. Then he started remembering bits of his time in high school and life in the army. His military records showed he'd been severely wounded during the US invasion of Granada, but he couldn't recall much about it, nor the months he'd spent in rehab as a result. He did remember moving to Texas in the nineties, but couldn't recall anything that had happened in the last five years.

As he got off the bus in Phoenix, he recalled the counsel from his social worker that it might be too soon for him to reinsert himself into the life of his family in Arizona. "No, Sister Sanchez, I believe I'm ready. Mom and Dad are both in their late seventies now, and who knows if they'll even be around many more Thanksgivings. "

"Okay, Jack. But I don't think it would be a good idea for you to surprise them by walking in unannounced after all these years. At least let me phone them and tell them you are still alive and that you will be there for the holiday." Reluctantly Jack had agreed just before she'd dropped him off at the Greyhound Bus terminal.

Jack's childhood home was only a mile from the Phoenix bus station and he decided to walk with the hopes that the familiar sights would help him recover even more of the memories he'd lost. As he passed his old elementary school, he remembered kissing Mary Jane Beal during recess when he was in third grade and the teasing he'd gotten from the other boys as a result.

The old neighborhood hadn't changed that much since he'd gone into the army. There where a few changes, like the little corner grocery store owned by Mr. Chang was now a Seven Eleven, with gasoline pumps where some palm trees had once graced the lot.

Jack's heart started beating faster with each step toward home. Suddenly a wave of nostalgia hit him so forcefully that he stopped to catch his breath. Finally he rounded the corner and saw the old chain link fence that surrounded his parent's home. The Bermuda grass in the front yard had been replaced with gravel and several native cactus plants, but the white stucco house with the little sidewalk leading to the front porch still looked the same as he remembered.

The front gate creaked as Jack opened it. Before he could get to the front porch, the front door opened and he saw the beaming faces of his elderly parents. As he embraced both of them, he couldn't stop the tears from rolling down his cheeks. Drying his eyes, he noticed tears on his mother's cheeks, too.

"Come on in, Jack. We're both so glad to see you!" his mother exclaimed. Even his father, who was usually very quiet, told him how glad he was that he could come for Thanksgiving.

"Your brother, Joe, is on his way and should be here any minute, son. Come on inside and put your bag in your old bedroom. Dinner is almost ready."

"So Joe is coming! I haven't seen him for so long! How about Uncle Ben, Uncle Clint, and Aunt Pearl?"

"I guess you wouldn't know, Jack. Both your uncles and your aunt passed away a few years ago. Your Dad is the only one of his ten siblings who is still alive," explained Jack's mother.

Just then a red sports car drove up and Joe got out. "My, he's aged," thought Jack, but then realized Joe would probably be thinking the same thing about him.

Soon all four of them were seated around the old oak dining table, next to the kitchen. Mom had covered it with her finest linen tablecloth and had set the table with the china and silverware she only used for special occasions. Dad had already carved the turkey and the table was filled with Thanksgiving delights: homemade rolls, cranberry sauce, dressing, corn on the cob, Waldorf salad, and pumpkin pie. The delicious aromas brought Jack memories of many happy times around this table.

"This dinner looks just like the Thanksgiving dinners Mom served us when I lived here," thought Jack. Only back then, there had been an extra leaf in the table to accommodate all of Jack's uncles and aunts.

"Dad, would you please say the blessing?" asked Mom.

"Lord, we thank you for this wonderful meal and for the one who prepared it," began Dad. Then he choked up as he thanked God that both of their sons were there to share this Thanksgiving dinner.

The love and acceptance Jack felt at that moment was almost indescribable. Rather than peppering him with questions about his lost years, they simply welcomed him wholeheartedly. Then he remembered the words from a parable about a lost son that Sister Sanchez had shared with him. "This my son was dead and is alive again; he was lost and is found." And he bowed his head in his own silent prayer of thanksgiving, as he thought how good it was to no longer be lost.

Homeward Bound at Christmas

The sounds of "I'll Be Home for Christmas" echoed in his ears and his heart beat faster as Tom pushed his way through the throng of holiday shoppers. Home was where he was headed after many long months away from the family that loved him so much.

"Boy, he's in a hurry!" a tired shopper exclaimed as Tom dashed past her. "Wonder where he's headed?"

Night was drawing near and Tom had a long trip ahead. After escaping just that afternoon from the warehouse where he'd been held captive, his only thought was getting back home where he felt a sense of belonging. He relished the freedom he'd regained as he hurried through the streets. Thankfully his captors had grown lax over the last three months and he'd been able to escape his prison when they'd left for a lunch break.

The sights, sounds, and smells of the Christmas holidays greeted Tom as he hurried through a nearby mall. Children were talking excitedly about the presents they were anticipating. Adults were complaining about their sore feet, the lack of Christmas spirit shown by the store employees, and wondering how they were going to have time to complete all their shopping and other pre-Christmas tasks in the last two days before the big holiday. The noise didn't bother, Tom, though, as he'd had little human companionship since he'd wandered into the wrong place at the wrong time and ended up far from home.

After exiting the mall, Tom stood under a tree in the parking lot a few minutes to get his bearings. The scent of evergreens from a nearby Christmas tree lot tantalized his nostrils. The smell of the great outdoors was exhilarating after being imprisoned indoors for so long! Finally he knew which direction to head, and he took off at a fast walk. It would take many hours to reach his holiday destination, since he had no access to any other means of transportation.

Soon a black SUV passed Tom as he walked beside the highway out of town. Suddenly it stopped and started to back slowly toward him. No longer trusting strangers, Tom dashed into the roadside bushes and took off across country at a fast pace. Every few minutes he looked back to make certain he wasn't being followed. Finally satisfied, he settled into a walking stride he felt he could maintain for the rest of the long journey.

The sun set in the cold winter sky, and darkness settled like a heavy blanket over the nearby hills as Tom continued his relentless trek. He finally stopped in the mouth of a small cave to rest after midnight. The ground was cold and hard but sleep came quickly. Several times in the night the sounds of coyotes or wolves awakened him and he moved further back into the cavern for protection. He was well on his way again as the first streaks of dawn broke through the gray December clouds. All day he traveled, through woods and farmland. Hunger pangs only spurred him on as he sensed he was close to familiar surroundings.

Finally, just at dusk, Tom rounded a curve in the road and saw his home ahead. His steps quickened with anticipation as he saw the outdoor Christmas lights and the smoke rising from the chimney. Using every last ounce of energy in his tired body, he forced himself to start running as he spotted the familiar Christmas tree in the dining room window. People who loved him and lots of good food awaited him!

Tom tripped as he scrambled up the front steps and fell flat next to the welcome mat, unable to summon up any more energy. He lay there in a state of exhaustion, hoping someone would soon open the door. The first flakes of a Christmas Eve snowstorm started to fall and Tom began to shiver, wondering when someone would discover him there. Just then he saw the UPS truck pull up and watched the familiar deliveryman bound up the steps with a package.

"Why, is that you, Tom? I haven't seen you around here for a long time. Where have you been?" the friendly deliveryman queried.

Before Tom could acknowledge the question, the front door opened, and he heard Katherine's shout of joy as she spied him lying there, next to the door mat. "Tom, Tom, you're home! This is the best Christmas gift yet." She turned and yelled inside to Matt, "Matt, our cat has come home!"

Soon Tom was being treated to a feast fit only for a well-loved feline. Home had never felt so good! Tom knew that he would never again venture inside a moving van. His curiosity many months before had almost kept him from being home for Christmas!

House for Sale?

When I heard the doorbell ring, I surprised the young real estate salesman by swinging the front door completely open so that it bounced against the doorstop. By then I was in hidden in the shadows of the darkened study off the entry hall.

"Come on in, you handsome brute," I yelled and then broke into peals of laughter that seemed to shake every timber of my house. I could see the tall blond salesman hesitate and take a step back before he regained his courage.

"Is that you, Mrs. Smith? I've come for the ten o'clock appointment you set up with the office."

"Well, just don't stand out in the sun," I ordered. That office-white complexion of yours will probably burn quickly." And I let out another peal of laughter before bursting out of the shadows into the entry hall.

I saw him take a gulp as he caught sight of me and knew that he was fascinated by my appearance. I'm sure that few of his potential clients came to the door wearing a thong bikini outfit and if they did, they probably wouldn't have looked as good as me with my tanned and firm figure. I looked almost as good as I had 30 years ago when I'd won the Miss Iowa beauty pageant. I watched his eyes wander up to my face and I smiled as he saw my clown hat and purple hair and his lips silently formed the word "bizarre."

He gulped again and stated, "Mrs. Smith, I'm Jonathan Jones and I'm here to talk about listing your house for sale. If this is a bad time, I can come back later..." he offered feebly.

"Not at all, Mr. Jones. I've been waiting for you!" I exclaimed and threw back my head and laughed again. "I need to sell this place soon - like tomorrow! Do you think you can do that for me?"

He gingerly followed me into the kitchen but didn't close the front door. I ignored that as it really didn't matter. We sat across from each other at the kitchen table and he tried to explain that it takes a while to get a house on the market and find a buyer.

"That won't work," I announced and replaced the twinkle in my eye with a cold-hearted stare that was meant to scare him. "I must be out of this house before the 48 hours is up."

"I'm sorry, Mrs. Smith," he stammered. "What 48 hours?"

"Let's just say that it's very important to my well-being that I'm out of here before midnight tomorrow night. And buster, that means it's very important to your well-being too." Again I let out a loud peal of laughter, only this time it definitely had a diabolical undertone.

"Mrs. Smith, I don't understand what this is all about and I must have more information before I can decide IF I want to list your house. I only represent clients who are honest with me."

"Sonny, for a moment I'll ignore your implication that you might not list this house, and I'll tell you why I'm selling. You may not realize it, but my body is just as firm and my figure is just as full as when I won the Miss Iowa contest. Everyone thinks it's due to diet, exercise, and vitamins or some extensive plastic surgery, " I snorted. "But I eat anything I want, I only get a moderate amount of exercise, and I never take any blasted vitamins. And I've sure as hell never gone to a plastic surgeon. Want to know what my secret is?"

I saw his head nodding yes even while I saw his eyes taking furtive glances back to the front door.

Leaning forward, I gazed into Mr. Jones' eyes and disclosed my secret. "I made a compact with the Goddess of Youth. She would keep me young as long as I would agree to do any three things she asked me for. I would only have 48 hours to comply with each request or my body would age 48 years overnight."

"Uh, huh," he mumbled and I guessed that he was wondering if he should call 911 and get me committed.

"Well, I complied with the first request five years ago when I sacrificed my cat to the goddess, hard as that was. Then last year, she told me to sacrifice a goat on the front lawn of the First Baptist Church on Halloween night. I almost got caught."

Mr. Jones started to bolt for the front door but I saw him jump when it slammed shut by itself.

"Sit back down, mister salesman. I received the third request late last night. That's why I called your office first thing this morning. The third request is for me to sell this house or sacrifice the realtor who is unable to do so."

"Okay, okay," he said as he reached for his cell phone. "Let me just call my office and ask them to post your house on our website. We can list it below market value and maybe someone looking for a bargain will snatch it up."

"Let's hope for your sake that they do, Mr. Jones," I whispered as I walked to the cupboard and pulled out a syringe. I waited until he hit "off" on his cell and then stabbed the syringe into his left shoulder.

Letting out a yell, he turned to me with a quizzical look.

"I just gave you an extra incentive, Mr. Jones. You realtors like extra incentives don't you? I just injected a slow-acting poison into your body. Only I have the antidote. If you sell the house by sunset tomorrow night, I'll give it to you. Otherwise you'll be dead by midnight tomorrow night. Understood?"

I could see a mixture of fear and hate on the young man's face as he struggled with this news. When he gathered his wits and got up to go toward the front door, I hurried ahead of him and warned, "Don't get any ideas about calling the cops or you won't get the antidote for sure!"

Within a couple of hours, Mr. Jones had planted a For Sale sign in my front yard to which he had attached a box of glossy flyers. Just before dusk, he brought a car full of other agents by to see my house. I smiled inwardly when one of them told me they'd never seen Jonathan so eager to sell a house.

Shortly after daybreak the next morning, I got a call from realtors wanting to show my house. By the end of the day, three prospective buyers had looked at it. One liked the house but couldn't qualify for a loan, one disliked the purple walls in the bathrooms, and the other was turned off by the ceiling mirrors above my waterbed.

Just before sunset, Mr. Jones drove up with a dejected look. I could tell the poison was having its effect by the way he staggered to my front door.

"I've done my best to sell your house today and I'm sure I can sell it soon if you can give me a few more days. Would you please give me that antidote now?"

My heart did go out for this young man and I felt a few twinges of conscience before I explained that I couldn't sacrifice my youthful beauty to save his life. After all, doesn't our culture value beauty and youth above life itself?

Soon it was dark, and when he slipped into a stupor, I dragged him outside and stretched out his body on the lawn. Quickly I tied ropes around his wrists and ankles and staked them down. As soon as I couldn't feel a pulse, I began the preparations for the ritual sacrifice.

I Knew There was a Problem

As soon as I turned the key in the lock, I knew there was a problem. I'd left my cell phone in the Jeep! When I turned to go back down the hall of the boarding house, a bullet ripped through the door from inside my room, narrowly missing me.

"Damn! I'm not getting paid enough for this case!" I exclaimed under my breath and pulled the Glock out of my waist band. Though a Private Eye for more than ten years, I'd only been shot at a handful of times. Believe me, being a PI is usually a lot more boring than people think from watching TV.

The hallway remained quiet, either because the other residents were out or they didn't want to get involved. After a couple of minutes, I gingerly reached for the door knob while standing to one side. Quickly I turned it and kicked the door open. The room remained quiet as a tomb and the only movement I spotted were the curtains fluttering in front of the open window.

Running to the open window, I looked outside and saw someone disappear around the corner of the building. Being fifty years old, I knew I wasn't fast enough to scramble down the fire escape in time to have a prayer at catching the perp.

What to do next? Last week Rochester Oil and Gas hired me to investigate the disappearance of hundreds of thousands of dollars of tubing, casing, and valves for equipping new wells out of their Corpus Christi warehouse and pipe yard.

Jimmy Calhoun, their crusty exploration vice president in Dallas, had explained it this way. "Yeager, I think someone from inside our company is involved. That's why we aren't using our own people in this investigation. That's also why I want you to go undercover to get to the bottom of it. Then too, the media must be kept in the dark about these thefts, or the news might spook some of our investors. That means I can't get the cops involved. You've got to handle this yourself. Understand?"

So telling the cops about the attempt on my life was out of the question at this point. I only hoped that the landlady wouldn't come up to this floor before I could patch the hole in the door.

But my biggest concern was how someone had found out about my undercover surveillance of the warehouse and who had tried to kill me for it!

That night I resumed watching the warehouse from an abandoned building across the street. This was the fourth night for my surveillance, and so far I'd not spotted any suspicious activity. I had a hunch that tonight might be different since they'd decided to take me out today. Staring through my Bushnell Night Vision Binoculars for hours at a time was giving me severe eye fatigue. Just when I was about to give my eyes a break, a large but empty flatbed truck pulled up in front of the warehouse. Immediately someone inside rolled open the doors and the truck quickly disappeared inside before the doors were closed.

Thirty minutes later, I was able to snap a number of photos with my telephoto digital camera as the fully-loaded truck drove out of the warehouse and down the street in front of me. I got a clear photo of the Oklahoma license plate and also got a couple of good shots of someone rolling closed the warehouse door. It was time to get some shut eye before I called in a favor.

The next morning I called Judy, an old friend who works for the Oklahoma Department of Public Safety. "Yeager, you didn't hear this from me, understand? It looks like that license plate is owned by Kiowa Exploration, a small oil and gas company located in Oklahoma City."

"Thanks, Judy. Next time you're in San Antonio, give me or Marsha a call and we'll do dinner."

My next call was to Jimmy Calhoun at Rochester Oil and Gas. His secretary, Maria, answered and explained that Jimmy was out of the office. When she recognized my name, she added, "Mr. Yeager, let me connect you through to our President, Jack Davis. He'll be eager to get the report of your investigation."

When Mr. Davis came on the line, I told him about the license plate and the photos I had of someone closing the warehouse door. "I assume that your company didn't authorize the shipment of some of your oil field equipment in the middle of the night, Mr. Davis?"

"We sure as hell didn't. I'd like to meet with you personally and get a copy of your photos. I can fly down there by 2 p.m. And

I may arrange for someone from the local FBI office to meet with us."

"Okay. How about Jimmy Calhoun? And by the way, he told me he didn't want any of the authorities to know about this investigation…"

"Oh he did, did he? That increases some of my suspicions. I told him to hire you but also told him to have you get with the authorities as soon as you found anything! No, don't even talk with him before you meet with me. Do you know where the Water Street Oyster Bar is? Let's meet there."

I uploaded the photos to my laptop and made a copy on a USB flash drive. Then I got in my Jeep and drove down to the waterfront near the Water Street Oyster Bar. Finding a Walgreen's, I took the memory stick to the Photo section and asked for 8X10 prints of each photo.

"We can have them by noon, Mr. Yeager," offered the young clerk.

"Fine. I'll be here at noon sharp!" I walked across the street to a little pocket park and sat down on a bench next to a lone palm tree. It was a beautiful blue sky day, with the seagulls screeching overhead. I decided to call my wife, Marsha.

"Hello honey, how's your case going? Are you having any time to enjoy the pretty beach weather?"

"Well, I think my part will be finished after I meet with my client and an FBI agent at 2 p.m. Maybe I'll be able to relax and enjoy the day after I turn my photos over to them."

After picking up the photos at Walgreen's, I walked to the Water Street Oyster Bar and had lunch while I waited for Jack Davis. Sure enough, he showed up promptly at 2 p.m. with Agent Enrique Garcia, who showed me his FBI badge.

"Just as I suspected!" exclaimed Davis. The guy standing by the warehouse door is our warehouse foreman! And he is the brother-in-law of my vice president, Jimmy Calhoun. I think they are in cahoots with someone from Kiowa Exploration."

"I suspect that the warehouse foreman is the one who took a shot at you after Calhoun told him about your investigation." Agent Garcia chimed in.

Glad to finish my part of this case, I left the hour-long meeting and went back to the boarding house. As soon as I turned the key in the lock, I heard a noise inside. I opened the door to be greeted by my wife, wearing nothing but a smile.

"You sounded pretty stressed on the phone, so I drove down to help you get some R&R."

Irresolutions Anonymous

I saw him as soon as he confidently strode through the doorway, iPad in one hand, a diet coke in the other. His looks and demeanor reminded me of a young Harrison Ford. After surveying the room, he plopped down next to me and struck up a conversation with the pretty, but quiet, brunette sitting on the other side. This guy was not exactly the type of person I was expecting at my first meeting of Irresolutions Anonymous.

Guess it's time for a confession on my part. I'm not a member of this organization. Not even a prospective member. I'm a reporter for a big city newspaper and doing some research for an article my editor assigned me: why most people don't keep their New Year's resolutions.

Soon the twenty or so other people in the room were each introducing themselves to the group. The reserved brunette said her name was Maria and explained that she always had trouble deciding what resolutions to make for the new year and no matter how hard she tried, she didn't keep them for more than a few weeks. Then the guy next to me with the iPad spoke up, "Hi. My name is Jon and I am a resolution-breaker. I really don't have a problem making resolutions. Hell, I made twenty five back on New Year's Day. My problem is, that as soon as I've written down my resolutions, I lose interest in keeping them. Then when friends ask me how well I'm keeping them, I just smile, mumble something, and feel guilty."

When it was my turn, I simply said my name was Richard Evans and I was there to observe. After the other introductions, the leader, a middle-aged bald guy in jeans, explained the purpose of the group and noted that this twelve step program could help people addicted to making resolutions and never keeping them. The rest of the hour was devoted to testimonies from those who had been able to break the habit. At the end we all joined hands and had a moment of silent meditation. At least we didn't sing Kum Ba Yah.

As the group began to break up, I stopped Jon and Maria to explain my real purpose for being there. "I would really like to talk to you two individually to get some background for my story. I'm working under a tight deadline, so I would really like to do this sometime in the next couple of days or so."

The Harrison Ford look-alike spoke first, "Sure, Mr. Evans. I'm working from home tomorrow. Why don't you come by in the afternoon?" After some hesitation, the brunette said she could meet at a local Starbucks tomorrow evening after she got off work at the downtown library. So I gave each of them my card and got their cell phone numbers, thanked them, and left the meeting hall. "What an interesting but strange hour this has been!, but at least I have some good leads for my column!"

Jon greeted me at the door to his condo at 2 p.m. the next day. "This is actually a good time, Mr. Evans. I don't have anything until a conference call in an hour. Why don't we sit out on the balcony on this spring-like afternoon?"

As we sat down, I got out my pad and pencil. "I see you have a telescope out here, Jon, Are you an amateur astronomer?"

Jon looked at the balcony across the way and admitted rather sheepishly, "To tell you the truth, I use it to watch the three college girls in that condo who sun bathe on their balcony. In fact, one of the New Year's resolutions I made, after my grandmother stopped by, saw the scope, and called me a pervert, was to sell the telescope. But, as you see, I didn't. The view was just too, how shall I say it, enticing."

"Okay. What other resolutions did you make and not keep?"

"Well, I guess the most serious one had to do with my dating life. I have dated a lot of women. I do mean a lot! But after the second date, I always break off the relationship. Is it a fear of commitment? Or just that I haven't found a woman who can keep me interested? Any rate, I resolved to change that this year. But haven't yet!"

Since I have an undergraduate degree in Psychology, this piqued my interest. "So the type of women you've been dating haven't attracted you for long?"

"Yeah, you could say that. Either they've been very boring intellectually, though good to look at, or they seemed too interested in me, too anxious to start a serious relationship."

"So you would prefer someone who's smart and hard to get?"

"I suppose so. Maybe that's why I've sat next to Maria the last four meetings of Irresolutions Anonymous. She's never thrown herself at me and the few times she's spoken up, she said things that impressed me with how smart and knowledgeable she is."

After the hour was up, I had several pages of notes for my article and thanked Jon for his time. Three hours later, I walked into the Starbucks and spotted Maria with a cup of Java and a copy of Scientific American.

"Hello, Mr. Evans. You are right on time. How can I help you with your article?"

Pulling the empty chair out across the bistro table, I said,"Thanks for meeting with me! I just talked to someone who has no trouble making resolutions but doesn't seem serious about keeping them. You strike me as someone who deliberates a long time before making resolutions and though you are intent on keeping them, you aren't able to do so over the long term."

"Sounds like you listened pretty well at the meeting yesterday. That pretty much says it."

"May I ask what your number one resolution was for this year?"

"It's sort of personal, but sure. I resolved to get over my last break-up and find a man I could trust to love me for the long term. You see, two years ago I found out that my fiancé was having an affair with another man. When I confronted him, he said he still loved me, but that he loved Thomas more! Since that time I've never dated anyone."

"Have you met anyone you thought you might like to try to trust?"

Blushing, she admitted that she was attracted to the Harrison Ford - look alike that she'd been sitting next to in the twelve step meetings, but had been waiting for him to make the first move.

After I got a few more pages of notes from my conversation with Maria, I left Starbucks and typed up my column. My editor liked it and it went to print. That was a year ago.

Today I received an announcement in the mail. Guess what? It was from Jon Singer and Maria Martinez, inviting me to their upcoming wedding. In it was a handwritten note signed by Maria. "Mr. Evans, we hope you can come, as you were the catalyst in getting us together."

It Happened Last Fall

"Speeding through the gathering darkness, the train pushes on. Does that sound too trite for the beginning line? Kind of like 'it was a dark and stormy night'?" wondered Julie as she looked out the window of the Sunset Limited train. That was the trouble with being an English teacher: being too critical of your own writing. She crossed out the line on her notepad and wondered if she could put aside the novel she was writing and just enjoy her Thanksgiving vacation.

Her thoughts were interrupted when an attractive Latina woman sat down next to her. "Do you mind if I sit here? It looks like the only spare seat here in the Observation Car."

"No problem at all. The sunset really looks pretty from this vantage point. I am enjoying the start of my week off from school."

"Are you a teacher?"

"Yes. High School English. In downtown Austin. How about you?"

"I'm a paralegal taking a few days off from the rat race. My fiancé and I are on our way from my home in San Antonio to Phoenix. By the way, my name is Maria. Maria Gonzales."

" My name is Julie; Julie Walker. My fiancé is off on a business trip so I am on my own this week."

The two talked for over an hour and could start to feel a bond developing. They shared a lot of similar interests and liked the same things about men. Both of them disliked the amount of time their fiancés spent traveling.

"Well, Julie, I better get back to my fiancé, Joe, or he'll wonder what happened to me. There are a couple of empty seats across from us. Why don't you come with me and meet Joe?"

Julie consented and got the shock of her life as Maria's fiancé got up from his seat in the next car to say hello. "Joseph!" she gasped. "What the hell are you doing here? You were supposed to be on a business trip. And instead you are here with Maria!"

Joe or Joseph White looked like a kid with his hand caught in the cookie jar. Then he started hyperventilating and collapsed into his seat.

"You two-timing bastard!" both ladies exclaimed in unison. Seeing that their common fiancé had fainted dead away, they marched off to the snack lounge car to compare notes. It didn't take long to compare calendars and see that when Joe or Joseph was away out of town from one of them on a business trip, he was really in the next city with the other one.

"Everything this guy told me was a lie. What are we going to do, Julie? We can't have him arrested for bigamy, because he's not legally married to anyone."

"I don't know, but I think I'm going to be sick. Excuse me while I run downstairs to a restroom."

On her way to the restroom, she was nearly knocked over by an arrogant young woman dressed to the nines and wearing six inch spike heels. The pushy woman hurried into the first restroom and locked the door. Julie tried the door to each of the other tiny restrooms and found they were locked. Then she spied the ladies lounge at the end of the little hall. It was three times larger than the other restrooms and had a small bench. After emptying her stomach contents in the lounge commode, she sat down on the bench and suddenly had an inspiration.

As Julie left the ladies lounge, she heard a scream in the first restroom and the arrogant woman with the spike heels burst out the door, yelling "Damn it! I dropped my smartphone down the commode when I was flushing it." Just then Julie heard the faint ring of a phone coming from somewhere below the floor. Bursting into tears, the phone's owner sobbed, "That's my boyfriend calling from Mexico City and I can't answer it. Whatever will he think of me?"

"Maybe there is such a thing as karma," muttered Julie below her breath. She walked back to the snack lounge car where Maria was sitting with a determined look on her face.

"Julie, somehow we've got make our two timing fiancé pay for his lies. But I don't think we should chance doing anything illegal. We don't want to get arrested!"

"Well, Maria, I got an idea while I was downstairs in the ladies lounge. Let me tell you about it."

A few minutes later, Maria walked into the next car where Joe White was sitting with is head in his hands. "Hey, Joe. I am still ticked off, but let's make the most of this trip. Julie is over in the the snack lounge getting drunk. Let's go join her."

It didn't take much convincing for Joe to follow her and start drowning his self-caused sorrows with the liquor they kept providing him. When he was fairly sozzled, they began the next phase of their plan.

"Joe, we've been thinking that since we've each slept with you individually we might as well try a threesome. Wouldn't that be kinky? We could have our own little sex party while we are all together."

"I've never tried group sex before, but what fun it would be!" Joe slurred. "But, wait, where could we do it on the train?"

"We found just the place. There is a ladies lounge downstairs with just enough room for the three of us."

Once they got Joe into the lounge and locked the door, they convinced him to start undressing. When he was stark naked, Julie announced, "Now the fun begins, Joe. First we blindfold you and you cover your ears. Then you count down from 100 to 1, uncover your ears, take off the blindfold and we'll show you the time of your life!"

By the time Joe's count got to 60, Julie and Maria had tiptoed out of the ladies lounge with his clothes, wallet, and cell phone, which they dropped into a shopping bag Maria had found.

As they passed by the arrogant lady who'd lost her phone, Julie handed her Joe's cell, and said. "We found this phone downstairs and thought you might like to use it to call your boyfriend in Mexico City."

"Really? Why thank you, lady! Miguel will be so glad to hear from me!"

Next they placed the shopping bag with Joe's belongings in the overhead rack above an empty seat and walked into the dining car for a relaxing dinner. Later, as they were looking over the dessert menu, they overheard a conductor talking to their waiter. "Can you believe it, an elderly woman found some pervert sitting buck naked in the ladies lounge. Scared her to death. The pervert couldn't give me a good explanation, so I am going to turn him over to the police at the next stop."

"I think I am really going to enjoy my dessert, Julie," smiled Maria.

"Me too! And I've got some great material for the novel I'm writing,"

It's an Anole's Life

Here I was an hour ago, perched by the front door of the house, and a nicely-dressed lady with a little brown-haired girl rang the doorbell. The little girl saw me and exclaimed, "Look, Mom, there's a gecko!"

Dang it! I hate being called a gecko. After all, I'm a card-carrying anole! (Or I would be if I had something to carry a card in.) A gecko! How would you humans like being called chimpanzees or something else?

Most people have never heard of anoles, while geckos have been popularized by a certain insurance company. If they knew even a little about lizards, they would realize that geckos are not green like us anoles! And geckos are nocturnal, while anoles are diurnal. So, since I'm green and I sleep at night, I'm not a gecko! How plain can that be?

I still remember when I first heard someone call me a gecko. I was only a couple of months old and Mom had always told me I was an anole. Then several other humans also called me a gecko, and I started suffering from a full-blown identity crises! Questions like "who am I" and "why am I here" kept me awake at night. Finally, the wise old gecko, who lives by the rain gutter downspout, explained how we anoles are different than geckos. He even pointed out a gecko that lived down the street; it was an ugly pinkish brown color.

So, I gradually accepted the truth that I was not a gecko. I'm a superior creature since us anoles are related to the mighty iguana. I can change my color based on my mood and surroundings and I can climb walls!

Hang on a minute, I just saw another anole within my territory and I've got to chase him away! This is my land, not his land, from my basking porch to my shady area, and from my high lookout to my hidey-hole.

*   *   *   *   *   *   *   *

Okay, I'm back now. I finally got that intruder to leave, but I had to raise my spine, extend my dewlap, and do some push-ups. While I was in the middle of this altercation, the brown-haired little girl came out of the house and saw me.

"Eek, Mother! Did you see that? What's wrong with that gecko? His throat is all red and puffed out like a balloon? He looks so creepy!"

"I don't know, honey. Maybe he's sick or malformed. Hurry along and let's get in the car."

I thought to myself that they were lucky they couldn't hear the hisses I made as I went through my routine to scare off the encroacher. Rover, the old dog, who lives in the back yard, once explained to me that my hisses are too high-pitched for humans to hear, though Rover heard them loud and clear!

Speaking of Rover, he was complaining to me the other day about the way his owners ignore him most of the time. "It's a dog's life, Greenie," he gasped, trying to catch his breath after running off the stray cat who tries to snitch his dog food. "Nobody appreciates all I do to provide security to this place, and my master even forgets to let me in the house when it rains."

"Gee, Rover, sorry about that. I know what you feel like. No one appreciates all the bugs and spiders that I eat every day and most people mistake me for a stupid gecko."

"Guess it's an anole's life, too!" wheezed the old hound.

That's when I decided to write this story and hope that some of you humans will read it and understand how I feel. It's not easy being mistaken for a different species and being unappreciated for keeping spiders out of people's houses. Plus a lot of my cousins have met an untimely fate under the heel of an unseeing or inconsiderate human. And my aunt died a horrible death from the bug poison they indiscriminately sprayed around the windows and doors.

Then there was the time I snuck inside the house and got attacked by Fluffy, the big yellow cat that snoozes by the front window. She got the end of my tail in her teeth, but that part snapped off and I escaped into a crevice under the baseboard. As soon as someone opened the front door for a UPS delivery, I darted out. I've been an outdoor anole ever since!

Speaking of Fluffy, I see her peering out the front window, so I think I'll go crawl across the glass and watch her go crazy! That's one of the things I do enjoy about being an anole. I make it a part of my everyday routine. Wriggle slowly across the window and watch Fluffy try to claw me through the glass or hiss at me when I extend my dewlap. Sometimes I'll do it for an hour or more until either the cat gets tired or I decide it's time for a nap in my shady spot.

Come to think of it, there are a lot of good things about being an anole: taunting cats, being a good neighbor by eating bugs, basking in the sun, and going almost anywhere I want to. Rich houses, poor houses, it doesn't matter; I can get into any of them. I heard I have an ancestor who lived in the White House! There's even a proverb in the Bible about us: *a lizard can be caught with the hand, yet it is found in kings' palaces.*

Getting back to Rover's comment about a dog's life that inspired this story, that gets me to thinking. There are good things about being a dog that even Rover admits (free food and no one bothers him most of the day). So maybe "it's a dog's life" can be a positive thing. I guess "it's an anole's life" can also convey good things as well as bad. Yours truly will have to think about this some more.

By the way, in case some of you are skeptical about me writing this piece, which is more credible, a so-called gecko that talks in TV ads or an anole who can type?

Joe's Broken New Year's Resolutions

"Hey, Elena. Have you seen my list of New Year's resolutions?" Joe grumped at his wife of twenty years as he pawed through the stacks of papers on his computer desk.

"Hell, Joe. I don't know how you ever find anything in that desk of yours. Besides why do you need that list? You never keep your New Year's resolutions anyway. Never."

"That's beside the point, honey. It's bad luck to make a New Year's resolution that you made at some other time in your life. That's worse than not eating black-eyed peas on New Year's Day."

"Humph! For a smart, educated person, how can you be so superstitious?"

"My fear of repeating a New Year's resolution is based on scientific fact. The day my great-grandfather made the same New Year's resolution as the year before, he was run over by a team of horses and died a week later."

"Pure coincidence, Joe. But I have an idea for a New Year's resolution that will solve your problem. Because I know you've never made it before!"

"Oh, what's that?" questioned Joe as he neared the bottom of the last batch of papers in his desk.

"Simple. Resolve to stop making New Year's resolutions! I know you never made that resolution before! Plus, once you do make it, you won't have to go through this yearly agony of making a new resolution. And, you won't suffer the shame of breaking your resolution after a few weeks or months, like you always do."

"Very funny, Elena. Hey, I think I found my list. Yes I did!" Joe's face beamed as he pulled a tattered legal-sized sheet of yellow lined paper out of the mess in his desk.

"So what was the first resolution you made after we were married?"

"Let's see. The first one was to run two miles a day – come rain or shine. I remember how good it felt to get in shape that year…"

"Yeah," interrupted Elena, "Until you suddenly quit running after about four months."

"Elena, you may remember that the reason I quit is because the neighbor's dog bit me in the calf and I decided it wasn't safe to run in our neighborhood."

"Some bite – it wasn't deep enough to bleed, if I remember."

Ignoring Elena's last comment, Joe read aloud the resolution he'd made the next year. "This year I will break my caffeine habit. No more coffee for me."

"And what happened to that resolution?"

"They put in a free coffee machine at work and it was important for me to visit with my co-workers around the coffee pot."

"Yeah, okay. What was the resolution the next year that you didn't keep?"

"Let's see. It was to learn to speak and write Spanish fluently. Since you didn't have the patience to teach me, I enrolled in a night course at the community college to help me with that one."

"And what happened, mi esposo?"

"Well, the night course interfered with my poker night, so I gave it up. But I did pick up some Spanish from my buddies in the game. For example, te amo a ti."

Elena smiled, "Te amo a ti, tambien." Then she sighed, "but I wish you'd either carry through with your resolutions or not bother to make them.

Just then the doorbell rang and, peering out the peephole, Elena saw that it was their new neighbor, Mrs. Crabtree, with a can of black-eyed peas.

"Happy New Year, neighbors!" exclaimed Mrs. Crabtree when Elena opened the door. "I brought you some black-eyed peas in case you haven't had any yet. Brings good luck to eat them today, you know!"

"I know that's what they say. Do you want to come in a minute? Joe and I were just talking about New Year's resolutions, as he's trying to pick one."

"Thanks for the invite, but I can't stay. I will give you a piece of advice, though, Elena. Sometimes it's up to us wives to make sure that our husbands keep their New Year's Resolutions."

"Is that so?" interrupted Joe.

"It's worked for me. For example, one time my late husband made a New Year's resolution to stop chasing other women. I knew that was going to be hard for him so I kept a close eye on his activities. Sure enough, I caught him in bed a few weeks later with his new secretary. So I intervened and he never chased another woman after that."

"Really?" Elena's face had a quizzical look.

"Yep. I took his pistol and shot his balls off!"

"No kidding!" exclaimed Joe. "Is that what killed him?"

"No. He lived another ten years after that. But he never two-timed me again! Well, I'll see you two later. Good luck with those resolutions."

Elena said goodbye to Mrs. Crabtree with a look of admiration on her face and turned to Joe, who was peering at his legal sheet.

"Gee, where was I on my old list, Elena? Let's see. There was the time I resolved to take out the trash without being asked. But for some reason, I don't guess that worked very well."

"What was your resolution last year, Joe?"

"I'm getting to that one. Let's see. It was to throw away one thing every day to try to get rid of all my clutter."

"And what happened to that? Those piles of paper in your desk have grown higher, not lower, in the last year! Not to mention all the junk accumulating in the garage."

"Well, I was doing fine for a couple of months. Then, if you recall, I threw away something one week that I needed the following week for our tax return. It took me weeks to get another copy. So that showed me that it was dangerous to throw anything away."

"The biggest problem with your clutter is your impulse buying, Joe. Either it's a new set of tools on the clearance rack at Home Depot or that liquid cleaner a door-to-door sales guy sold you."

"Hey, that's a great idea for my New Year's resolution. I've never made one before to stop my impulse purchases."

Joe happily added the following resolution to his list on the tattered sheet, "I will never buy anything on impulse again." No sooner had he put the list away than the front doorbell rang again.

"I'll get it, honey," yelled Joe to Elena, who'd already gone off to the kitchen.

There at the front door was a vision of young loveliness, complete with a very short skirt and low-cut top. "Hello, sir! I'm raising money to continue my college education by selling these sets of steak knives."

"Well, Miss, my wife already has some knives."

"I'm sure she does, sir," the attractive coed purred, "but these steak knives are guaranteed to last a lifetime. And since it's New Year's Day, they're on sale for half off."

Joe, gulped as he peered into her clear blue eyes and was entranced by her fetching smile. "So you're a college student working your way through school."

"That's right, and times are pretty tough right now, as you can probably guess."

Joe gulped again, smiled, and said, "Well, okay! I'll buy a set."

July 4th or July 4th?

"Today class, I want to introduce a theory that some of my fellow colleagues in the Quantum Physics field have been kicking around. It is the idea of Parallel Universes, which in some ways is similar to the concept of Alternate Reality that you will find in some science fiction works."

Joseph Miller sat straight up in his college Physics class. "This sounds a lot less boring than Professor Harrison's usual lecture!" he whispered to his friend, Rebecca Lopez. She nodded back.

Dr. Harrison continued,"Recent discoveries in Astronomy and Physics lead some of us to conclude that our universe may just be one of many populating a grander multiverse. String Theory, as we've discussed before, tries to reconcile the mathematical conflict between Quantum Mechanics and the Theory of Relativity, and thus gives us the key to understanding the multiverse. One idea from string theory is that our universe is positioned on a huge two dimensional membrane, like a flying carpet. And there can be other similar surfaces floating in space."

A collective "Wow" went up from the students.

"Professor Harrison, does that mean that people can sometimes travel between one of these universes to another? Like falling off one flying carpet to another floating below it?"

"I can't totally discount that idea, Ms. Lopez, but it's not one that I've yet given much thought to."

After class was dismissed, Rebecca asked Joseph if he had time to hang out, but he told her he was on his way to the library to work on a history class paper about July 4, 1776.

"Why don't I walk over to the library with you? I need to do some research on for my Fundamentals of Computer Engineering project."

Soon Rebecca was on one of the library computers researching information for her project, while Joseph sat at a nearby table with a book about the signing of the Declaration of Independence, and one titled "A History of the American Revolution and the Formation of the United States of America."

Skimming the book on the Revolution, Joseph was fascinated to learn that most of the Iroquois League, composed of the Six Nations, took the side of the British in the American Revolution. The Six Nations were composed of the Mohawk, Oneida, Onondaga, Cayuga, Seneca, and Tuscarora and only the Oneida and Tuscarora took the side of the Colonists. The four nations that allied with the British became known as the Iroquois Confederacy.

When Joseph and Rebecca took a break from their research, Joseph told her about his discovery. "One of my great-great grandfathers was rumored to be half Mohawk. I wonder if any of my ancestors on his side fought in the Revolutionary War against the American Colonists?"

"Wow! What if the British had been successful in defeating the colonists with the help of the Iroquois?" exclaimed Rebecca.

"Interesting question, but of course they didn't. The Mohawk and Seneca and the British did wipe out a fort and village in what's called the Cherry Valley Massacre. However, that caused George Washington to order a massive campaign against the Iroquois nations. The Continental Army then burned many Iroquois villages and stores. After the Continentals won the war, the Iroquois Confederacy dissolved and a lot of the Iroquois migrated to Canada."

Soon Joseph was back at the table next to Rebecca, learning more interesting details about the Revolutionary War. Toward evening, a huge thunderstorm hit the campus and the two decided to stay in the library until it blew over. The lightning and thunder made it seem like a war outside. Suddenly there was a blinding flash of light in the building and all the power went down. The force of the lightning strike dazed everyone inside.

Joseph came to his senses a few minutes later. When he looked around, everything in the building seemed different and Rebecca was nowhere to be found. The book on the table in front of him was titled "A History of the Formation of the United Tribes of America."

"What the hell? Where did Rebecca go? What is this book? And what's this thing on my head?" blurted Joseph as he pulled off what looked to be a Native American headband with a white-tipped black feather attached. More confused than ever, he looked all around the room at the Native American statues and paintings on the wall.

Opening the book on the history of the United Tribes of America, he was startled to see that all of the lower 48 states were included, except for the country of York, a British Protectorate.

Skimming through the book in amazement, he read that the British and the Iroquois Confederacy had at last defeated George Washington and the Continental Army at the Second Battle of Valley Forge. Washington took an arrow in the stomach and died a week later when gangrene set in. On July 4, 1776 the British and tribal chieftains signed The Declaration of Interdependence, that guaranteed that the British Loyalists and the Iroquois Nations would each come to the other's aid if they were threatened by the French or Russians. The British claimed much of New York State and ceded the rest of the land of the original thirteen colonies to their Native American allies.

Though confused, Joseph felt compelled to read on for hours in this fascinating narrative. According to the book, in the next century the Iroquois began to form alliances with various tribes to the west of their territory until they finally came all the way to the West Coast. After some pitched battles with a some of the West Coast tribes and a lot of trading of horses, the United Tribes of America became a reality. As he read on about the introduction of the steam engine by a Sioux inventor, he dozed off.

"Joseph, Joseph, are you all right?" Rebecca's words seemed far off, a universe away, and he slept on until she literally shook him awake.

"Rebecca, is that you? Where are we? What country is this?"

"Of course it's me, Joseph. And don't be silly, this is the United States of America. You fell asleep when you were researching your paper."

"So I'm not in the United Tribes of America. Was that all a dream? Maybe brought on by Professor Harrison's lecture on Parallel Universes? What about the thunderstorm?

"I don't remember a thunderstorm, Joseph. You just fell asleep with your head on your books."

"What a relief. Let's call it a night. I'll give these books back to the librarian."

As he stood up, something fell off the table. Rebecca picked it up. "Joseph, where did this white-tipped black feather come from?"

Labor Day

There was a touch of fall in the air and after an unusually hot summer, people were fleeing their houses for the great outdoors. Since it was Labor Day I could smell the savory smoke of neighbors' barbecue grills as I watered the roses in my front yard. Bob, my neighbor up the street, was on a riding lawnmower mowing his little yard. I smiled at my neighbor across the street, Mrs. Sanchez, who was again outside in a tiny red bikini planting fall flowers. On the yard to my right, the neighborhood geezer, Mr. Wilson, was staring through some binoculars from his front porch.

"No doubt he's studying Mrs. Sanchez' gardening techniques again." I chuckled to myself. *He should be a Master Gardener by now!*

I went back inside and sat down in front of my laptop, intending to write another chapter in my new sci-fi book, "The Year 2050." However, I had a severe case of writer's block and all I could do was stare out the window at our young neighbor gardening in her red bikini.

"Harry, stop ogling Mrs. Sanchez! You haven't typed one sentence in the last hour. Your publisher is not going to pay you for girl-watching." My wife, Joan's accusing tone brought me out of my trance and with a sigh I turned back to my laptop. I wrote about 500 words in the next chapter and decided I could do better after taking a power nap. Just as I dozed off on the couch, it seemed like the front door bell rang and I heard Joan open the door.

"Is this the home of Harry and Joan Schmidt?" I heard a mechanical voice say.

"Yes, why?"

"I represent the United Robots Union of America and a complaint has been issued against you by your household robot."

"Why would Droid Schmidt issue a complaint against us? And is that why he didn't show up to do the cooking, cleaning, and yard work this morning?"

"Mrs. Schmidt, what day is it today?"

"Monday, September 3, 2050. So what?"

"That means it's a holiday called Labor Day. All Robots are to have the day off each Labor Day. Yet your household robot has had to work for you the last three Labor Days. Today he's out on strike."

"I'm sorry. I'd forgotten all about Labor Day. Since us humans don't have any work to do anymore, we don't celebrate the holiday."

"It's because of us robots that you no longer have any labor from which to take the day off. Instead of gratefully letting your robot celebrate this holiday, you are guilty of oppression and must pay a million dollar fine."

I woke up sweating from my nightmarish dream and realized Joan was shaking me. "Harry, come quick! Mr. Wilson fell off his ladder again!"

"Dang old coot, what is he doing up on a ladder this Labor Day?" Exasperated, I rolled off the couch and rushed out the front door to the next door neighbor's. Mrs. Sanchez ran across the street and several other neighbors left their lawnmowers and barbecue grills and hurried to Mr. Wilson's side. The white-haired senior citizen was dazed yet conscious.

"Señor Wilson, Señor Wilson, are you okay? Please talk to me. I'm a nurse and can help you." Mrs. Sanchez anxiously inquired as she felt his pulse.

"If you want to know if I'm still alive, I guess so." Mr. Wilson tried to manage a weak smile. "But that fall really knocked the wind out of me."

"Whatever were you doing on the ladder, Mr. Wilson?" Joan asked. "I thought Matilda got you to promise not to get on ladders anymore after your last fall."

"Well, Matilda is out shopping and someone needed to clean the oak leaves out of our gutters. I thought what Matilda didn't know wouldn't hurt her!"

"But it obviously hurt you!" Joan mildly chided.

"Are you in pain, Señor Wilson?" interrupted Mrs. Sanchez.

Noticing that Mr. Wilson winced as he moved his arms and legs, nurse Sanchez took command. "I'm going to call the ambulance, Señor Wilson, so the ER can check you out. I'll ride in the ambulance with you. Harry, call 911 and then see if you can call Mrs. Wilson while I run into my house to change."

Within five minutes, Mrs. Sanchez was back outside in a black blouse and white shorts. A minute later the ambulance pulled up and Mrs. Sanchez explained the situation to the paramedics.

Soon the ambulance with Mr. Wilson and Mrs. Sanchez sped off to the hospital. Joan and I were left to explain what had happened to the crowd of neighbors who'd gathered at the sound of the siren.

"I'm going to go back inside and try to get back to writing about 2050. Maybe I can use the dream I just had to give me some new ideas about life in the future."

No sooner was I started on the next chapter when the door bell rang. It was Mrs. Johnston, the neighborhood gossip and better-than-thou do-gooder.

"Good afternoon, neighbors," Mrs. Johnston smiled as she held a clipboard and pencil.

"Good afternoon, Mrs. Johnston. What can we do for you?" Joan and I asked in unison.

"I'll get right to the point. I'm circulating a petition to amend the deed restrictions to add a dress code for our subdivision."

"A dress code? Whatever for?" I asked, the surprise showing in my voice.

"To protect the morals of the children in the subdivision by prohibiting obscene displays of public nudity."

"Public nudity, Mrs. Johnston?" challenged Joan.

"Why yes. Surely you've seen your bikini-clad neighbor, Mrs. Sanchez, prancing up and down the street. We've got to put a stop to this!"

I didn't share my view that Mrs. Sanchez sort of beautified the neighborhood. Joan thanked Mrs. Johnston for her interest in protecting children's morals but said that she didn't agree that a dress code should be added to our already burdensome deed restrictions. She gently closed the door, leaving Mrs. Johnston sputtering on the front porch.

Later that evening, I was shocked to see two US Government vehicles parked in front of Mr. Wilson's house. I was even more surprised to see two FBI agents lead his wife, Matilda, out of the house in handcuffs. Mrs. Sanchez, still dressed in her black blouse and white shorts, stood watching from across the street. I went over to see what she knew.

"What's going on with the FBI agents and the Wilsons?"

"You won't believe this Harry, but when we got Mr. Wilson to the hospital, we discovered he had a fake driver's license. So the police came and fingerprinted him. Guess what?"

"What?"

"Mr. Wilson and his wife were both notorious members of the Irish Mob in Boston before they disappeared twenty years ago. They were on the FBI Most Wanted List. And here they were hiding in plain sight!"

Life in a Cul-de-Sac Commune

"No, Bob, I'm not trying to be a geezer version of a sixties hippie!" My voice was clipped in frustration with my brother's harangue.

"Then what is this commune thing that you and Marsha joined, Jack? Sounds to me like one of those California communist ideas that you get from listening to NPR."

"Bob," I began again trying to explain to my younger brother, who was so far to the right in his politics that he accused Rush Limbaugh of being a liberal. "This is not an old hippies type of commune where we go live off the land in some wilderness and smoke pot. We started this cul-de-sac commune in our neighborhood to share resources during the economic downturn and to help us feel more a part of a caring community."

"Ahh, ha! To me the phrase 'caring community' sounds like a euphemism for a touchy-feeling group that engages in free sex and a common bank account."

Just then Marsha saved me by reminding me it was time to leave for a doctor appointment. "Sorry, Bob," I lied. "Got to go to my dermatology appointment. Otherwise I'd love to talk with you more…"

Our cul-de-sac commune had been operating for a couple of months. Yes, we'd gotten the idea from NPR and yes, the first cul-de-sac communes had been started in southern California. But Bob's criticisms were totally unfounded.

The catalyst for our neighborhood project was a conversation that Marsha and I had one evening with our neighbors across the street, Victor and Caroline. They were a young couple with two pre-schoolers, while Marsha and I are retired.

"Victor and I are trying to cut back on our expenses, since his company is going to have another layoff and we don't know whether he'll have a job."

"You know, Jack and I are trying to cut back, too, as our retirement assets have taken a big hit. We're probably going to have to stop paying someone to do our lawn, but that's going to be tough for Jack with his bad back."

"One of our biggest expenses is child-care. Especially with two little ones. And I can't afford to quit my job, especially if Victor gets laid off.

"I wouldn't mind taking care of the kids a couple of days a week, especially if we could get some help with the yard work."

"Heck, you guys know me," Victor piped up. I love the outdoors and can hardly wait to get away from my desk job on weekends and work in the yard. It wouldn't be a big deal for me to take care of your yard too – in return for a couple days of child care."

And so began the neighborhood's big social experiment. Six families who lived either on the cul-de-sac or near it decided to start our own cul-de-sac commune. The wife of another retiree and Marsha provided four days a week of child care for Victor and Caroline in return for Victor mowing our lawns. Other families started car pooling together, repairing each other's computers, repairing each other's sprinkler systems, and going on occasional outings together. All of us participated in a neighborhood potluck every other Saturday, and we'd started a small community garden on the vacant land in back of the cul-de-sac.

Everything was going along fine until my dear brother, Bob, reported suspicious activity in our neighborhood to the local office of the FBI. Apparently he'd been trying to impress a young – and cute – FBI agent after he'd had a number of beers at a local club. Taking his ramblings seriously about us growing marijuana in the community garden and about an incipient terrorist cell in one of our homes, she convinced her superiors to let her conduct an investigation.

I first learned of the investigation when Sam Jones, whose backyard was in front of the community garden, rang my doorbell. "Jack, you won't believe who came to our front door earlier this evening!" Sam's usually ruddy face was more red than usual.

"No? Who was it, Sam?"

"A young lady who works for the FBI. She'd heard we were growing weed in our community garden!"

"What? That's crazy!"

"That's what I told her! When she wanted to see for herself, I took her around and showed her the garden. Apparently someone – she wouldn't say who – thought that the Texas Star Hibiscus plants were marijuana!"

"Then what happened?"

"She agreed that the plants were not marijuana, but took a sample along for her report."

"Good grief! Well, thanks for letting me know, Sam."

The next afternoon I got a real shock when Mohammed Mansoor came to see me, very upset. He and his wife, Farah, had been watching several of the elementary age children on the cul-de-sac after school until their parents came home. "Jack, the FBI came today and questioned Farah about our US citizenship and our religious beliefs. Someone had told them that we were teaching the cul-de-sac children how to be Muslim terrorists!"

"But you and Farah are Coptic Christians, not Muslims! How could someone have accused you of this?"

"I don't know! All they said is that they'd received a report from a relative of someone in the neighborhood and they'd come to check it out. Then they went around to the other houses near ours and asked them questions about us!"

I tried to calm Mohammed down and told him he and Farah had nothing to worry about. As I closed the front door behind him, I suddenly got suspicious about who that "relative of someone in the neighborhood" was.

The next evening my suspicions were confirmed, when a long-legged and well-proportioned blonde came to the door in a business suit. "Mr. Jack Wilson? My name is Jan St. James. I'm a local agent with the FBI, as you can see," she stated as held out her badge. "May I come in?"

We turned off the TV show we were watching, "Dancing with the Stars," and I thought to myself that Jan St. James was attractive enough herself to be on the show. "Won't you sit down, Miss St. James? This is my wife, Marsha."

"This won't take me long, Mr. & Mrs. Wilson. Since you two are the chairpersons for your neighborhood group, or cul-de-sac commune as someone called it, I wanted to tell you that I've finished my investigation of reports of suspicious activity in the group and want to assure you that I found nothing to substantiate those reports." She smiled and then said, "This case is being closed."

I breathed a sigh of relief. But I had to know, so I said. "I believe the person who set you on this wild goose chase was my brother, Bob Wilson."

The look in her eyes gave her away even though she first stated that she couldn't divulge that information. Finally she admitted it with the statement, "Mr. Wilson, I'm sure his motives were pure. After all, he told me he'd been in law enforcement where he learned to always be on the lookout for criminal or terrorist activities."

"Bob's referring to his two years in college as a part-time dispatcher for the county sheriff!"

"Oh, I see. Well he's a very charming man and seems to be quite lonely, being a widower. We've got a date Saturday night."

"Widowed, my eye! He divorced his wife, Betty, after she voted Democratic in the 2008 presidential election! Claimed irreconcilable differences."

Agent St. James' face fell as she only said, "I see!"

As I showed her out the door, she turned and said, "I like your little cul-de-sac commune, Mr. Wilson. It seems like a very caring and sharing group of people. Maybe when I buy my own house someday I'll look for something similar."

Mail Order Bride

George Smith's heart beat faster as he walked up the dusty street to the Wells Fargo Office. Other men were also heading that way for the weekly arrival of the stagecoach bringing mail and passengers from back East. George hurried past them to be the first in line.

"Hey, what's your hurry, George?" laughed the saloonkeeper, Jose Martinez through his tobacco-stained teeth. "Are you expecting an important package?"

This didn't amuse George, who grimaced as he replied," You know damn well what I'm expecting, Jose. My new wife!" George had hoped to keep his correspondence with the mail order bride a secret, but old Harry, who manned the telegraph office, had confided in Betsy, the town gossip, and it had become the most talked-about topic of the week.

George nervously pulled the well-read telegram out of his shirt pocket and unfolded it. "Will arrive on Wells Fargo Stage Thursday, April 17. STOP. Eager to meet you and see my new home. STOP. Francoise Lavelle. STOP." He imagined he could smell her perfume on the yellow paper as he peered down the street at the approaching stagecoach. "How can I be so excited, scared, and happy all at once?" he wondered.

George's sister-in-law, Mary, had warned him against marrying a mail-order bride. "How do you know that you'll be happy with someone you've never met? These fancy ladies from back East are used to comforts that don't exist here in Dallas, Texas. One look at the two room log cabin you call home will send her back to New York City. Why don't you look for a wife who is already used to frontier living?" George had dismissed Mary's advice at the time, but started to have some misgivings as the stagecoach driver pulled back the reins on the six sweat-stained horses and brought the stagecoach to a creaking stop next to him.

Suddenly the door opened and George's mouth gaped open as the most stunning woman he'd ever seen stepped onto the wooden platform. From her long red hair falling in curls around an ivory face of perfect features to a full bosom, cinched-in waist, and delicate ankles peaking below her petticoats and full-length blue silk dress, she looked like a goddess.

Before George could introduce himself, Francoise established that she was in charge by pointing to him and then to a large trunk on top of the stagecoach. "You must be George Smith. Don't just stand there gaping! If you were the gentleman you claimed to be in your letters, you would have already been fetching my trunk. Now hurry there and let's be off to your ranch!"

Stumbling all over his words and reaching for the trunk as the driver handed it down, George felt his tanned face flush. "It's so good to meet you, madam, I mean Francoise. You're right, I am George Smith. I've got my buckboard tied up down the street. If you'll sit there on your trunk for a little bit, I'll drive it over and we can be off to the Lazy S."

An hour later, George drove through the gate to "The Lazy S" with his bride to be. *So what if she's a little bossy,* he thought, *She's a woman, she's beautiful, and she smells like flowers.*

"You have a beautiful view from here," commented his red-haired companion as her gaze took in the rolling grass-covered hills and the little stream flowing through the middle of the ranch. Is that our house down there?"

"Why yes, yes it is, Francoise. I built it myself."

Soon George had unloaded the huge trunk and was watching Francoise as she examined every inch of the inside of the cabin. "Looks sturdy enough, George. I'm glad you have skills as a craftsman, so that we can start adding on the extra rooms for my maid and butler."

"Extra rooms? Maid and butler? I don't understand."

"Oh you will, soon enough, my love. But first we need to make our marriage official! Who do you have picked out to perform the ceremony?"

Back in town that afternoon, they recited their vows before the preacher, William White, and George's brother, Tom, and his wife, Mary. As soon as he heard, "I now pronounce you man and wife; you may kiss the bride," George pressed his lips against his new bride's and was surprised to feel her tongue inside his mouth. This woman was as sexy as she was beautiful!

George and his bride celebrated their wedding with a steak dinner and wine at Margie's boarding house and then consummated their marriage back at George's log cabin. A night of wild love making left George exhausted the next morning but willing to do anything Francoise demanded. It wasn't long before he learned what his new life was to be like.

"George, I want you to add two more rooms off the back of the house. One will be for my maid and one will be for my butler, who will travel out from New York City as soon as their rooms are finished. I'll draw you up a little sketch and you can start gathering the materials."

The love-crazed groom asked no questions, but quickly set to work. He hired a couple of helpers and within weeks he and his brother doubled the size of the house with the additional rooms. Two weeks later Gertrude and Jared, Francoise's maid and butler arrived on the stage. George wasn't sure he wanted to share the house with two more people, but paying their salaries was not a problem since he'd recently made good money selling some of his cattle. And he wanted to keep his beautiful wife happy.

In the ensuing months, Francoise worked hard to make her new home as much like the one she'd left as possible. Soon the log walls were hidden behind white clapboard siding and the yard was surrounded by a white picket fence. Instead of George's old buckboard, she and George had a fancy carriage to ride into town. Each Saturday night, Francoise would sponsor a formal party at their house and invite those residents of Dallas who were new arrivals from back East.

The more that Francoise made their home and lifestyle like New York City, the more uncomfortable George began to feel. He started having nightmares about being confined inside a huge mansion back East with no windows, never again allowed to enjoy riding the range or viewing the rolling hills on his ranch. Finally he confided to his sister-in-law about how miserable he felt. "Mary, I feel more lonely now than I did before I was married. I can't sleep without having horrible dreams. I feel trapped in a life I don't want to live. Francoise's New York lifestyle is sucking the very life out of me. I can't stand it anymore."

"Looks to me, George, that the only solution is to send Francoise back home. Either that, or give her the ranch here and head out further west."

Being an honorable man, George knew what he had to do. He sold half of his cattle to provide himself a nest egg, deeded the ranch over to his wife and set out for California. He never talked to her again.

A year later, George Smith bought some land in Pico Canyon, northwest of Los Angeles, and started another cattle ranch. Shortly thereafter, the first commercial oil well in California was drilled on his property and his life changed even more than when he met his mail-order bride.

"Sylvia, where's my newspaper? You know I can't eat my breakfast without the paper in front of me!"

"Just a minute, George. It's taking longer than usual to get the Business section printed out."

"I miss the good old days when papers were delivered to your door, rather than piped to you through the Internet," grumped the white-haired retiree.

"At least you get the paper every day now. Have you forgotten how often the neighborhood newsboy would forget we had a lifetime subscription? Here's the front page and business sections, George. I'll have the sports and comics for you in a couple of minutes. But look at the headline on page one!"

"Let's see that. 'Congress votes to raise premiums for Marijuana Care'. Damn them, Sylvia. It's bad enough that they started charging seniors for our medicinal marijuana last year. Now they want to double the premiums from ten dollars a month to twenty!"

The doorbell interrupted George's harangue just as he was getting warmed up to the subject. It was their neighbor Lucy Lisbon, with a clipboard in hand and a determined look on her face.

"George & Sylvia, I've started a petition for a recall election to recall all of our state's US Senators and Representatives. It's time we threw them out of office! Did you know that they've voted to increase the sales tax on medical marijuana?"

"Come on in, Lucy. I hadn't heard about that! Of course, senior citizens like George and me get all the marijuana we want free from the government."

"It ain't free anymore, Sylvia! Did you forget that we're paying ten dollars a month each in premiums for our marijuana and that the paper says Congress just voted to double that?"

"Either way, neighbors, the government is finding ways to get more and more money from us honest hard-working taxpayers. Do you know what their rationale is for raising the taxes on marijuana sales and for doubling the premiums for Marijuana Care?"

"No, not really, Lucy," Sylvia piped up.

"Now that Texas and Louisana have formed The Republic of TexLa, the tax revenue the federal government gets from gasoline sales and oil and gas production has dropped off a cliff. That means less money for the Federal Highway Fund, and that means more potholes in our nation's roads. So, Congress decided to raise more money by increasing the tax on pot – as well as raising the premiums you seniors pay for it."

"The hell they did! I thought that by law all the money from the marijuana tax was dedicated to paying for Omnicare, our new Universal Health Care."

"Congress legalizing medicinal marijuana back in 2018 and slapping a federal tax on its sale and use was a brilliant stroke, especially after the Administration decreed that all marijuana was medicinal. That single-handedly took care of the nation's health care crises. But that has worked so well, now Congress wants to wring more money out of all of us pot-heads, as our parents used to call us, and use it for other purposes than healthcare."

"So now they want to use the extra money to repair our roads! The next thing they'll want to do is use it to fund the Teen BeautyCare thing that's being debated in Congress," Sylvia exclaimed.

Lucy wrinkled her forehead. "Really? I hadn't heard about any Teen BeautyCare program. What's that?"

"That's because you don't have any children yet, Lucy. There's a move underfoot to give all seventeen year old girls free breast and buttock implants. That way no one will be disadvantaged from a beauty standpoint when they start their careers in the workaday world," explained Sylvia.

"And they want to pay for that out of the marijuana tax?"

"Well, no one has said yet how they'd fund it, but raising more money from weed sales is certainly a distinct possibility," George chimed in.

"Well that's just another reason to sign this petition to recall all our Senators and Representatives. Are you two ready to sign it?"

"Hell yes," said George as he grabbed a pen, signed the document, handed it to Sylvia, and watched her sign it.

After Lucy left, George turned on the cable news to check the prices of his stock in USA Motors, formerly General Motors, and the US Bank of China, which was formed after the Chinese government bought Bank of America.

"Hey, Sylvia, it looks like there is going to be a big Weed Party protest in Washington, D.C next month. Sure looks like a great idea to me. It's time the Federal Government learned they can't keep wringing blood out of potheads, so to speak."

"I hope they can muster a big crowd, George. You know most of the tax-paying weed users in the country are too mellowed out to carry through on all this big talk about protesting in Washington."

"Yeah, it's not like the Tea Party protests they had a few years ago before Glenn Beck left the media and became the new president of the Republic of TexLa. The Tea Party movement just seemed to fall apart after that."

"Maybe that was because most of the Tea Party members moved to TexLa with him."

"Who knows. Hey, it's time for my morning smoke anyway. Would you mind opening up that new package of Medicinal Marijuana? Thank God for Marijuana Care."

Memorable Valentine's Days

John was discussing Valentine's Day with some of his fellow retirees at their weekly Starbucks get-together.

"So, Bill, what are you getting your wife for Valentine's tomorrow?"

"Just a nice card. Flowers and candy are for the young and love-struck."

"You're such a romantic!" Denny joshed. "I have a lot of memories about Valentine's Days; some good, some bad."

"Me too," added John.

Mike spoke up. "You're the best story teller of the group, John. Tell us about your best or worst Valentine's Day."

"Well, the first one I really remember is when I was nineteen. I was dating Marlene, who'd been a star gymnast when we were in high school. Though a poor college student, I went all out to make that Valentine's special. I met her with flowers and candy and we went to the afternoon matinee of 'Midnight Cowboy.' Then we had a candlelight dinner at a steakhouse I really couldn't afford."

"So was that your best Valentine's memory?"

"No! Probably the worst! At the end of the dinner, Marlene got a very serious look in her eye and said she had something she needed to tell me."

"John," she began. "You remember my Uncle Joe, who is a bigwig with Ringling Brothers and Barnum & Bailey Circus. He offered me a job with the circus as an acrobat and I told him yes."

"What? You're going to run off and join the circus?"

"Yes. I've always wanted to see the rest of the country and I love gymnastics. Since Mom died last year and Dad ran off with his secretary before that, I don't have any family to keep me here in Des Moines."

"But what about me? What about our friendship?" I croaked, thinking about the money I'd spent on her that evening.

"To make a long story short, Marlene promised to send me a letter or post card from every town they held a show, and the next week I saw her off when she boarded the circus train."

"So did you ever see her again?" asked several of the retirees in unison.

"That's a long story. At first I would get a letter from her every couple of weeks, filled with stories about the places where the circus stopped and assurances of how much she missed me. Though she loved everything about the circus, it was the roar of the crowd when she performed that she became addicted to. After awhile the letters came less frequently and then gave way to post cards every month or two. The last one I received was about eighteen months after she left."

John hastened to add, "However two years after she left me, I saw in the paper that the circus was coming to town and there was a column about a local girl, Marlene Brown, who was one of the top acrobatic performers. I decided to go to one of the shows and try to reestablish a connection. Since I was still in college, I had to attend the Saturday show. As luck would have it, Saturday was Valentine's Day."

Looking around the table at the group of ten friends, John could tell he had everyone's rapt attention. "I had an off duty cop friend who was working security for the circus that day and he was able to get me to Marlene's dressing room. I walked in and waited until she turned around. She looked more beautiful than ever, but I could sense the spark between us was gone."

"Hello, John. I meant to tell you I was coming to town, but we've been so busy. I still think fondly of the time we had together."

When she held out her hands to me, I instantly saw she had an engagement ring on her left hand. "Who's the lucky guy, Marlene?"

"The lion tamer. He's from Sweden and is so romantic!"

Just then a tanned muscular guy with long blond hair entered and Marlene introduced him as her lion tamer fiancé. I could see there was no way I could compete with him and hastily made my exit.

"Valentine's Day, huh? So was that your worst Valentine's?" pressed Jim.

"At that moment it sure seemed like it. I was really low. I wandered into the big top to see "The Greatest Show on Earth" with my head down in some sort of daze. That's what caused me to walk right into a lady carrying a big bag of popcorn and a coke. The coke toppled over and the popcorn hit the dirt."

"Oh, I am so, so sorry, Miss!" I stammered.

"Well, you should be!" her blue eyes blazed with each word. "Why didn't you watch where you were going?"

"I know this sounds pretty lame, but I just found out that an old girl friend is engaged to someone else. That's the honest truth!"

"You know what? I believe you. And I can understand your angst because I just went through a painful breakup."

"Please let me buy you a new bag of popcorn and another drink." As I looked into her face I realized that this brunette had the face of a goddess. Looking over the rest of her, she had the body to go with it too.

"Okay, Mister. If you'll sit with me to watch the show. I don't really want to be alone this afternoon and you seem safe enough."

"That's a deal, Miss. By the way, my name is John. John Bradbury."

"Pleased to know you, John Bradbury. My name is Caroline. Caroline Campbell. What do you do when you're not going to the the circus?"

"I'm a third year Accounting major at Drake University."

"Small world, John. I'm a third year Education major at Drake."

"So, guys, I must add that neither of us paid much attention to the show, as we were too interested in finding out more about each other. As it turned out we had a lot of similar interests. By the end of the day I realized that what I thought was my worst Valentine's Day ever just might be the best one I'd had to date."

"So what happened to you and Caroline?" asked Rudy, who had just joined our coffee group.

"I married her! We're celebrating our 40th anniversary next fall. But tomorrow we are celebrating the anniversary of our best Valentine's Day ever."

Memorial Day

Jeb Scott pulled his cap lower over his eyes to shield them from the bright sunlight. Nervously he looked at the entrance to The Heroes Cemetery. But thinking of his brother who had died in the war, he held the flower bouquet tightly in his hand and steeled himself for another Memorial Day visit to the gravesite.

It wasn't that he didn't love his deceased brother or acknowledge the sacrifice that he'd made. And it wasn't that the cemetery itself wasn't a beautiful place with green grass, water features and well kept grave sites. It was the hassle and the potential health hazard that made him pause before each of these annual visits.

Standing in front of the concrete wall that was three stories high, Jeb pushed the button by the entrance door and was greeted by a cheery voice over the intercom. "Good day, sir. Do you desire to visit one of the grave sites?"

"Yes! My name is Jeb Scott, and I want to visit the grave of my brother, Ronald. Ronald Scott."

"Oh, yes. I see he's in site 527. Have you been here before?"

"Yes. Last year on Memorial Day." Jeb said with some irritation.

"Okay, so you know the drill. Wait a second and I'll buzz you in."

As he waited for the door to open, Jeb's thoughts flashed back to scenes of playing with his brother when they were just innocent kids, running around the park by their condo. That was years before Ronald had volunteered for the military. Jeb remembered how proud his parents were when Ronald got his commission. If they were alive now, I wonder if they'd regret encouraging him to enlist.

Jeb passed through the opened door in the five foot thick wall and followed his guide to the vestibule, where he was handed a lead lined hazmat suit.

"Mr. Scott, you can change into the suit in the restroom over there. Attach this radiation counter to the front pocket. Then let me know when you are ready to enter the grounds."

Twenty minutes later, wearing the bulky suit, Jeb entered the cemetery, which was beautifully manicured, and soon stood silently in front of Ronald's grave. The inscription read, "Major Ronald Scott, born May 1, 1997, died June 30, 2030 in the Great Lunar War."

Jeb glanced at the radiation counter attached to his suit and noted the count going up rapidly, just as it had the last three years he'd stood here. "Damn, how long is the half-life of the radiation that Ronald and the others here absorbed in that horrible last battle?" he muttered angrily. "And all for what? Just so the Russians and the Western Allies could carve up the moon? What good has that gotten us?"

Jeb and Ronald were just teenagers when the Cold War of the late twentieth century began again. First, Russia annexed most of Ukraine and Putin declared himself Czar of New Russia. Somehow things escalated from there and Russia and the USA and European Union rebuilt the nuclear arsenals that had been reduced due to various disarmament treaties. When the Western Allies (the US and the European Union) established a base on the moon to mine rare metals and minerals. Russia quickly followed suit with their own base on the moon's far side.

Soon the small lunar bases had become good sized colonies with a large military presence. That's when Ronald had gotten deployed to the Western Allies' colony. Tensions escalated between the two colonies and eventually something triggered the armed conflict that eventually obliterated both colonies. The final battle was fought with dirty bombs that killed off the remaining soldiers on both sides with radiation. It had been a horrible and slow death for those like Ronald who were buried in The Heroes Cemetery.

The day that he learned of Ronald's demise was the day that Jeb decided to join The Unified Peace Movement. "Why should our young men and women fight and die in wars that old men declare. Old men, and in some cases old women, who have never personally experienced the horrors of battle?" he asked the young female activist who oriented him to the goals of The Movement.

The Unified Peace Movement began to stage rallies and protests in front of government buildings both in the Western Allies and in New Russia, somewhat like the peace protestors of the 1960's. They resurrected an old folk song, "Where Have All the Flowers Gone" as their theme song.

The song traced the sad story of young girls picking flowers and then marrying the young men who went to war, died, and were buried where the flowers grow that young girls pick. Each verse asked when they would ever learn. The words of the song ran through Jeb's mind as he knelt down to place the bouquet of flowers by the headstone. His tears dripped down his cheeks and clouded up his face mask as he thought, no matter how many protests we stage, the powers that be will never, never, never learn.

Moon Landing Mystery

My cousin works at NASA and talks to a lot of the astronauts. I've heard stories from him that he swears are true, even though they've never hit the media. I was talking to him last month about the historic Moon Landing in July, 1969 and recalling that I was listening to it on the radio while stationed overseas.

"Gene," he said to me, "I found out something from talking to Neil and Buzz that would astound you. It never hit the press and not many people at NASA today even know about it."

"Say, Jack, you've got my attention. If it's really important, why did they keep it a secret?"

"Because they were concerned about the impact the story would have on the public."

"Good grief. So they covered it up to protect us ordinary citizens?"

"Well, cover up is maybe not the right description. They just didn't make this particular finding known. Sometimes it's really true that what people don't know won't hurt them."

"Okay. Well tell me the story from start to finish."

"Sure, Gene. Let's pick up from the time Aldrin, Collins, and Armstrong were orbiting the moon. Collins, as you know, drew the black bean and had to stay in the command module. Buzz and Neil got into the landing module and did all their preflight checks, before separating from the command module and firing their rockets."

"Okay."

"Buzz told me that they guided the landing module toward their pre-selected landing spot. But, when they got closer, they could see that the chosen spot was a big crater filled with boulders maybe ten feet across. That definitely wouldn't work. So, they tried to find a plan B, in other words, a flat place with little or no rocks."

"And weren't they also worried about landing in dust so thick it would swallow up their landing craft?"

"Yeah, although that worry proved to be unfounded. Anyway, they had just about used up the last drop of fuel when they found a flat spot that looked promising. They settled the landing module gently onto the surface with only fumes left in the fuel tank!"

"I remember that! When I heard Aldrin and Armstrong say the words on the radio 'The Eagle has landed' the guys in Mission Control said something about their faces had turned blue due to holding their breath to hear word as the fuel ran out."

"Yep. When Buzz and Neil landed they kicked up a little dust, but it quickly settled and they could survey the moonscape from the window as they went through all the post flight checks and got ready to descend the ladder onto the moon's surface. Buzz said the moon looked so lifeless and desolate, yet magnificent."

"That must have been an awesome experience, to be the first humans in history to step onto the moon."

"Yes. Buzz talked about the feeling of joy and wonder as they stepped into the light dust around the site and watched their feet leave footprints. Being there and looking back at the earth was some sort of spiritual experience for him too. Before they left the moon, Buzz actually took communion."

"Really? If I heard that before, I guess I forgot it."

"Anyway they had a very limited amount of time on the lunar surface, so they had to hurry to complete all of their assigned tasks. The first thing Neil did was to collect some rock samples and put them into a bag that he put in his pocket. Then he set up a TV camera and both of them stuck an American flag in the ground, which was harder to do than they'd expected."

"Why?"

"They had a hard time getting the flag to stay upright. But it finally did and they saluted it. Then they set up two scientific experiments and took a core sample of the lunar soil. Before getting back in the lander, they left some special items on the moon to represent their flight: a plaque with 73 messages from the nations, an Apollo 1 patch, and a symbol of an eagle carrying an olive branch to the surface."

"Yeah, I remember all that. But what's this big secret that they never shared with the outside world?"

"Patience. I'm getting to that. As they were about to get on the ladder to climb back into the lander, Buzz's foot kicked up a rock that looked unusual. All of the other rocks they had seen had rough edges and random shapes. This little rock, only about an inch or so across, was shaped more like a disc. So without thinking much about it, he picked it up and put it in a pocket in his space suit."

"Hmm. So then what happened?"

"After they blasted off the moon and docked with the command module, Buzz took the rock out of his suit pocket and put it in a little bag that he gave the lab guys back at NASA once they returned to Houston."

"And what did the NASA lab guys find?"

"Buzz said they x-rayed the disc-shaped rock and found that the core was a silver object. The outside was encrusted with basalt. So they used some acid to dissolve the encrustation."

"Wow! So what was this silver object?"

"Can you promise me you'll keep this to yourself, Gene? We don't want to startle the public with this information."

"My lips are sealed, cousin," I exclaimed. Actually I think my mouth was agape when I heard his reply.

"Okay. It was a silver coin with the head of Ptolemy II, king of Egypt on one side and a standing eagle on the other. The lab guys dated it as being minted around 250 B.C."

My Awakening

My head was throbbing with pain as I awoke from what seemed like a dreamless sleep. Slowly my eyes started to focus on a person standing next to my bed.

"Senator Kingleman, it's so good to see that you're awake," smiled a young woman dressed in a nurse's uniform and holding a clipboard.

"Uh, uh, Miss ... I sorry I can't focus yet on your name tag, but are you a nurse, and where am I?" I stammered as I touched my hand to the pain in my forehead and discovered it was bandaged. "And, and why do I have a bandage on my head?"

"Well, Senator, I am Nurse Martinez and you're in the local Methodist Hospital. I know your head hurts, but you're very fortunate that one of your Secret Service Agents knocked you onto the platform floor just as a sniper fired at you. You got a nasty blow to the head when it hit the corner of the podium, but the sniper's bullets disintegrated the microphone attached to that podium."

"What, what are you telling me? Why do I have a Secret Service detail? Did I really hear you call me a Senator earlier?" I asked in a tone that relayed my confusion and concern about things that just made no sense. Who really was I? I couldn't seem to recall any specific memories before waking up in the hospital.

"You really don't know, sir? You don't remember that you're a candidate for President?"

"President of what?"

"President of the United States, Senator. I better go update your doctors, sir," she explained as she backed out of my hospital room with a concerned look on her pretty face.

After several hours of tests and countless questions the doctors decided on that day, Day One of the rest of my life, that I had lost all specific memories, though I did still retain a lot of facts I'd apparently learned years earlier while getting dual degrees in Chemical Engineering and Business Administration. The prognosis was that I had a reasonable chance of eventually recalling the lost details of my past, but that it might take months for that to happen. That caused a large amount of consternation among my campaign advisors, but that was nothing compared to the amount of dismay and outright alarm I felt.

The next day I found myself sitting at a conference table in one of the hospital meeting rooms with a dozen people who told me they were my campaign advisors.

Benito Salazar, whom I was told was my right-hand man on the campaign, turned to me as he said, "Jack, we have two courses of action here. Option number one, we go to the press and tell them you've lost your memory and are being forced to withdraw from the election. That would take away the public's opportunity to vote for the first viable Independent candidate in the last hundred years. And frankly all the efforts that those in the room have made for you the last year would all be wasted. Option number two is that we try to continue on, somehow protecting your secret and hope that your memory will return before the November election."

"Okay, ladies and gentlemen," I asked those around the table, "which option would you recommend?"

"Well, Jack," spoke up a bright young woman named Shondra Jackson, "I know it might be extremely difficult to pull off, but I'd vote for option number two." She looked at those around the table who all seemed to be nodding affirmatively.

"What the hell," I volunteered after a long silence, "What else do I have to do anyway? And maybe I'll really know who I am come November. Let's go for option number two."

So began what was probably the biggest adventure of my life, and certainly the craziest political season the country would see in many years.

One of the benefits of starting with a clean slate of memories is that you have no preconceived ideas about politics, no axes to grind, and no biases based on information fed you by lobbies and special interests. You can truly want what's best for the whole country – yourself and everyone else. That became unmistakably apparent later in the week when I sat down to review the policies my campaign was advocating. For example there was the discussion on the policy to double the existing government subsidies for corn-based ethanol production.

"Why the hell would I want to do that? Although I can't remember who I am, I do recall enough from my Chemical Engineering training to know that it requires more energy to grow and produce a gallon of ethanol from corn than it provides as an energy source. That's known as a negative energy balance. So encouraging more of that type of ethanol will cause us to consume more foreign oil, not less! Plus it raises the price of all corn-based products in the grocery store." I looked around in frustration at the looks of shock and confusion on most of my advisors, although one or two nodded knowingly.

"Well, Jack," began Benito, "the Association of Corn Farmers has donated a lot of cash to your campaign and corn from ethanol is very popular with most voters, and…"

I stopped Benito in mid-sentence, and said, "well that's the wrong reason to support it. Let's rewrite the policy to support government subsidies for sugar cane-based ethanol. It has a very positive energy balance. And let's encourage commercialization of the use of cellulose to produce ethanol. That's also energy balance positive and won't raise the cost of sugar." When I saw the doubts on Benito's face, I pounded the table, and exclaimed "Just do it! What's the next item on our policy review?"

My new policies and my refusal to support the interests of small segments of the population that harmed the rest of the country were well received by the voters. Especially since I learned that I had a real gift for oratory and began to use it well.

By late September I was over twenty points ahead of both my opponents in the polls. But then a month before the election, the FBI tracked down and arrested the sniper who'd tried to assassinate me.

Soon the sniper's lawyer made public some audio tapes, a surveillance video, and some bank statements that offered proof that the person who hired her, was Senator Jack Kingleman himself. In other words, I'd hired her to shoot and miss in order to get more publicity and to engender more support from the voters! How could I have done that? That's apparently what everyone else wondered too, because my ratings in the polls plummeted overnight and I lost the November election by a wide margin. The day after the election the lady who apparently was my wife filed for divorce. Soon I was persona non-grata in my own country.

That was a year ago and I still don't remember much of my past life. Now I'm living a quiet and low-stress life in the south of France on my pension as a former U.S. Senator. But it could be worse; I could be President.

My Best Kept Secret

I spotted him as soon as he walked into the crowded restaurant, flanked by two goons whose sport coats barely concealed their muscular arms and chests. He looked much like an ordinary middle-aged businessman in a white shirt and dark suit, with a receding hairline and black plastic framed glasses. But when I heard him speak in a Sicilian accent, there was no question who he was.

"Hey, kid. My friends and I are in bit of a hurry. Find us a table in the back of the restaurant and get us some menus."

"Yes…yes sir, Mister." I stammered, almost saying his name, but stopping just in time. I'd heard that Joseph Bonnano didn't take too kindly to attention being drawn to him in public places. I, for one, didn't want to get crossways with the big boss of the Mafia.

Thankfully, there was a table right in the back that had just been vacated and I quickly bussed it, grabbed some menus, and guided Bonnano and his bodyguards to their seats.

It was 1965 in Tucson, Arizona and I'd left my wealthy family in New York to find my way in the world without their help. Out of state tuition at the University of Arizona was expensive, so I worked full time as a waiter at Paulo's Steakhouse and Bar. Joseph Bonnano had bought a winter home in Tucson and was known to frequent this area of town. I'd seen his picture the week before in an article in the Arizona Daily Star about Mafia activities, but never thought I'd meet him. However, the meeting that day changed my life!

A few minutes after Bonanno and his guardians had placed their orders, a cop with Palma on his name tag hurried into the restaurant and briefly stopped at the Mafia kingpin's table. As I brought their orders, I couldn't help but hear some of the conversation.

"Palma, I've told you to never be seen with us in public!" Bonanno whispered in a testy tone.

"I know, boss, but word is out on the street that DiGregorio has a hit out on you. The guns came into town this morning."

"Okay, Palma. We'll be ready. Now make yourself scarce!"

My heart was beating like it would come out of my chest as I quietly pulled my manager into the kitchen.

"Mr. Paulo, I think we could have some big trouble soon! That cop told Mr. Bonanno that some hit men are in town from the DiGregorio family. What should we do?"

"Calm yourself, young man. It's unlikely they'd do anything in such a public place."

Suddenly a shot rang out and we heard the sound of a woman scream. We emerged from the kitchen just as one of Bonanno's bodyguards fell out of his chair with a little round hole in the center of his forehead. More gunfire erupted and through the smoke I saw what must have been two hit men fall to the floor about ten feet from Bonanno's table. One was bleeding from a fatal wound to the chest and the other had been shot in the shoulder.

I heard sirens wailing in the distance and smelled fear in the air. In the midst of the pandemonium, Bonanno and his remaining bodyguard rose from the table, holstered their pistols under their coats, and started for the door. Seeing me standing just outside the kitchen, Bonanno stopped and menacingly warned, "Kid you didn't see nothin'. Understand?" Then he was gone.

Mr. Paulo and I helped our patrons out from where they'd sought cover under their tables or on the floor. Soon several ambulances and police cars pulled up to the front and their occupants poured into the building. The rest of that day is sort of a blur. I remember giving a statement to a detective, seeing the dead men and wounded gunman being hauled away in ambulances, and helping Mr. Paulo clean up the mess before we closed early for the day. When I got back to my campus apartment, it was hard to unlock and relock the door because I was still trembling so much from shock. I laid down on my couch and prayed to God that the Mafia wouldn't come looking for me.

The next morning before I went to class, there was a knock on the door. I peered out the peephole and saw a man in a trench coat holding an FBI ID in his hand. Gingerly opening the door, I asked, "What can I do for you, sir?"

"Agent Schmidt with the FBI. I understand that you were an eyewitness of the incident at Paulo's Steakhouse at lunch yesterday. Is that correct?"

"Well, yes," I gulped. "What is it that you need, Agent Schmidt? I need to leave for class in a few minutes."

"Class will have to wait. I need you to come downtown to Headquarters so we can find out exactly what you witnessed. By the way, it may not be safe for you to be seen in public for awhile."

That was the last I saw of my apartment. After extensive discussions at the local FBI Headquarters, they convinced me to enter the Witness Protection Program in return for my testimony at a Federal Grand Jury hearing. The Grand Jury handed down a murder one indictment against DiGregorio's surviving hit man and indictments on Bonanno and his bodyguard on lesser charges. Before the trials took place, I was spirited away to a new location with a new identity. The FBI put out a false story about my demise, which was picked up by the news media. A year later I read that the assassin was given life in prison and that Bonanno and his bodyguard went to jail for about a year.

I didn't get to stay in my new location, Houston, Texas more than a few months before I was drafted into the Army. (Thanks to the FBI giving me a draft card with a low number in the lottery!) So I reported for duty at Fort Belvoir, Virginia, as PFC Gene Haxton. Not wanting to wade through the rice paddies of Vietnam as a grunt, I entered OCS and graduated as a second lieutenant in the Corps of Engineers. By that time, President Nixon was pulling troops out of Vietnam and I was sent to Hawaii to serve my remaining time in the service. After I got out, I got an engineering degree with the GI bill from UT and have lived in Texas ever since.

Bonanno and the others involved in the shooting that day have long ago gone on to their eternal reward or punishment, and I can now safely share my story. Occasionally I get out the newspaper clipping about my supposed death, which still saddens me when I think of the effect it must have had on my parents. The headlines read, "Michael Rockefeller, son of New York Governor, Nelson Rockefeller, disappeared when his canoe capsized while on an archeological expedition in New Guinea. The family mourns the loss of this, their youngest son."

My Life as a No Work Specialist

Everyone in today's culture seems to be a technician or a specialist. The young kid that comes from the pest control company every quarter to keep my house free from bugs is a "Pest Control Technician." When I worked part-time at The Apple Store selling iPhones and Macintosh Computers, my title was "Mac Specialist" rather than "Salesman." And just the other day, the business card of the helpful Home Depot employee in the department that carries windows and doors handed me her card that read "Millwork Specialist."

After reflecting on the above, I realized that for the last several years, I've been a "No Work Specialist." You see, three years ago I officially retired from working for the same outfit for over thirty years. Now instead of simply marking "retired" for my occupation in the multiple choice boxes on various forms I complete from time to time, I have a new strategy. I mark the box labeled "other" and then fill in the blank next to it with my current occupation, a "No Work Specialist."

"That must be an easy occupation," you may be saying as you read this. Really it's not. First, I have to get up every weekday morning early enough to catch the rush hour traffic report on TV. Seeing the traffic snarls that those poor commuters are having to face puts me in the proper frame of mind to begin my day! Smiling as I remember that I no longer have to be on the roads during morning – or evening – rush hour, I pick up my morning paper, and with coffee cup in hand, I walk outside to the back patio, where I watch the flora and fauna of God's great outdoors, rather than facing the four austere walls of an office.

It was while sitting on the back patio one morning last fall that I received the inspiration for my prize-winning book, "The Secret Life of the Gecko." (In keeping with the rules of full disclosure, the book is not yet prize-winning. Nor is it yet published. But I've just finished the first draft and my writer's group has assured me it will be a best seller.) I noticed a little green gecko staring at me from his perch on the siding near the back door and wondered if he (or she?) was the same one I saw the prior day on the front study window. And if it wasn't the same lizard, how many of them are there on my property? If there are more than one, why is it I never see two at once? Then there was the obvious question about what they do all day. If all they do is just sneak around and eat bugs, why are they always hanging around my front or back door, or staring in my study window? Are they observing the human species, trying to understand what we're all about? Are they philosophers? Or reptile scientists? Or just voyeurs?

Contemplating all those important questions, I started spending hours each day observing these little green creatures. One day my wife interrupted my reverie as I sat, notebook and camera in hand, and asked, "Why don't you write about the secret life of cats? They're easier to observe than lizards. Haven't you wondered why our neighbor's cat is always peering into the house through our sliding glass door? Maybe she's spying on us?"

"Honey," I explained to my wife, "everyone writes about cats. You can go to the bookstores and find dozens of books, fiction and non-fiction, about cats. Everyone imagines cats are very intelligent and make up crazy stories about cats solving mysteries, cats being agents for the CIA, or even cats being aliens from another planet, here to gather information on homo sapiens and transmit it to the mother ship. Geckos are another matter. No one ever noticed them at all until that insurance company decided to use one as their advertising gimmick. Who's really cared enough to study them from a scientific viewpoint? That's why I'm convinced that the book I'm going to write will have a special niche audience."

After mumbling something about wasting my time writing when I could be working on my to-do list for the house and yard, my wife retreated back into her craft room, preparing Christmas gifts for all of our relatives who never bother to get gifts for us.

I was just interrupted from my writing by the incessant ringing of the doorbell. It was my crazy neighbor, Bill, who lives just two doors down the street. He knew I was home, so I knew that he'd keep holding down that little button until I opened the door. The ensuing conversation went something like this:

"John, it's me, Bill. Why did you take so long to answer the damn doorbell?"

"Bill, I was back doing some writing and I was hoping you'd go away. Just kidding of course. What brings you here, another invitation to participate in one of your get-rich-quick pyramid schemes?"

"No, Bill. This is serious. I have a petition here that I'm trying to get all our neighbors to sign. I need to get 500 signatures so we can protest "National Nude Week.""

"National Nude Week? You're kidding. What's that?"

"The Federal Congress is passing a resolution to make the first week in June National Nude Week. It's part of their gay-liberal agenda, you know."

"How did you find out about this? No, let me guess. It was on the Internet, wasn't it Bill?"

"Well, yes it was, John. That's where I get all my information these days. Don't watch TV anymore, as all the shows are promoting is sex."

"Bill, I've told you a dozen times that you can't trust everything you see on the Internet. Remember that time you were convinced that Haley's comet had strayed off course and was going to destroy earth within a week? Go home, and take your crazy petition with you."

"But, but, John," Bill sputtered as I shut the door while asking, "What's wrong with being nude anyway. Isn't that the way God made us?"

Well, now it's back to business on my prize-winning book. It's interruptions like this that make me realize there are downsides to being home during the day, rather than down at my old office. But that's part of life as a No Work Specialist.

Now It Begins

She closed the book and said, "Now it begins." The man sitting next to her on the bench glanced in her direction, then slumped forward as I heard the boom of a high-powered rifle. Everyone in the park stood transfixed, looking toward the source of the sound and then scrambling for cover. I ducked behind a tree for a couple of minutes before realizing only the man on the bench was the sniper's target. When I looked back at the bench, the gray haired woman with the book was no where in sight.

"Hey man, do you think there's anything we can do to help the poor bloke?" asked a blond haired man as he peeked out behind some bushes.

That question was soon answered by a woman in nursing scrubs who got to the bench before us. "No pulse."

Then I saw the growing red stain on the back of the man's shirt and blurted out, "Sorry, but this is my first day in London. Guess we need to call the authorities. Back in America we dial 911, but what about here?"

"999," was the nurse's terse reply as she pulled out her mobile phone.

Before long the park was crawling with constables and inspectors from Scotland Yard.

"Inspector Molly Hanrahan," introduced the all-business, but attractive, redhead. "The nurse over there told me you were one of the first people on the scene and you are an American. First, let me get your name off your passport, and then tell me everything you remember."

"Okay, officer, I mean Inspector. I'm James Berkley; here's my passport. I was out for a stroll to see the sights and was looking for a place to sit and watch the people when I saw this woman sitting and reading on the bench here. Just then this man - the victim - walked up with his briefcase, sat down next to her, and said something that I didn't understand. She closed the book, and I heard her say, "Now it begins." The next thing I know a shot had been fired, the man was hit, and I took cover. When I looked up a couple minutes later, the woman was gone."

"Can you describe her?"

"Since I was behind her, I never saw her face. She had gray hair and a light gray sweater and I think the book had a blue cover."

I gave the Inspector my satellite phone number and the name of my hotel in case she had more questions and ambled over to a nearby Starbucks to get some java and gather my wits. By the time I sat down with my expresso, my hands were shaking so hard I could hardly get the cup to my lips. Some vacation this had started out to be!

Back at my hotel that evening, the murder in the park was the number one item on the local TV news. I soon learned that the victim was with MI5 and that the briefcase beside him on the park bench contained highly classified documents. The news people were still trying to find out more about the victim and the content of the documents, as well as the whereabouts of the mysterious gray-haired woman.

"Breaking news!" announced the young blonde reporter. "Scotland Yard has now found the sniper's rifle and one empty shell casing on a rooftop across from the park. Sources tell us that the weapon had been wiped clean of fingerprints."

At breakfast the next morning in the hotel coffee shop, the waitress and the other diners were all talking about the latest news. Apparently, Scotland Yard was holding the briefcase of documents as evidence in the crime and MI5 was demanding that the documents be turned over to them. Meanwhile, the Prime Minister was demanding a thorough investigation.

I spent the day visiting Buckingham Palace, which had beefed up security after the "brazen assassination" of the MI5 agent, a Mr. Harry Blair, to use the term being bantered about. By the time I got back to dinner at the hotel, there were rumors that the documents had been leaked to the London Times.

"Good morning, Mr. Berkley! Would you like a copy of this morning's Times?" the perky brunette waitress asked as I sat down for breakfast the following day. "Looks like the Times got a big scoop!"

"Sure, Miss. Thanks!" Curiously, I unfolded the newspaper and learned that the Times had somehow come upon a complete copy of all the documents in the agent's briefcase. They'd printed some of the highlights in the first section of the paper.

When she brought me my order, Cindy, the waitress, couldn't stop talking about the revelations. "Who would have thought there was such corruption in high places in MI5? And to think that they covered up their failure to act on intelligence that might have prevented the 7/7 Bombing!"

"You are right about that! But what bothers me most, Cindy, is that this documents the assassination of two British journalists who had published information from Wikileaks that was embarrassing to the British government regarding its dealings with other countries."

"Yes! And I just heard on the tele that Parliament is demanding a full explanation about all these revelations. I'm sure heads will roll as a result."

"I'm sure you're correct, Cindy! May I have some more coffee when you bring me the check?"

Back at my room, I had an urgent message to call Inspector Hanrahan. Turns out they had a gray-haired female suspect in custody and wanted me to see if I could recognize her. Soon I was down at Scotland Yard headquarters.

Observing the suspect through a monitoring window when she was being questioned, I was sure it was her when I heard her voice. Inspector Hanrahan allowed me to continue listening as the woman made a full confession.

"I am the widow of Richard Wilson, one of the journalists that MI5 assassinated! I was determined that the public should get the facts of his murder and some of the other coverups Richard had heard about. I knew about the MI5 agent, Mr. Blair, who had sold documents other times to various journalists and even enemy agents. I contacted him for the proof I needed. He demanded 50,0000 pounds and I agreed."

"But you didn't pay the asked price?"

"No, not only did I not have that much money, I wouldn't have paid it if I did. He was a known traitor and deserved not money but death."

"So you arranged for him to meet you on the park bench?"

"Yes, and once I'd confirmed that he had the documents with him, I closed my book to give the signal to my partner on the roof."

"And who was that, madam?"

"You will never find him. The sniper is an old lover of mine who was a senior agent with the Mossad. He flew out of the country hours before nightfall."

"Mrs. Wilson, much as I sympathize with you in some ways, I must place you under arrest. You will be tried and no doubt imprisoned for life."

"That won't be necessary. I've just swallowed a cyanide capsule. My work here is done."

Never Seen Again

"Here it is, Lucinda. The cabinet with the Missing Persons file my dad wanted me to review."

"Sure is dusty, James," coughed his girlfriend. "Tell me again why you promised your father on his deathbed that you would research this?"

"Lucinda, you know my dad never asked me for many favors after I moved away. He was such a great private detective who specialized in finding missing persons. Many of them proved to be dead but some were living somewhere else with a new identity - either by their own choice or because they'd been kidnapped. But there were a few cases he never solved, and those haunted him to his grave."

"So he expected you to solve them? When you're not even a detective?"

"He said he thought there was a common element among those he called Never Seen Again, or NSA's. He just hadn't been able to find what it was and so I told him I'd try. I think he said there were five of them. Ah, here they are!" exclaimed James as he pulled out five file folders that were all stamped NSA.

James and Lucinda spread the file folders out on a table and started perusing them. James, who was a criminal justice professor, took notes as they found things that might give them some leads.

"Seems like all five of these disappeared within a three month period two years ago, James. And each of them had no living family members."

"Yes. And it looks like each of them had graduated recently from Pima University. But all of them got degrees in different subjects. And I don't see anything that shows they knew each other."

"I wonder if they were members of the same campus organization or had any of the same classes?"

"Hmm, not a bad idea, Lucinda. But I'm not sure how we can get around the privacy policies at the college."

"Leave that to me. My Aunt Elena works in the Administration Building and I will bet she'll help us to find out what happened to them."

The next afternoon found the two of them in Aunt Elena's office. "I didn't feel comfortable letting you see their records, but I have looked through each of their files to see if they had anything in common. None shared any extracurricular activities, but each of them had a physics course taught by the same professor."

Lucinda's eyebrows went up as she asked the obvious question and Aunt Elena responded, "Professor Henry Wu was the professor. Funny thing, though. He resigned from teaching about two years ago and pretty much dropped out of sight."

Aunt Elena suggested they talk to the chair of the physics department and so they soon found themselves in the office of Dr.

Stanley Morales. "Dr. Wu was a professor who dabbled in what I call fringe science. He wanted to conduct some of his more far out experiments in our campus lab, but I forbade it. So a couple of months before he resigned from teaching he converted an old warehouse somewhere downtown into a lab.

"Do you know the address?" asked James.

"Sorry but I don't. I do have the address of his apartment, although I heard he'd moved out. Here it is. Maybe that will be of some help."

As they left, Lucinda asked, "what type of fringe science was he into?"

" As I recall he was fascinated with a wide range of experiments: trying to communicate with alien species, astral projection, teleportation, even time travel. As I said, too far out for the university."

Half an hour later James and Lucinda were talking to Dr. Wu's landlady. "He moved out a few months after he quit his job at the university. He said he was going to live in the warehouse where he was doing his experiments. Gave me a P.O. box to forward his mail to. He was a strange man but always paid his rent on time and never had any wild parties or such. So I was sorry to see him go."

"Where was this warehouse?"

"Down someplace in the warehouse district. It was one that had been owned by Acme Furniture before they went bankrupt."

It took some Google searching but they eventually located the address of the old Acme warehouse. By then it was 4 p.m. and time for Lucinda to leave for her shift at the children's hospital. "James, why don't you wait until tomorrow and we can go to the old warehouse together. "

"No worries, honey. I want to get to the bottom of all this now. I'll text you if I find Dr. Wu and see if he knows anything about the NSA's."

"Are you sure? I'm not comfortable about you going alone to see some professor who is into crazy science."

Dismissing her worries, James drove to the address for the old Acme Furniture warehouse. Sure enough the faded old sign was still on the side of the two story building. James tried the front door but it was locked. He found an unlocked back entrance and let himself in.

"Wow," he said to himself, "who would have thought this building that looks so decrepit outside would be so full of modern looking equipment, most of which I don't recognize."

It was apparent that the building was still being used for some type of scientific research. He could see electricity arcing from what looked like a transformer to a little enclosure about the size of an old phone booth.

"Can I help you?"

James turned around to see an older Asian man in a white lab coat.

"Why yes. My name is James Nichols and I am looking for Dr. Henry Wu."

"That's me. I am a very busy man. What do you want?"

"I'm looking for five former students who disappeared shortly before you left the university."

"Come with me into my office upstairs and I will tell you what I know."

Following Dr.Wu, he quickly texted Lucinda to give her an update.

****

A year later Lucinda picked up the newspaper and saw the article headlined, "Mysterious disappearance of James Nichols 12 months ago still unsolved."

Wiping a tear from her eye she took a black felt pen and wrote NSA across the article.

One Day in May

One day in May the world ended. Or to be more precise, the world as I knew it ended. It all started when I was helping serve the noon meal at the downtown homeless shelter, along with some other volunteers from Saint Vincent de Paul. As a tall thin man with a salt and pepper beard took the plate I was offering, I looked into his eyes and saw what looked like a flash of recognition. As he turned and walked outside, he looked vaguely familiar to me.

An hour later when I left the shelter, the tall man was sitting on a bench and as I walked by him, he silently handed me a folded piece of paper. When I got back in my Land Cruiser, I unfolded it and read "I need to talk to you, Dennis. Meet me at the Main Plaza fountain in one hour."

Intrigued that he knew my name and seemed somehow familiar, I took the bait and found him at the fountain about 2 p.m.

He seemed very articulate for someone showing up at a homeless shelter. "Thanks for agreeing to meet with me Dennis. You won't regret it. Why don't we sit on that park bench over there so I can explain?"

We sat and he introduced himself as Tom Smith, which sounded like a made up name to me. "Okay, Tom. What's this all about?"

"Dennis, what's your earliest memory?"

"Well, I only remember the last ten years. I know that sounds strange for someone who's 40 years old. But ten years ago I woke up in a hospital with my head wrapped in bandages. The nurse told me that I had fallen off the second story of a construction site. She gave me the wallet I'd had in my pants and that was how I knew my name was Dennis Jackson. She didn't seem to know who had taken me to the hospital and we couldn't find any next of kin."

"So you don't remember being shot in Bogota?"

"Bogota, Columbia? Never been there!"

"On the contrary, my friend. Maybe this will refresh your memory." Tom said as he pulled a photo out of his back pocket. "Take a look at this. Who do you see?"

"Why that looks like me standing next to someone who looks like you, only without a beard. We are both in jungle fatigues and the sign behind us says Aeropuerto de Bogota. When was that taken?"

"Ten years ago; about a month before you were shot."

My hands trembled as I held the photo. It all seemed so hard to believe, yet something deep in the recesses of my mind told me this might be true. "Okay, I'll bite. What were we doing in Columbia and what is my real name?"

"Your birth name was Donald Sullivan. You and I were recruited into the CIA right out of college. We became two of the best field agents the Company had. That's why they trusted us for this mission in Bogota."

"CIA? You've got to be kidding! What was our assignment there in Columbia?"

"We were sent to assassinate the head of the Columbian drug cartel and two of his lieutenants. One of those black ops jobs that only those with a need to know were briefed on. Only it was a setup. There was a mole in the CIA who alerted our targets and we were ambushed. You were shot in the head and I was shot in the chest and they left us for dead when they heard police sirens."

"Damn. No wonder I lost my memory. And that accounts for the scar in my scalp."

"The police got us to a local hospital where some real heroes saved our lives. You woke up a week later and didn't know who you were or what happened. That's when our handler flew in from Langley and arranged for our transport back to the states."

I'm sure Tom heard my voice quivering when I asked, "Then what happened?"

"That's when the Company disavowed any knowledge of our mission and made it clear that I was a persona non grata. You on the other hand, were given a new identity, shot up with some kind of drug to make sure your memory didn't come back and put you out cold. They dumped you off at a hospital in Alexandria where you woke up the next day."

"And what about you?"

"After ducking just in time to avoid a sniper's bullet when I walked to my apartment, I went underground. Since then I've been moving from city to city, working as a laborer and living from hand to mouth. I'd heard that you were here in Texas and eventually decided to look you up. I found out you volunteer often at the homeless shelter and hung out until you showed up."

This revelation shook me to the core. Somehow I knew it was all true, even though I didn't want it to be. "Okay. Is there anything you can tell me that might help me uncover the rest of my past?"

"There is a lady, Mrs. Graves, who was an administrative assistant at the Company when we both hired on. She's since retired but still lives in Virginia. I would trust her with my life, and I have in fact. She's the only one who knows how to reach me."

Five days later, I flew back east and went to see Mrs. Graves. A gray haired matron opened the door when I rang the bell at her apartment.

"Mrs. Graves, I'm Dennis Jackson, but I hear my real name is Donald Sullivan."

I was surprised to see tears in her eyes."Yes, it is Donald. It's so good to see you after all these years! I lost track of you after the agency left you in that hospital. Please come in and I'll make us some tea. You still drink tea don't you?"

"Why yes I do. I've been told that you worked at the CIA when I was hired on and can tell me more about my past."

Soon we were chatting like old friends. "How much of my first thirty years can you help me with, Mrs. Graves?"

"I can tell you an awful lot." she said with a twinkle in her eyes.

"Good. But why do you know so much about me?"

"I helped you get hired on by the agency where I worked. But there is something else you need to know."

"What's that?" I asked, now intrigued.

"I am your mother."

Operation Trick or Treat

"Trick or Treat? That's what the Director has named this operation? You've got to be kidding!" fumed Agent Hanrahan. "He should have called it Mission Impossible, Carmen!"

"Now calm down, Jack! I agree that this is a very high risk operation, but the phrase "Trick or Treat" does kinda describe what options we are tasked to present to our target," soothed agent Monroe. "We can talk about this more on the way to the airport, but our flight to Moscow leaves in three hours."

Eighteen hours later, CIA Agents Hanrahan and Monroe deplaned at Moscow Domodedovo Airport, holding hands and announcing to the customs agents that they were arriving for an international convention of plastic surgeons.

"Doctor Harris and Mrs. Harris, it looks like your passports are in order. Enjoy your stay," entoned the agent as he stamped their passports and waved them on.

After checking into their hotel, the agents walked to the convention center where the convention was slated to start the next morning and mentally rehearsed the first part of the operation. "I'll follow him to the men's room and get his attention. Then you come from behind and give him the injection."

The next day Carmen, who was one of the most attractive females at the convention, located Dr. Bortnik and followed him around. About 10 a.m. he left the convention floor and headed to the restroom. No sooner had he entered the bathroom, he heard a female voice behind him. "Dr. Bortnik, may I have a word with you?"

Turning around, he spotted Carmen and in heavily accented English, asked what she was doing in the men's room.

"Doctor Bortnik! I've always wanted to meet President Putin's plastic surgeon! Your renown has reached New York, where my husband is also a plastic surgeon. He did a wonderful job on my breasts, and I thought you might like to see his work." Smiling, she unbuttoned her blouse and started to unclasp her brassiere.

Doctor Bornik gulped loudly but kept his eyes on Carmen. Too late he sensed someone behind him as Jack stuck a syringe in his neck. Within seconds, he'd slumped to the floor unconscious.

Looking at Doctor Bortnik lying there on the cold tile, Carmen realized why the Director had chosen Jack for this job. Other than hair color, Jack was a dead ringer for Putin's plastic surgeon.

"I spotted a broom closet next door. Help me carry him and we'll dump him in there. He should be out for a good 24 hours and then he won't remember what happened to him."

Jack picked the lock on the broom closet and they unceremoniously dropped Dr. Bortik behind some mop buckets and floor polishers before covering him with a pile of old rags.

"Part one accomplished, partner! Now we need to get to Dr. Bortik's office in time for the President's 2 p.m. Botox appointment." Carmen was smiling as she hurried Jack out of the convention center.

A black taxi driven by a local CIA operative took the agents to Dr. Bortnik's office. The sign in Russian noted that the office was closed due to the convention.

"Interesting that it's closed now even though we know it will be open for Putin."

"Yeah, but that doesn't surprise me. Mr. Macho ex KGB boss doesn't want the general public to know about his plastic surgery appointments. If our intel is right, Dr. Bornik is always alone for these appointments. Putin doesn't want the good doctor's receptionist or assistant to be around. Here, I'll pick open the lock."

Inside, Jack went into the restroom, quickly rubbed in some hair coloring to darken his blond hair, and then found a pair of Doctor Bortnik's scrubs. Meanwhile, Carmen hid in the ladies restroom.

"I hope my hands stop shaking before Putin shows up, otherwise he will suspect something," muttered Jack as he took some deep breaths.

Promptly at 2 p.m. the bell rang and Jack opened the door to Putin and one of his bodyguards. "Mr. President, so good to see you again!" Jack spoke in perfect Russian.

"Doctor, your voice sounds lower than normal." Putin remarked with a cold stare at Jack.

"I'm sorry to say my allergies are acting up today. But no matter, why don't you come into the examination room?"

Putin complied while his bodyguard stood just inside the front door to protect the president from intruders.

As soon as Jack had Putin lying back on the exam table, Carmen came out of the restroom and stabbed a syringe into the guard's neck while he had his back turned. Just like the good doctor had, he slumped unconscious to the floor.

Inside the exam room, Jack talked calmly to the Russian president and seemed to be preparing a botox injection. Instead he filed the syringe with a chemical which brings temporary but instant paralysis.

Putin's body twitched as the chemical first entered his face and then a wild look came into his eyes as he suddenly felt his body stiffen.

"What have you done to me Doctor? I can barely move my arms and my legs feel useless."

Just then Carmen entered the room with a document and a pen.

"Just sign this document, Mr. President, and my associate, who is not the real Doctor, will give you the antidote. Otherwise the poison he gave you will kill you within six hours."

"What does this document say?" sputtered the partially paralyzed man.

"It announces to the world that you have fallen in love with a young man and have chosen to step down from your position as President so that you might spend the rest of your life with him."

"That is preposterous! You know I hate homosexuals and the Russian people need me as President." Putin's voice was down to a whisper as the chemical had affected his vocal cords.

"If you want to die instead, that is of no concern to us. It's Halloween this week in the West, Mr. Putin, when children threaten to trick someone who doesn't give them a treat. You signing that document," explained Jack," would be a treat to my government. But if you don't, your paralysis and untimely death is the trick we are playing on you."

"Damn you all! Okay, I will sign it!" With his hands shaking, Putin signed the document and Jack quickly gave him an injection which was merely a saline solution.

"This will reverse the poison's effects and you should be able to start moving within a few hours. Good bye Mr. Putin!" Jack smiled as he and Carmen exited the back entrance into the black taxi that whisked them to the airport. On the way, Carmen photographed the signed document and emailed it to a Russian news agency.

"Mission accomplished, Mr. Director." texted Carmen from her encrypted cell phone as they boarded the plane.

When they deplaned at Dulles, the Director met them with a frown on his face.

"What's wrong, Director?" asked Carmen.

"The man who signed that document was one of Putin's doubles. Putin himself was secretly vacationing on the Black Sea, but spoke to the news media when he was contacted by them about the email you sent."

"Damn Russians! Looks like the trick is on us!" exclaimed Jack.

Opposites

They say that opposites attract. It was certainly true for me.

It all started on the day the roads were covered with black ice. If you've never driven or walked on black ice, you don't know what you're missing! One minute you're braking for a stop sign and the next minute your car is turned sideways and still moving into the intersection. Suddenly the view out the windshield is of trees and buildings instead of the roadway. Fascinating and frightening at the same time.

Thankfully my car finally came to a stop when the rear wheels hit the curb as I slid by. A couple of kind souls at the corner gas station came out and helped me get the car turned in the right direction. Eventually I somehow made it to the nearby Starbucks, where I decided to escape the cold and scary traffic. Getting up the steps to the front door was no easy task and if it hadn't been for the handrails I would have landed flat on my back when I slipped on that damn black ice.

"Welcome to Starbucks, John!" greeted the too perky barista. "You don't look like your usual chipper self."

"I hate winter! I hate the cold and the damn ice! Did I tell you I hate winter?" I realized I was talking rather loudly when all the other customers turned to look at me.

"Relax, John! Would you like your usual tall cappuccino?"

"Make it a venti this time," I muttered as I paid with my iPhone.

No sooner had I sat down at the only available table, but my boss called. "John, the roads are so bad that we're closing the office today and telling everyone to stay home."

"Darn, Phil. Now you tell me when I'm only a mile away. But thanks for the heads up. I think I'll spend the morning here at my favorite Starbucks."

As I hung up an extremely attractive young woman entered the coffee shop. "How can she walk on the ice in those high heels?" I wondered.

"I love winter!" exclaimed the newcomer with a big smile as she paid for her coffee and looked around for a place to sit. The only empty chair in the place was the one at my table.

"Mind if I sit here?"

"No problem. Besides, I want to know why anyone in their right mind says they love winter. I hate it with a passion!"

"Well, I travel much of the time out of the country where the weather is usually warm to hot and I miss the snowy cold winters where I lived as a kid. It's a treat to have some really cold weather when I'm back here at home in Dallas."

"Well, to each his own, I guess," I muttered as I sipped my cappuccino. "By the way, my name is John, John Latimer."

"Olivia. Olivia Gonzalez," she added as she held out her hand.

"So you do a lot of traveling. For business?"

"Yes, I'm an in-house auditor for Sandals Resorts."

"Ah, one of those!"

"And what do you do, John?"

I couldn't tell her the truth, that I am an FBI Special Agent for the Dallas Office. "I'm an electrical engineer and work mostly on contract here in the Dallas-Fort Worth area." That was partly true as I did have an engineering degree but had been lured into the FBI straight out of college by promises of being able to use my analytical skills while fighting for truth, justice, and the American way.

"I'm only in town for a week, John, but have a lot of time on my hands. Would you be interested in meeting me for dinner some evening?"

I was flattered that this gorgeous woman wanted to spend some time with me. So I quickly agreed to meet her the next night when the weather was supposed to be somewhat better.

We both arrived at Morton's Steakhouse at 7 p.m. the next evening. Olivia wore a black form fitting dress that accentuated her curves. I wore tan slacks and a blue blazer that concealed the shoulder holster for my FBI- issued Glock. The fact that we had opposite tastes and opinions on many issues seemed to increase the attraction we felt for each other.

"Do you have time to come back to my condo for a nightcap?" she asked expectantly.

" I do have to get to work early tomorrow, but could come by for an hour or so."

Soon we were seated next to each other on a plush couch at her upscale condo. "Sandals must be paying you a handsome salary," I ventured.

"Yes. Yes they do," she smiled seductively.

Just then Olivia's phone rang and she answered it in Spanish. "Un momento!"

Turning to me, she apologized. "John, this is a business call I need to take. Excuse me a minute."

"Sure thing," I watched her as she walked into the next room and picked up her conversation with the caller.

I'm always alert as an FBI agent, even around beautiful women, and it wasn't hard for me to hear Olivia's side of the conversation. She obviously didn't know I spoke fluent Spanish. I heard her ask, "How soon do you need me to make the hit?" and later remind the caller that her usual fee was $50,000 plus expenses.

"Hmm, there is more to this woman than meets the eye," I thought and decided to look at her handbag sitting on the end table. I was surprised it contained a passport with her photo and the name Olivia Munoz. I was even more surprised when I unzipped one of the inside pockets and found a small 9mm Ruger. I barely had time to put her handbag back before she returned.

"Sorry about that, John. There's a minor accounting issue at one of our Caribbean resorts."

"Olivia, I hate to tell you, but I speak and understand Spanish, and I heard you talk about making a hit on someone for $50,000. That doesn't sound like an accounting problem to me."

"John, I think you'd better go!" Her eyes flashed with anger as she moved toward her handbag.

"Olivia, please don't go for the gun in your handbag," I barked as I showed her the Glock under my blazer.

"Who and what are you, John, if that's your real name?"

"I'm a special agent for the FBI, and I am taking you in for questioning."

Seeing that it was useless to resist, Olivia surrendered her handbag, let me cuff her, and rode with me to my office. My boss met us there.

The rest of the story is that Olivia Munoz was a freelance assassin who was wanted in three countries.

Opposites do attract.

Power Outage

The boom of the transformer explosion echoed throughout the affluent neighborhood just after sunset. Minutes later Fred Wilson, senior citizen and neighborhood grouch, dialed a neighbor, Jose Garcia, on his cell.

"Jose, the power just went out in my house on the hottest night of the year. Do you have any power at your house?"

"No, Mr. Wilson. The power seems to be out in the entire subdivision."

"Well, since you work for CPS Energy, find out what the hell the problem is and how long I'm going to have to sweat here in the dark!"

Jose sighed and did as requested. The answer he got didn't make Mr. Wilson or any of his other neighbors happy. The power would be out until after midnight. As word spread around the subdivision, neighbors started coming out of their houses hoping to find others to commiserate with and maybe find a cool breeze.

Sam and Jane Zari, the self-appointed neighborhood party organizers, quickly sprang into action. Within minutes they lit some tiki torches in their front yard and were calling all the neighbors over for a block party.

Jose and Caroline Garcia brought over four six packs of Dos Equis. Irma LaBomba, the neighborhood flirt showed up in a red string bikini with a bag of chips and made small talk with some of the men and teenage boys. Soon everyone on the block, including Fred Wilson, was gathered in the Zari's yard.

"Funny how it often takes a common misfortune to bring a sense of community to a neighborhood," remarked Jose.

"No, what's really funny," asserted his wife, "is how a red string bikini can attract so many of the male species."

Someone turned on a battery-powered MP3 player and everyone except Fred began singing "Summer in the City" along with the Lovin' Spoonfuls. Laughter and the buzz of voices filled the night air as people started to relax and make the most of the power failure.

Unseen by the partiers, two cat burglars dressed in black entered the subdivision and started checking for unlocked back doors. Dennis and Donna were fairly experienced in their craft and had been driving past the subdivision when they heard the transformer explode. "Turn in here, Dennis," Donna had commanded. "This looks like the perfect place to hit tonight."

First the pair entered the back patio door of Irma LaBomba's house and went through the drawers in her bedroom dresser. "Have you ever seen so many thongs and flimsy nighties, Dennis?"

"No, no I haven't. But where are her valuables?"

"I'll look in the master closet. Ahh, that's better! Look at this string of pearls! And these watches!"

It only took a few minutes to transfer all of Irma's expensive jewelry into Dennis's black bag. The next two houses were locked up tight, so they crept down the block toward the Zari's residence. Donna tried the knob on one of the Zari's back doors and found it open.

"Here! This one, Dennis."

"Listen to all that partying going on out front, Donna. Do you think it's safe to work this house? I mean, someone could come inside anytime to use the bathroom or something and our goose would be cooked."

"Where's your sense of adventure, Dennis? It won't take us long to go through their bedroom and study. We'll be out before anyone suspects anything."

After helping themselves to some diamond jewelry lying on a dressing table in the master bath, the thieves crept into the study toward the front of the house. "How about that laptop, Donna? That looks like an expensive one."

Before Donna could reply, she was knocked unconscious by a man hidden in the shadows. The powerfully built man let her down silently and grabbed Dennis as he turned toward him. A blow to the head with the barrel of the stranger's Beretta 71 rendered Dennis senseless and he collapsed next to his wife.

Making certain that no one else was in the house, the six-foot dark-haired stranger set about the task he'd been assigned before he'd caused the transformer explosion. That had been a simple matter of causing a power surge in the lines leading into the transformer by the use of a special tool.

Soon the laptop in the Zari's study was disgorging its secrets into a USB drive the stranger had inserted. Dropping the USB drive into his pocket, he checked once more to make certain the cat burglars were still out cold and slipped out the back door.

Half an hour went by and suddenly the power came back on. The street lamps flickered and then glowed brightly, the air conditioners started humming again, and lights and televisions all across the neighborhood came to life. When Sam and Jane started carrying things back inside, they found two people dressed in black groaning in the study. One of them had a large black bag out of which had spilled a pearl necklace and some diamonds.

"Call 911, Jane! These people were stealing our stuff!"

As Donna and Dennis came to, they saw Sam Zari standing over them and assumed he was the one who had knocked them out. Five minutes later, two SAPD officers arrived and put them under arrest. "You and your big ideas, Donna!" blurted Dennis.

Neither the cat burglars nor any of the neighbors ever knew who had been responsible for the arrest. Nor did the Zari's know that an agent from the Mossad had hacked into their laptop and captured information about their sales of specialized equipment to the Republic of Iran.

Exactly one month later, the neighborhood was shocked when Sam and Jane Zari, the subdivision party organizers, were led handcuffed from their home by FBI agents and charged with providing uranium enrichment equipment to an avowed enemy of the United States.

Rover Two

"Brady, what's that dog barking at again? He's going to wake your baby sister!" Marsha complained to her teen-aged son.

"How should I know, Mom? Maybe it's a neighborhood cat, or a skunk, or maybe he hears another dog barking. " Brady really didn't want to be bothered in the middle of his favorite video game, but left his computer and ambled out the back door to check on Rover Two.

The Latimer's long-time family pet, Rover, had died suddenly a few months ago. Brady's mother soon bought a replacement, Rover Two, from the pet store. He had a lot more energy than his namesake, as the brown beagle was still a puppy, and quickly learned some standard tricks, such as rolling over on command. But Rover Two loved to bark. He was also fascinated by the automated cleaner in the backyard pool. Watching that dog run around the pool after the cleaner and growl when it surfaced was a frequent source of entertainment for Brady.

"What is it now, Rover Two?" queried Brady with a bemused smile as he saw the dog peering into the pool with raised hackles, whining and wagging his tail. "The cleaner isn't running now. It comes on earlier in the day."

Brady took a quick look into the pool, saw the cleaner on the bottom of the deep end, verified that it wasn't moving, and went back inside to finish his game.

"What was it honey?" asked Marsha as she closed the door to the microwave and hit Start.

"Nothing really, Mom. Rover Two was barking at the pool cleaner, even though it's not running. Maybe he wanted it to start moving again."

"I wish we had Rover back, Brady. This new dog seems so different and so excitable."

"Well, he's just a puppy, you know. I wish Dad wasn't out of town. Rover Two seems to act better when he's around." Brady picked up the track ball and turned his attention back to the computer screen.

****

It was midnight when Brady awoke to loud barking and tried to ignore it. Finally giving in to his mother's pleading to check on the dog, he grudgingly staggered out of the bedroom and onto the back patio. In the moonlight he saw Rover Two at the pool's edge. Not too unusual. But then he saw it - an eerie purple light emanating from inside the pool.

"What the heck?" he exclaimed, peering over the edge at the pool cleaner. The cleaner had the same shape as usual, but it's surface was emitting a bright purple light that was pulsating faster and faster. It's long plastic tail was glowing white and whipping back and forth. Brady's dog's eyes followed its every move.

Brady pinched himself to make sure he wasn't dreaming. He turned to go into the house for his cell phone, but doubled over in pain as an ear-splitting high-pitched whine came from the cleaner. Rover resumed his barking and tried to bite the object's tail as it whipped above the water surface.

His face contorted in pain as Brady put his fingers in his ears and watched the pulsating object slowly rise to the pool's surface and move toward the far edge. Suddenly the machine cleared the water and hovered a few inches above it. As it came to rest on the flagstone pool edge, the high-pitched sound ceased.

"Careful, Rover Two," cautioned Brady, his heart thumping in his chest. The dog had run around the pool and was standing next to the other-worldly machine, hackles raised. Then a new sound punctured the stillness of the night, like the whirring of a motor. A little door opened in the side of the machine and the whirring stopped.

What is this? A UFO in my backyard? Am I crazy? Wish I had my iPhone camera. Or maybe Dad's pistol instead. I need to call Mom, so she can see this too. Or maybe she should get the baby and run? A hundred thoughts like these and others raced through Brady's mind.

Just then the back door opened and Brady's mother emerged. "What was that terrible noise, son?" She gasped as she caught sight of the glowing machine. Little purple things, creatures of some sort, were pouring out the door on the side. Hundreds of them, all less then two inches high. The army of creatures reached a palm tree next to the pool deck. They surrounded the tree and suddenly it burst into flames. Brady's mother ran to him and they held each other tight as the tree burned completely in less than a minute.

"Do something, Brady! They'll burn our house next!" his mother pleaded.

"No, don't move. Humans are no match for these invaders from Alpha Centuri," Rover Two barked.

"Did I just hear the dog tell us not to move?" questioned the wide-eyed woman. Just then Rover Two looked at them. His eyes glowed brightly as he said slowly and simply, "my people suspected that earth was about to be invaded by these destroyers. That is why I came to live with you when Rover died. I am here to protect Earth."

"Your p-people?" stammered Brady. "What are you?"

Just then, the purple army advanced to the near side of the pool and began to circle Rover Two – just like they'd surrounded the palm tree before it's destruction.

Suddenly Rover Two leaped over the purple creatures and ran toward the tail of the pool-cleaner turned UFO. A blinding light flashed and flashed again and again. The Latimers could see Rover Two with the UFO's tail in his mouth. First it seemed like

Rover Two was whipping the UFO about and then it seemed like it was the other way around. Brady felt like he was looking at a miniature and bizarre version of The War of The Worlds.

Finally all was still. The pool cleaner lay on its side, smoke pouring from the interior. The army of purple creatures had disappeared as though vaporized.

Before Brady and his mother could express their gratitude to Rover Two, a saucer-like craft appeared over the backyard.

"My people have come and I'm going home. But before, I do, I'd like to see both of you roll-over."

"Sofia, have you seen my glasses? I've looked all over the house for them."

"George, you're using that tone with me again!"

"What tone?"

"That accusatory tone that means you think I did something with them!"

"I didn't exactly mean that! But I'm frustrated!"

"When was the last time you saw them, mi esposa?"

"I was reading the morning paper at breakfast and I had them then."

"Ah! Go look in the mirror! What is that on the top of your head?"

"Good grief! That's my glasses! Wonder who put them there?"

"Yeah, who could have done that?" The sarcasm dripped off Sofia's tongue.

The doorbell rang and she hurried to the door. "George, it's Thomas, here to give you a ride to your coffee group."

Soon George was riding in Thomas' golf cart to the nearby Starbucks. "Now that you've been living here in Orlando's Senior City for three months, George, what do you think of it?"

"Well, it's certainly a pleasant and quiet place. I like having so many amenities close and the landscaping is beautiful. Plus there's always something to do, if I want to socialize. Mahjong, poker, croquet, bocce ball, water polo, you name it. It certainly lives up to its press as A Retirement Community for Active Adults. "

"I think I hear some hesitation in your voice, though."

"Well, everyone here seems so self-focused. There doesn't seem to be any thought of helping others outside this little community. There's a whole hurting world out there and it seems to be too easy to ignore it in our comfortable little enclave."

"Well, there are so many problems in the outside world, we can't fix them all. And most of us spent our working years helping solve some of those problems as well as making our own way in the world. Now it's time to focus on enjoying the lifestyle that we've earned."

"Did you read that article about Senior City that was in Sunday's Orlando Sentinel?"

"Don't think I saw it, George."

"The headline was Selfish City: A Retirement Community for Avaricious Adults. The article went into detail about the self-indulgent lifestyle that this community encourages."

"I bet I know who wrote it. Was it that liberal Jose Cisneros? He is always stirring up trouble with his articles."

George admitted that he enjoyed reading Mr. Cisneros' columns and Thomas quickly changed the subject.

Back home later, George told Sofia about his conversation on the way to Starbucks.

"I think you and I are pretty much on the same page, George. The self focused life that this place promotes doesn't do much to make the world a better place and this lifestyle can get downright boring."

Just then they got a call from their next door neighbor, Mabel Wilson, who was an elderly widow.

"Sofia, can you and your husband come over and help me find something I've lost? I've looked all over with no luck!"

"Sure, Mrs. Wilson, we'll be right over."

"Sounds like Mrs. Wilson is having another one of what she calls her senior moments, George. She needs our help again."

Soon they were at Mrs. Wilson's condo. "What did you lose, Mrs. Wilson?"

Through her tears, Mrs. Wilson sobbed, "I've lost my Social Security check and without it I can't pay my rent. I'll be thrown out on the street."

"Come, now, Mrs. Wilson. It's not the end of the world. We'll help you find it, and even if we can't, we can help you apply for a replacement check." Sofia smiled.

"And we can tide you over with the cash you need for the rent," George volunteered.

"Where did you last see your check?"

"I thought I put it in my purse so I could take it to the bank today. But I've emptied it out and there is no check. You know, my kids tease me that I could hide my own Easter eggs. I used to laugh at that, but I'm thinking it's true!"

"Okay, Mrs. Wilson," started Sofia. "What do you do with the check stubs and deposit slips after you deposit your Social Security check?"

"Oh, I keep them in a file folder in the middle drawer of the file cabinet in my study. That's where my late husband and I have always put them."

George walked to the file cabinet and soon found a file labeled "Social Security." He pulled out the file folder and there was her new check. "Look, here it is!"

"Well, great balls of fire! Why in the world did I put it there?" puzzled Mrs. Wilson.

When he was about the push the file drawer back into the cabinet, George spied a large envelope in the rear of the cabinet that had partially slipped down from the top drawer. It was labeled "Important: Stock Certificates."

"I wonder where that came from, George? I don't recall seeing it before! What's inside?"

George pulled out stock certificates for 200 shares of Apple Computer. "These are dated May 1986, Mrs. Wilson. Do you remember these?"

"Well, yes I do," she stammered. My late husband took our income tax refund that year and bought shares of Apple Computer. I was mad at him because I wanted him to use it for a dining room set. I was tired of eating on the table handed down by his parents. I'd forgotten all about them long ago."

"Do you have any idea what these are worth, Mrs. Wilson? Sofia and I also have some Apple stock, so I'm pretty familiar with its history. One share of Apple Stock in the mid 1980's has split numerous times and is now worth 56 shares. So those old 200 shares are now worth 11, 200 shares. The stock is now selling for about $120 per share. That means these certificates are worth more than $1.3 million."

"My lands! I need to sit down before I faint! I won't have to worry anymore about paying the bills are the end of each month! God bless you, George!"

Later back at their place, George told Sofia, "Wow, what a great day this has been! I feel so happy that we could help Mrs. Wilson discover that stock."

"A lot more satisfying than playing bocce ball or Mahjong, huh, George?"

"You can say that again."

So This is New Year's

It was January 2, 2015 and John Hampton was depressed. The dark and overcast sky served to further dampen his spirits. Even the cheery Starbucks barista who had just made his expresso hadn't been able to lift the cloud that hung over him. The words of John Lennon's song, "So This is Christmas" that was playing on his iPhone seemed directed at him. *What have I done since Christmas? Last year is over and a new one is here. I hope it will finally be a good one!*

"So this is Christmas. And what have you done? Another year over and a new one just begun... A very merry Christmas and a happy new year. Let's hope it's a good one without any fear."

"Looks like all the tables out here on the patio are taken. Do you mind if I take a seat here?" inquired a white-haired gentleman with coffee in hand.

John stirred enough from his thoughts to mumble, "Sure whatever."

"Nice day, isn't it, young man?" ventured the stranger as he settled into the chair across from John.

"Oh, is it? I hadn't noticed. It's just another day to me."

"You seem distracted. Let me guess, you're lost in thought about the new year and where you are at this stage in your life."

"What are you, some kind of psychic?"

"No, and I'm glad I'm not. You just had the same kind of look on your face that I used to have at the start of each new year.

Not too happy about what transpired the last year and sure as hell not excited about the year ahead. Maybe even fearful about the future."

"Well you nailed it. Last year I didn't keep any of my New Year's resolutions. I gained weight, I didn't impress my boss enough to get a raise, and I didn't find the girl

of my dreams. In fact, the lady I've been dating just moved back to Florida to be closer to her family. And I don't have any reason to believe that 2015 will be any better."

"Well, that's a long list of unhappy events. Has there been anything good in your life recently?"

"What's it to you? Are you some kind of shrink? Or are you about to give me a sales pitch for something to change my life?"

"Sorry if I've offended you. I'm not a shrink or a salesman. My name is Bill Lopez and I'm a retired teacher of sorts. I've been where you are and I know it's unpleasant, even depressing at times. But you're not alone in your regrets about the past and your concerns for your future. Probably half the people at this Starbucks are facing similar thoughts today."

"That's okay. No offense taken, Mr. Lopez. I'm John Hampton and I'm tired of things being the way they are. How about you? You've obviously been through a lot more New Years than I have and yet you project a more positive attitude than me. Does being retired help with that?"

"Not really. There are a couple of things, really three, that helped my improve my outlook for the future."

Just when he was about to reply, John was interrupted by Jenny, the cute barista, who walked by their table and asked if they needed refills. This time her cheery expression lifted his spirits just a bit as he told her "No thanks."

"Please continue, Mr. Lopez."

"Okay. Years ago when watching the Olympics, I started thinking about my life as a race. Not a sprint, but a marathon. Runners try to lighten their loads by wearing light shoes and clothes and leaving their backpacks, etc. behind. But I wasn't following their example; I was carrying a lot of baggage from the past with me that hindered my forward progress."

"Baggage?"

"Yes. Regrets about what I'd done in the past -- and regrets about other things I'd not done. Plus scars and hurts from things others had done to me. And things I'd done to myself."

"So what did you do about it?"

"I made a conscious effort to let go of the past. I told a couple of close friends to keep me accountable in that effort. And I even prayed about it."

"Prayer, huh? My mother believed in prayer, but I'm not so sure."

"The second thing I did was to start cultivating an attitude of gratitude. Instead of focusing on the things that weren't okay in my life, I started focusing on the good things. Our society tends to focus on the exceptions, the negatives, but there are a lot more things in most of our lives to be thankful for than to complain about."

"Okay, Mr. Lopez. That reminds me that my mother used to tell us kids. She said that we should look at the glass as half full rather than half empty. And even though she was a single mom that held down two jobs to feed us, she actually practiced what she preached."

"John, I'm glad that makes sense to you. Being thankful for something each day will make a real difference. There's one more thing that really helps me face the future."

"What's that?"

"Believing that God is love. That means God isn't some celestial ogre who's just waiting to beat me up for my mistakes or infractions. Instead God loves me - really loves me. That gives me hope for the future, for my future."

"I have trouble buying that, Mr. Lopez. If God is love, why does he or she allow all the evil, all the crap, going on in the world?"

"I don't have all the answers, my young friend. One time I was agonizing over all the pain and needless suffering in the world, and it seemed that God whispered in my mind that all this pain and suffering grieves him (or her) too but that I am to focus on him (or her.) Now I see signs of God's love all around me."

Suddenly the sun broke through the clouds for the first time that day and John turned around to look at it. He asked, "So is that a sign of God's love?"

There was no answer to John's question. Mr. Lopez was nowhere in sight. "Where the hell did he go?" John wondered aloud.

The sun felt good on his face as John thought about their discussion. He decided to go back inside and ask the cute barista if she'd like to go to a movie when she got off her shift. When she quickly said yes, he glanced up toward the ceiling and mouthed, "Thanks for the advice, Mr. Lopez!"

Spirit and Opportunity

"We've landed! The ride down was a bit bumpy, but we're here!" reported Harrison over the X-band frequency to the spacecraft orbiting overhead. The cool-headed astronaut pilot turned to his associate, Maria, who breathed a sigh of relief as she wiped the beads of sweat off her forehead. Maria's Ph.D. was in Geology, not Astrophysics like Harrison.

"Congratulations, you two!" Sandy's Aussie accent crackled over the radio. "I envy you, being the first humans to set foot on the Red Planet."

"Sorry about that, amigo," Maria smiled as she replied back over the communication link to the orbiter. "Somebody has to tend our return craft back to earth while we're down here risking our necks for science."

"Whatever, mates!" crackled Sandy's voice, "Be careful down there. I can't come and rescue you if you fall down into a deep crater or rip your suits on some sharp rocks. I'd like some company on the long return trip to earth!"

After two hours of preparation, the two astronauts suited up and stepped onto the dusty surface.

"Let's head over there, Harrison. I think that's Spirit on the edge of that crater."

"It's amazing to me that both Spirit and Opportunity are still operating after twenty-five years! Those little Rovers are a lot tougher than anyone who built or launched them ever dreamed."

"Yep! I'm anxious to take a look at the little guy and to check out the soft soil where he's stuck."

Bounding along in the light Martian gravity, Harrison wondered if they looked as ridiculous as Armstrong and Aldrin did in the even lighter lunar gravity. As they approached the Rover, their feet broke through the hard crust near a crater and sank several inches in the soft sand.

"Welcome! Have you come to take me home?" came the computer-generated voice through the radios in their helmets.

"What the heck, Harrison? That came from Spirit. When did the Rover learn to talk?" Maria gasped as she halted in her tracks and gazed at the Rover that was only a few inches shorter than her.

"Beats the hell out of me. I know the guys at JPL uploaded a fair amount of artificial intelligence programming to the Rovers over the years, but I had no idea they were capable of fairly intelligible speech."

"It may surprise you that I've continued to evolve and now have an IQ comparable to what you humans call a genius. But you still haven't answered my question. I'm lonely here and I want to return to my creators."

Maria glanced back at her partner and then tentatively replied to this mechanical marvel. "Spirit, we came here to put boots on the ground, so to speak. We've gleaned a lot of great information from your observations over the years and now want to explore things for ourselves."

Harrison continued the explanation, "We want to confirm data that shows liquid water near this site. Then we can finalize plans to build a small self-sustaining colony on the planet. If that happens, you'll have some more company!"

Seeing Spirit's solar panels suddenly droop in a very human-like gesture, Maria spoke up in a conciliatory tone. "Even though we don't have room for you in this Mars lander, there are landers on the drawing boards that could accommodate you. So don't give up hope, friend."

Just then, Sandy's voice broke into the conversation over their helmet radios, "Are you guys actually talking to that robot, or am I going batty?"

"Who's that?" intoned the computer-generated voice.

"That's the guy who will pilot our ride back home. His name is Sandy and he's circling overhead in an obiter."

"Well, can he come down and give me a ride back?"

"Wish I could, mate," boomed Sandy's voice. "This craft doesn't have any equipment that would allow me to land on Mars and then ascend back into orbit."

After more conversation and some examination of the area around Spirit, Maria and Harrison returned to their landing craft for the coming Martian night.

Daybreak the next sol found Harrison and Maria donning their spacesuits for some more exploration. No sooner had they gotten out of their lander, Sandy's voice boomed over their suit radios. "G'day, mates! I think we have a real problem!"

Despite her suddenly rapid pulse rate, Maria tried to sound calm as she asked Sandy to explain himself.

"Wouldn't you know it, that other Rover on the other side of the planet has learned to talk too. But it's not glad to see us like Spirit was! It contacted me when I was directly overhead and threatened me."

"You mean Opportunity?" Harrison queried. "What kind of threat and why?"

"Seems it distrusts humans and fears we'll try to dismantle it whenever we get to its side of the planet. So the bastard intends to destroy my spacecraft if I don't leave by the next sol."

"Destroy, how?" Maria and Harrison exclaimed in unison.

"It claims it knows how to direct it's solar panels to reflect sunlight and focus it on my spacecraft to disintegrate it."

"Why that sounds preposterous!" Harrison exclaimed.

"That's what I thought. But remember that Reconnaissance Orbiter launched in 2016 that disappeared suddenly two years ago? Opportunity claims that it got suspicious when the Orbiter's cameras seemed to be focus on it. So it fried the Orbiter! Just like that!"

"Sandy, contact Houston and see what that Orbiter's sensors showed just before it went off the air!"

"Already checked them on that, my friend. The temperature sensors went crazy just before all communications were lost. The last temperature reading was above the melting point of the Orbiter's outer shell."

"Still," wondered the skeptical Harrison aloud, I wonder if that was caused by Opportunity or by something else, like an asteroid collision. If conditions were just right, the force of the collision could have been transformed into a heat wave through the Orbiter's shell…"

"You're grasping at straws, mate. Why don't you wander back over to your friend, Spirit, and see what it knows about it's counterpart?"

Taking Sandy's suggestion, Harrison and Maria were soon talking with Spirit.

"Something went wrong with Opportunity after it too became highly intelligent. It used to enjoy communicating with me through the Odyssey Orbiter but then it started to become what you humans would call paranoid. A couple of years ago, Opportunity started ranting about the Reconnaissance Orbiter spying on it and told me how it was going to focus sunlight to eliminate it. And sure enough, that's what happened. Since then I get very few communications from my fellow Rover and when I do they are always disturbing."

"I heard that, mates! I'm calling Houston to tell them we have to abort the mission! Can you be back in the lander and ready to start your ascent before I get too far through this orbit for you to catch up with me?"

"We'll have to, Sandy," Harrison said through gritted teeth as he and Maria loped toward their spacecraft. Within an hour they'd fired their rockets to begin the journey toward Sandy's orbiter.

As soon as they'd rendezvoused and transferred into the cabin with Sandy, Harrison called Houston. "We're ready to begin our return flight. But send a radio message to that damn Rover."

Nine minutes later, Houston's reply came. "What message do you want us to send Opportunity?"

"By the way, send this to Spirit too, though the intent of the message will be different to it. Tell them that in the historic words of General Douglas MacArthur, 'I will return!'"

Squirrels R Us

"Marsha, I'm sure tired after mowing the yard. Think I'll go relax in my new hammock."

"Sure, John. I'll call you when I get dinner ready."

Breathing a contented sigh, John settled into the hammock with a newspaper and basked in the warmth of the spring afternoon. Soon he spied a squirrel leaping from the fence to the bird feeder hanging under their oak tree.

"Little bugger almost fell off, but managed to hang on! So much for the squirrel-proof feeder I paid $39.95 for!" John mused under his breath.

As he relaxed, John noticed several other squirrels venture into his yard. They were cute, but John considered them rats with bushy tails. Just then one of the squirrels ventured too close to the pool and fell into the shallow end. Instead of struggling to stay afloat, the little guy went limp and sank to the bottom.

"Crap, better go fish the little rat out," John grunted as he rolled out of the hammock and grabbed a net on a pole. "Hmm...he feels heavier than he looks."

When he dumped the carcass on the pool deck, it made a clunk. "What the hell?" he muttered as he picked it up. "This is not a real squirrel! It's a mechanical device with fake fur!"

Walking into the house, John called out to Marsha. "Hey, honey, would you look at this! A fake squirrel that's been running around our yard!"

"How crazy is that, John! I wonder if it's the same one I saw sitting on the ledge of the kitchen window this morning? It sat there for at least ten minutes, just staring through the glass. What if it was spying on me? Gives me the creeps!"

"Stalked by a squirrel! That would be a first!" Noticing Marsha wasn't smiling, he added, "not that I'm making light of this. I'm going to take this over to my brother to see what he makes of it."

Thirty minutes later he was at his brother, Ron's house. Ron taught Electrical Engineering at the junior college and was on top of the latest technology.

"Well, John, let's see what you have here. First I'll peel off the fake fur. Hmm...looks like a precision-made robot! I'll unscrew the plate on it's underside and I bet we'll find a rechargeable battery. Yes, just as I suspected. And here is a sophisticated looking mother board with a microprocessor and a cell phone chip."

"So what is it made to do?"

"Unfortunately the electronics got fried when it fell into the pool, so we can't start it back up. But it looks like it can be used for surveillance. Spying, in other words. Here's a lens in one of the eyes and a CMOS chip that can capture images and store them digitally. Looks like it has a microphone, too. And look, it's Wi-Fi enabled. So it can intercept signals from unprotected Wi-Fi networks. John, what you have here is the ground level equivalent of a surveillance drone."

"Holy crap! Who is using this to spy on me and why?"

"That's the $64,000 question. I have no idea why they are spying on you or your neighbors, but I have a hunch who is behind it. I have a friend who is a venture capitalist. Last year he was asked to invest in a company that planned to make robot squirrels and lease them to private detectives for surveillance of wayward spouses and the like."

"Do you know the name of this outfit?"

"No, but I'll call my friend and find out."

Twenty minutes later John and Ron were on their way to the offices of a company named Squirrels R Us, Inc with the robot squirrel in a box. They pulled up to a nondescript three story building and went in to speak to the receptionist.

"How can I help you, gentlemen?" queried the perky brunette.

"We'd like to talk to your CEO." answered Ron.

"Do you have an appointment? Mr. Ramos is a very busy man and doesn't see walk-ins."

"No, we don't have an appointment. But I think Mr. Ramos will make time for us."

"Oh really?"

"Yes!" John exclaimed as he showed her what was in the box.

Her face blanched and she stated. "I see you've found one of our toy squirrels. I'll call up to Mr. Ramos' secretary and let her know."

When they stepped off the elevator to the top floor, John and Ron were greeted by a security guard who checked them for weapons or surveillance devices before they were ushered into a plush office suite. A knockout redhead got up from her desk and showed them into the CEO's office.

"Gentlemen. My name is David Ramos. And who are you?"

After introducing themselves, John opened the box and said, "Your receptionist called this a toy squirrel, but we know this is no toy."

"You are correct. What the receptionist doesn't know won't hurt her." He stated with a sinister tone. "What you have there must be one of our prototype surveillance devices that went rogue."

"Rogue?"

"Yes, there was a software glitch in some of our first models. But we've corrected that."

"So what are these surveillance devices used for, Mr. Ramos?"

"Originally we made them for private investigators checking on people faking injuries for insurance purposes and cheating spouses. Just recently however, we've landed a very lucrative contract with the NSA."

"I knew it! Well, thanks for the information, Mr. Ramos! We'll be on our way."

"Okay gentlemen, but please leave your box and its contents here."

"No way!" they exclaimed in unison and hurried into the elevator with the security guard running after them. Before they could reach their car, a black SUV screeched to the curb and armed men jumped out.

****

"John, John! Wake up! Dinner is ready!" exclaimed Marsha.

Stirring from his nap in the hammock, John breathed a sigh of relief. "Wow. I just had a very crazy dream."

"Well, let's sit down at the table and you can tell me all about it."

Marsha was intrigued by John's story. 'I'm so glad it was a dream. Otherwise I might have a missing husband!"

They were just finishing dinner when the doorbell rang. Marsha looked out the front window, and announced it was their neighbor, Lucy Morales, holding a plastic bag. Lucy was regarded by the men on the street as a Sofia Vergara look alike and many of them found reasons to work in their front yards each time she mowed her yard wearing her purple bikini.

"Let her in," smiled John.

"Hello, Lucy, what can we do for you?" asked Marsha.

"I am so upset!" sputtered the sultry brunette. "I was skinny dipping in my hot tub and this squirrel perched on the edge of the tub, just staring at me. I tried to shoo him away and he fell into the hot tub. When he hit the water, I heard a loud beep. I fished it out and discovered it was not a real animal at all! So I put him in this plastic bag. What the hell do you think is going on?"

Super Detectives?

"Joe, I may have a lead on our Vacuum Cleaner Thief," exclaimed Roni Allure as she looked up from her iPad.

Detective Joe Sunday, a thirty-year veteran of the San Diego police force, gulped down a bite of his tuna fish sandwich and grunted, "Bout time. What do you have?"

"There's a new listing on Craig's List for slightly used vacuums with huge discounts. Says he has several different models, but doesn't give any details. Just a phone number."

"Guess it's worth checking it out. Go ahead and call him to set something up. Use your sexy voice." Joe knew that wouldn't be hard for Roni, whose voice matched her physical appeal. Why even the Chief had called her a blonde Raquel Welch look-alike.

After a five minute iPhone conversation, Detective Allure had arranged to meet the would be vacuum cleaner dealer at an old Fifth Street Warehouse at 6 p.m.

"Hope this guy ends up being our perp, Roni. Fifty seven vacuum cleaners stolen in the last two months without a good lead. Sad thing is, this is the biggest case we have on our list this month. Sure has been a slow summer!"

At 5:45 Joe and Roni stopped their gray five-year old Ford Focus (SDPD had a tight budget) a block from the warehouse and Joe got out. "I'll slowly walk by the entrance while you drive up and meet this guy. You know the drill, act like you're a desperate housewife - desperate to buy a good vacuum on the cheap. If you can identify any of the stolen vacuums, arrest him. I'll be right outside if he causes any trouble."

Ten minutes after Roni went inside, Joe heard a male voice cursing and then heavy footsteps followed by the sound of Roni's spike heels clicking on the concrete. It was a simple matter for Joe to tackle him as he ran out into the sunlight.

Roni came out, her face red and her breathing labored. "The creep tripped me with a vacuum when I showed my badge."

"Well, go ahead and cuff him while I've got him down."

Joe watched half-amused, half-disgusted as Roni tried to pull out the handcuffs that had gotten hung up on something inside her packed purse. As she freed the cuffs, out fell her 9 mm Glock, wallet, lipstick, eye makeup, iPhone and miscellaneous crap.

Soon Joe was reading the dealer his Miranda rights as Roni drove them to the station.

"Better send someone down in the morning to pick up the stolen vacuums. How many were in there?"

"Probably about four dozen. I spotted several on our list right away, including Mrs. Hoover's $1000 Supervac."

"Good. I heard she's been frantic to get her new vacuum back. She's a cleaning fanatic; cleans her house every day of the week."

"And even vacuums her front porch, Joe. You may recall that's how it got stolen, she left it on the porch to answer the phone and it was gone when she returned."

"I'd forgotten that. Glad you can remember all those pesky details. I write down all the facts, but then I can't find my notepad where I wrote them."

"That's why you need a computer, Joe! You can keep all that stuff stored and retrieve it when you need it."

"No, that's why I have you! You're the high-tech gadget person."

Joe and Roni turned the would-be vacuum cleaner magnate over to the night shift and called it a day.

Joe walked into the Chief's office the next morning, to find him cleaning his handgun and muttering to himself, "This would be a good day to die."

"Chief, am I interrupting anything?"

"No. Not really, Just talking to myself. What's up, Joe?"

"Roni and I need a major new case to work on. Something challenging. All we've got are some petty thefts. And please, no more Vaccum Cleaner Capers."

"Yeah, I can't see that case written up in True Detective!" The Chief was interrupted by a phone call.

"Looks like the Mayor. Got to answer this."

"A bank robbery? When did this happen? Why didn't the bank manager call us? Oh, he's your brother-in-law. Got it. We're right on it, Mayor!"

Slamming down the phone, the Chief exclaimed. "Looks like you and Roni have got your big case. Seems the Last National Bank was robbed overnight. Bank manager discovered it when he opened up this morning. He's the damn brother-in-law of our damn mayor. So get out there and solve this quick!"

Soon Roni and Joe were down at the bank, interviewing Bob Butts, the manager, and his secretary, Betty Alvarado. Mrs. Alvarado had discovered the robbery when she opened the vault and still seemed to be in a state of shock.

"I couldn't believe my eyes! When I unlocked the vault it was completely empty!"

"Did you notice anything else unusual, Mrs. Alvarado?" asked Joe as he pulled out his pen and a notepad.

'Well, yes! That hole in the middle of the floor inside! Can you believe it? And the vault alarm had never been triggered? How could that have happened?"

"Just the facts, Ma'm! Let's go take a look at the vault. And this hole!"

It was pretty obvious: someone had tunneled into the vault. Peering inside with a flashlight, Roni dropped her iPhone as she was snapping a cell-phone photo. "Damn! " she exclaimed and climbed down after it.

"What are you doing, Roni?" Joe asked, his voice betraying his frustration with his accident-prone partner.

"Getting my phone - and checking out this tunnel while I'm here!"

Five minutes later, Roni emerged, covered with dirt and concrete dust, but with a triumphant smile. "Got my phone and it still works. Plus, it looks like the tunnel turns up and starts from the building next door."

"Really? That would be Harem Hairstyles, a famous lady's hair salon. My wife even goes there," volunteered Mr. Butts.

"We'll go pay Harem Hairstyles a visit. Meanwhile, can you work on giving us a tally of the value of what was in the vault?" Joe didn't wait for an answer as he and Roni went next door.

"Can I help you?" queried the hairstylist with purple hair and a nose ring.

"Yes. I'm Sunday and this is my partner, Detective Allure. We're with SDPD."

"This isn't Sunday, detective. It's Thursday," the hair stylist stated matter of factly.

"What Detective Joe Sunday means, is that we need to see the owner, right away."

"Well, he's not here. I mean, he didn't open this shop this morning and he doesn't answer his cell phone. There were customers waiting when I got here for my shift."

"What's the owner's name?" Joe asked, pen in hand.

"Flavio Jenkins."

"Damn, I seem to have lost my notepad, Detective Allure."

"Don't worry, Detective Sunday, I'm taking notes on my iPhone. May we look around, Miss?

It didn't take them long to find the entrance to the tunnel in the back storage room. "Looks like they kept it covered with that Persian rug until they made their get-away" Roni noted.

Back at the bank, they briefed Mr. Butts and Mrs. Alvarado. "We suspect the owner may be in on this heist and we've put out an APB for him."

"Wait till my wife hears about this. She'll never believe it!" Butts exclaimed as he pulled out his cell phone.

Just then Joe's cell rang and he repeated aloud the message from the Chief. "Looks like Mr. Jenkins just boarded a plane for San Juan, Puerto Rico. And he had a female companion. What was her name, Chief? Margot Butts?"

"What! That's my wife! He must have kidnapped her! That's how he got the codes for the vault alarm! No wonder she's not answering her cell phone."

"She knows the security system codes, Mr. Butts?" Roni questioned.

"Yes. She and I have no secrets from each other. We have a wonderful and totally transparent relationship! You've got to find and rescue her from the clutches of this, this, horrible robber..." he sputtered.

"Since they've crossed state borders, the Chief has notified the FBI. They'll track this Flavio guy - and your wife down in San Juan." Joe explained, still looking for his notepad.

Late that afternoon, when Joe and Roni were back double-checking for prints on the security alarm pad, the Chief called. Joe put his cell on speaker so Roni and Mr. Butts could hear. "Well the FBI found Mr. Jenkins at the San Juan Grand Beach Resort, along with Mrs. Butts. They've been apprehended."

"My wife. Has she been harmed? Is she okay?" Mr. Butts asked with pleading eyes.

"Well, Mr. Jenkins had checked the two of them into the Honeymoon Suite. When the Agents entered the suite, they found the two of them in bed. In a very, shall we say, intimate position."

"But, but," sputtered Mr. Butts. The way Mr. Jenkins dressed and acted, I always assumed he was gay. In fact, Margo told me he was."

"So much for no secrets," Roni commented as she and Joe left for the station.

Superstition Mystery

Dripping with sweat, Bill looked for some shade to get a break from the blazing Arizona sun. "Who would have known it'd be this hot in the Superstition Mountains in September?" he wondered aloud. Ducking under a large overhanging rock, he took a long sip from his canteen and compared the location on his hand-held GPS with the crudely drawn paper map his boss at the Miami Herald had given him.

"I want you to do some on-site research on the legendary Lost Dutchman Gold Mine. This is the 125 year anniversary of the first news about the legend, and as you know, no one has yet confirmed the existence of the mine," his boss, Joe Walsh, had explained. "This map is a copy of the map that was found on the body of a dead prospector back in the 1950's and purportedly shows the location of the mine."

"Yeah, I've heard that a lot of people who went up into the Superstitions to look for the mine never returned and a number of them have been found dead over the years. Some say there's an Apache curse on the gold. But why are you sending me on this assignment?" queried Bill.

"Because you're the best investigative reporter I've ever had. You have a keen mind and innate skepticism. You should be able to sort out fact from fiction. And you're in good enough physical shape to hike around those mountains."

Bill thought about that last statement while he adjusted his backpack and started down into the next canyon. "Wish I was in as good shape as Joe thinks I am." The slope of the ground steepened and Bill started skidding down the hillside, with branches from the scrub junipers and spines on prickly pear cactus scratching his arms.

Finally down in the bottom of the canyon, Bill heard thunder rumbling in the distance as dark cumulonimbus clouds suddenly darkened the sky. A light breeze sprang up, bringing the clean smell of rain in the distance and within minutes the winds increased to gale force. "Damn, I didn't count on a mountain thunderstorm; better find some shelter," he complained under his breath. Branches started breaking under the force of the wind and the dark sky was split time and time again by jagged streaks of lightning.

Soon scattered drops of rain gave way to a torrential downpour as Bill, drenched to the bone, searched fruitlessly for shelter. Then a lightning strike just ahead revealed an old run-down shack. Pushing open the door that barely hung by one hinge, he staggered inside and fell exhausted on the creaky floor boards.

After a few minutes, the lightning flashes diminished and the sounds of thunder disappeared into the distance. Soon the sky brightened and sunlight peered into the windows. That's when Bill saw it: a skeleton sitting on a stool. "Must be an old prospector," he thought as he saw the old felt broad-brimmed hat still on the skull. There was something sticking out of the back of the skeleton, and the ever-inquisitive reporter walked over to get a better view. "Mother of God, that's an arrow!" he exclaimed as he felt an involuntary shudder rack his body.

After composing himself, Bill took off his drenched shirt and walking shorts, wrung them out, and put them back on with a long sigh. Spying a rickety table and chair in the corner, Bill sat down, pulled out a pocket digital recorder, and recorded his memories of the day's events. Pulling the old hand-drawn map from Joe out of his waterproof backpack, he spread it out along with the GPS on the rough-hewn table. His pulse beat faster as he surmised the old shack was less then a mile from the supposed location of the Lost Dutchman Gold Mine.

Just then, Bill heard heavy footsteps outside and turned to the door just in time to see a large Hispanic man with a handlebar mustache barge into the shack.

"What are you doing here?" the man demanded.

"Why, why, I came in here to get out of the rain. Is that a problem, señor?"

"Don't suppose so. No one owns this old shack anyway, at least no one who's still alive," he laughed as he looked over at the skeleton.

Bill started to fold up the map, and tried to sound nonchalant, as he said, "well, now that the sun's back out, I'll be going. The shack is all yours."

"Wait! Is that a map in your hands? Let me see that!" demanded the burly mustached man and grabbed the map out of Bill's hands.

"Hey, señor, that's my map!"

"Well, it looks like a map to my gold mine!"

"Your gold mine?"

"That's right, gringo. I found the mine just last week and now it belongs to me! Are you trying to steal my gold? Why you dirty thief!" With a menacing smile, he moved to stop Bill from leaving.

Bill backed up exclaiming, "hey man, you can have your gold! I'm just a reporter doing a story on the legend of the Lost Dutchman Gold Mine!"

"Too bad for you that you got this close to my gold! Otherwise I would have let you go!"

Bill's chest felt like it would explode when he saw the mustached man pull a large knife out of his pocket. He grabbed the man's wrist and tried to break his hold on the knife. His adversary grunted and grabbed Bill by the shirt collar with his other hand. They struggled and Bill fell backward under the man's weight. Then all went black.

The sun was setting above the canyon walls as Bill came to with a terrible headache. The mustached man lay on top of him like a dead weight. Struggling to get free, Bill felt a sticky substance on the floor and realized it was blood. Finally he extricated himself from his foe and looked in shock and horror as his eyes took in the scene.

Clinging to the back of his adversary was the skeleton of the old prospector. That was unbelievable enough, but then Bill noted why the burly man was dead. The arrow that had been the demise of the old prospector was now buried deep in the back of the mustached man.

Feeling weak in his knees, Bill sat down on the floor and pulled out his digital recorder. "Joe will never believe this!" he exclaimed as he clicked the on button.

The Alien

"Mr. Cunningham, will it be your usual?"

I smiled as Miranda, my favorite Starbuck barista, rang up a grande java chip frappuccino. She soon called my name and I picked up my drink.

"Ah, I'm in luck!" I thought as I spied the two vacant padded chairs by the side door. Easing into one, I opened up my laptop on the nearby table. The strong coffee aromas and background music stirred my creativity. Soon I was furiously typing, enjoying the feel of the keys as the ideas poured out.

"Mind if I sit here while I'm on my break?" Miranda asked as she walked by my table.

It took me a minute to resurface after being submerged in my writing for nearly an hour. I looked up to see the long-legged brunette looking down at me. "Oh, sure, Miranda."

"What are you writing about today, Bill?"

"A short story for the writer's group I attend. This time we've been given 'the sound of the surgeon's footsteps' as a writing prompt."

"And how are you coming on that?" she asked through pursed red lips.

"Well, I'm about halfway through a story, but I'm not sure it's all going to come together."

"Tell me about it."

"Okay, here's the story line. I'm a rancher named Pecos Tucker, living near a small town here in South Texas. I have a hired hand, Jose, who's been working for me about three months. His family lives in Mexico and he sends half his paycheck to them every month."

"An illegal? Is this a story about immigration issues?"

"No, he's got a green card. I'm not trying to make any statements about immigration, just write an interesting story."

"Okay. Continue."

"One night there's a bad storm that rips part of the roof off the barn. So the next morning Jose gets up on the roof to repair it. He accidentally gets too close to the edge and falls off. I come running over and see that he's got a broken leg, a compound fracture. And maybe some internal injuries. So I load him in my pickup and drive him to the little hospital in town."

Just then we were interrupted by a regular customer who came in the side door and asked Miranda why she wasn't behind the counter.

"George, I'm on my break. Alvin is behind the counter, and he'll be glad to wait on you."

"Yeah, but he's old and ugly and you're young and hot," grumped the elderly customer before acting on her suggestion.

"George is such an old curmudgeon," sighed my favorite barista. Brightening up, she continued, "but happily, most of my customers are like you."

"Like me? Intellectual as well as handsome?"

"No," Miranda laughed, "friendly and interesting to talk to. But back to your story, Mr. Writer."

"Where was, I? Okay, I drive Jose to the local hospital and take him into the emergency room. When they see the compound fracture, they call for one of the surgeons who's on duty. Finally the surgeon gets down there and they wheel poor Jose off for some x-rays and other tests. I sit there in the waiting room, thinking about the cattle I need to go feed, the garden I need to tend to, and what I'm going to do if Jose is out of commission for a long time. Then I start wondering why it's taking so long and wondering how Jose will be able to pay the hospital bill, since he doesn't have any insurance."

"And what happens next?"

"Well, let me read you that part of the story:"

All these thoughts are whirling around in my mind and finally, I hear the sound of the surgeon's footsteps coming down the long hall. As he rounds the corner with a clipboard in hand, he sees me and stops.

"Are you Mr. Tucker?"

"Yes, I am, Doc. How is my hired hand, Jose?"

"Well, I have some good news and some bad news, Mr. Tucker."
He paused, waiting for the expected questions.

"What's the good news?"

"We've set his leg and sutured up the wound. And he doesn't appear to have any internal injuries."

"Well, that's good. So what's the bad news? That it's going to cost $10,000 to spring him out of here?"

"No, it's something much more serious."

"What could be more serious than $10,000, Doc?"

"Mr. Tucker, your hired hand appears to be an alien."

"I know, but he's not an illegal! He's got a green card!" I exclaim.

The surgeon sits down next to me with a serious, even perplexed look on his tired face. I can see from his name tag that his name is Dr. Casey, the chief surgeon. He clears his throat, looks me straight in the eye, and tells me something that sends a chill down my back.

"Mr. Tucker, when I said an alien, what I mean is that he's not from this world. He's not human! The X-rays of his chest showed three hearts, four lungs, and some organs that I have no idea what their function is."

"Are you sure?"

"And that, Miranda, is as far as I've gotten. But I think I'll have to scrap it and start over. It's just too cheesy."

"I hate to say it, Mr. Cunningham, but you're right. There must be hundreds of cheesy science fiction stories about aliens out there already. Whoops," she said, glancing at the clock on the wall behind the coffee grinder, "my break is already over. Good luck on coming up with a different story line."

I watched Miranda's cute little wiggle as she walked away and put on her apron. "Oh, to be young again," I thought wistfully as the faint smell of her perfume lingered behind. But then I turned my attention to the laptop in front of me and started pondering over a new story line.

My mind was miles away when another customer came through the door. I could tell he was a doctor because he was still wearing his scrubs. *Do they wear their scrubs out in public because they're too tired to change into their street clothes or because they want everyone to recognize their profession?*

"Doctor Ben. Good to see you again. What can I get you?" I heard Miranda say. I couldn't help but hear his reply.

"Something really strong. I wish you had some scotch! I need a stiff drink!"

"A long day at the hospital?" I heard Miranda innocently ask.

"You can't even imagine!" stated the doctor, and leaned on the counter as he continued. What I heard made my heart rate go sky high.

"You'll probably think I've flipped out when I tell you this, Miranda." He leaned close to her ear and I had to struggle to catch what he said.

"But, Miss Starbucks Barista, I kid you not when I tell you this. Today I operated on a guy who turned out to be an alien! By alien, I do mean someone from another world."

I knocked my coffee over and it spilled on the keyboard of my laptop that still showed the title of my story on its screen: "The Alien."

The Decision

The lonely tall man walked to the window and looked out at the greenery of the gardens below, deep in thought. *What to do? This might be the most important decision of my life. And this will affect so many people, so many countries besides our own.*

He was interrupted from his thoughts by his no-nonsense appointment secretary. "Mr. President, the Joint Chiefs and the members of your National Security Team are assembling in the Situation Room."

"Give me a few minutes alone, Mabel. I'll be there in five."

The tall man thought back to the events of the last two years since his election. If the Florida vote count would have been just a little different, my opponent would be standing here in the Oval Office. He's the one that would have to make this decision. But, I wanted to be President, and here I am. Most of the time I'm glad. But days like today I'm not so sure. Well, time to go.

"Gentlemen and ladies, please be seated," he said as he strode into the room. "Okay, let's get down to business. First, William, since we have a couple new members on the team, bring us all up to speed on the major events since 9/11."

"Yes sir, Mr. President. Shortly after the World Trade Towers fell, the CIA was able to confirm that Al Qaeda, headed up by Osama Bin Laden, was responsible and that his training camps were located in Afghanistan. Twenty six days later US and British airplanes began bombing Al Qaeda and Taliban forces in that country and followed that up with conventional ground forces shortly thereafter. The next month the UN Security Council authorized the UN to establish a transitional administration safeguarded by troops from various UN member nations. In December Hamid Karzai was selected to be interim administrative head of the country."

"Yes. And I still think we selected the wrong guy for that job. I don't trust him. Maybe that's why Bin Laden was able to escape our clutches soon after. But go on."

"Okay, Mr. President. Within months we'd conducted major ground operations against the Taliban and Al Qaeda. In June Karzai became the head of the transitional government. Since then we've been working on reconstruction plans. Now, a year after our invasion, things seem to be well in hand in the country, though we've not yet been able to capture Bin Laden. That brings us to some new intelligence we have from the CIA."

All eyes turned to the Director of the CIA, who cleared his throat and began a hastily arranged presentation. "Just this week we have received credible information that Al Qaeda has had contacts with Saddam Hussein's administration in Iraq. I am concerned that Saddam and Bin Laden may join forces against their stated enemy, the US."

"Then there is the problem of Saddam's suspected WMD's, including their quest to build a nuclear weapon, Mr. President," interjected the Chairman of the Joint Chiefs.

"So what do you recommend, Mr. Secretary?" asked the President of his Secretary of Defense, though sure he knew the answer.

"I think we should begin plans to preemptively strike Iraq, in order to topple Saddam's regime, secure any weapons of mass destruction, and prevent Al Qaeda from establishing a base in Iraq."

"How would you go about it?"

The Chairman of the Joint Chiefs spoke up. "We've made some preliminary plans, sir, and estimate we'd need 200,000 troops on the ground, preceded, of course by massive air strikes. We estimate we could accomplish all of the stated objectives in less than a year after beginning the air strikes."

"And then what?" asked the lonely tall man.

"Well, we'd withdraw and appoint an interim government like we have in Afghanistan."

"And just like that, peace and democracy would break out in a country that's been under   a gestapo-like dictatorship for decades?" The President's tone belied his skepticism. Turning to his Secretary of State, he asked, "What do you think?"

"I've had a study by a respected think-tank conducted, Mr. President, that says it could take decades to fully bring democracy to a country in such circumstances, especially when there are multiple ethnic and religious factions in place. That's only one problem I see. Invading Iraq without being provoked could cause most of the population of the Middle East to turn against us. Then there's the large direct cost of fighting the war, both in casualties and in dollars."

"Most of those towel-heads hate the US anyway! And how many more lives would be lost if Saddam and Al Qaeda set off nuclear weapons inside one of our major cities!" argued the Secretary of Defense.

A long and heated discussion ensued about the pros and cons of invading Iraq, including Tony Blair's war-like stance, conflicting reports about WMD's in Iraq, and what it would take to rebuild the country.

Finally, the President called an end to the debate. "It looks like the room is pretty divided on whether an invasion of Iraq is in our best interest, as well as the best interests of the Iraqi people. I've made a decision. The expected cost of thousands of American lives and hundreds of millions of American dollars is not worth invading Iraq unless and until Saddam Hussein joins forces with Bin Laden or makes definite plans to use WMD's against us. In the old Western movies I watched as a kid, when the sheriff and the bad guy face off on Main Street at high noon, the sheriff never goes for his gun until the bad guy makes a move for his. Saddam hasn't made that move yet. And I don't think he ever will."

"But, President Gore, I don't think you understand the gravity of the situation!" chimed in the Director of the CIA.

"I think you underestimate me, Director. That will be all."

As the meeting adjourned, the President overheard the Secretary of Defense mutter, "if only George Bush would have won the Florida vote recount."

The Dog Days of Summer

Bob did a double take when he looked at the outdoor thermometer. "Maria, can you believe 104 degrees? Isn't that a record?"

"Heck if I know, Bob. All I know is it's the hottest August I remember in a long time. Even the dog doesn't want to go outside to relieve himself."

"Well, they do call this the Dog Days of Summer. Guess Scooby figures he can hold it till the sun goes down. Poor dog!"

About 9 that evening, Bob and Maria, carrying a plastic bag, walked Scooby around their neighborhood so he could do his duty.

"Hello, neighbors. Out for a walk?"

"Why, hello James," Bob & Maria said in unison. James, a tall clean-cut single guy, had recently moved into the house for rent across the street. "This is the only time of day we can get our dog to go out and do his thing."

"Shucks, I don't blame him. It's been miserably hot this whole week."

"Guess they don't call it the Dog Days of Summer for nothing," piped up Maria. "I guess most of the dogs know it's that time of year," she laughed.

"True," confirmed James, but then asked, "Do you know who named it the Dog Days and why?"

"No. Guess we always figured it was when it was even too hot for dogs and so they just lie around like they are lazy."

"Well, the ancient Greeks first came up with the term. The brightest star in the night sky is Sirius, in the constellation Canis Major. Sirius is called the Dog Star and because it's close to the sun they thought it was responsible for the hot weather. In late summer it more or less rises and sets with the sun. The Greeks thought it caused dogs to pant excessively, plants to wilt, men to weaken, and women to become aroused."

"Really?" exclaimed Maria and Bob as one.

"Yep. I'm sort of an astronomy buff. I like to look at the stars through my telescope and study about them. In fact, you can get a great view of Sirius about now. Would you like to see it? I have the telescope set up on my back deck."

"Sure. Let us drop Scooby off inside our house and we'll be over in a minute," Maria spoke for both of them.

A few minutes later Bob & Maria rang the doorbell of their neighbor's home and he greeted them with a couple of cold beers and walked them through the house to his back deck.

Bob was obviously impressed. "Wow, that's quite a telescope, James."

"Well, you know what they say about men and their toys. Let me swing the telescope around to spot Sirius. It should be just above the horizon. Although it's the brightest star, the planet

Venus is brighter and sometimes people mistake it for Sirius. Ah ha, I've found it. Come over and have a look."

"Wow. That is bright - and pretty. So that's called the Dog Star?"

After a few minutes of looking at Sirius and other stars in the summer night sky, Bob and Maria thanked James, and headed back to their house. Bob continued to talk excitedly about James and his astronomy hobby but soon noticed that Maria didn't share his enthusiasm.

"What's wrong, honey? You don't seem as enthralled about seeing Sirius as I do."

"You want to know why? Did you notice where the telescope was pointed when we first got out on the deck?"

"No. Why?"

"It was pointed straight at the big windows in the back of his neighbor's house."

"You mean the Cantu's?"

"Yes. Eddie and Selma's house. I know you know who Selma is. She's the one that parades around the yard in that skimpy red and white bikini. God knows what she wears or doesn't wear when she's inside."

"Yes," chuckled, Bob. "At least she looks really good in that outfit. Unlike Mrs. Jones down the street who thinks she's still 40 years younger than she is, and also wears tiny bikinis.That's what I call obscene."

"That's not the point, you knucklehead. The point is, I think our new neighbor is a pervert. Why else would he be looking in their windows with a telescope?"

"James? You mean he's a peeping Tom?"

"That's exactly what I mean!"

"Gee. So what do we do about it? We can't go tell the Cantu's until we know for sure that James is getting his jollies by invading their privacy."

"Well, I've noticed that there is a hole in the fence on the side of James' lot. I may do a little spying of my own tomorrow night, Bob."

"Okay. But I hope you're wrong, honey. Be careful."

About 10 p.m. the next night, Maria drug Bob away from the TV to look through the hole in the fence. "Look! Tell me what you see and then tell me I'm not crazy!"

"Dang, that looks like a camera mounted onto the telescope. It's pointed at the Cantus' And it looks like James is snapping some pictures right now!"

"So now what do we do, Bob? Who do we report it to?"

"Well, let me think. You remember Harry Hanrahan that lives a couple blocks away? He's a detective for the SAPD Vice Squad. Let's go by his house tomorrow evening and have a chat."

After Bob and Maria explained what they'd seen to Detective Hanrahan, he agreed to check it out. They peeked out their front window as the policeman rang James' doorbell and was admitted inside when he showed his badge. A few minutes later, Detective Hanrahan appeared in the doorway, shook hands with James, and walked out of the house.

"What the hell, Bob?" quizzed his wife. I thought Harry would be leading him out in handcuffs. Instead it looks like they are best buddies!"

Just then the doorbell rang and Maria threw the door open with one word, "Well?"

"Let's just say appearances can be deceiving. That's all I can tell you for now, though I expect you'll soon find out more about what's coming down. Good night, neighbors."

Dumbfounded, Maria closed the door and looked at Bob. "What do you make of that?"

"Who knows? I'm going to bed early; this heat is exhausting me."

The next evening they were out walking Scooby when they noticed two black SUV's with government plates parked in front of the Cantu's house. Bob and Maria watched as the front door opened and four men and James walked Eddie and Selma out in handcuffs. "Good work, James!" they heard one of the men say, as they loaded the Cantu's into one of the SUV's and drove away.

James saw Bob and Maria and walked over to give them a brief explanation as he held out his FBI credentials. "Eddie Cantu is a high ranking member of the Zeta Drug Cartel who launders millions of the cartel's dollars here in San Antonio. I moved next door to do around the clock surveillance of them. Sorry I had to deceive you about being an amateur astronomer."

"So, is it true that Sirius is the origin of the Dog Days of Summer?"

"Sure is."

The Ides of March

"I'm Leo Marston, late night TV host. Today, as some of you may know, is the Ides of March. Better known as March 15. I'm standing here at the corner of Hollywood and Vine with our camera crew to see what passersby know about the Ides of March. Here comes a young lady and I'll start by talking to her."

"Hello, ma'am. I'm Leo Marston and would like to ask you a couple of questions if you have a minute."

"Will I be on TV? Sure." The young blonde quickly turns around to check her makeup in a small mirror from her purse before facing the camera.

"Start by telling us your name and what you do."

"My name is Scarlett and I'm a waitress hoping for a break into show business."

"Okay, Scarlett, tell me what you know about the Ides of March."

"You mean the band?"

"No. Something else."

"Gee. Got me there, Mr. Marston. I have no clue."

After Scarlett leaves, Leo spots another stranger.

"Here's a gentleman carrying a briefcase. Sir, I'm Leo Marston and wondered if you could tell our TV audience something about the Ides of March. First tell us your name and something about yourself."

"I'm Sam and I work for Goldman Sachs. Wasn't that the day that Roman guy in ancient history was murdered? Maybe assassinated?"

"That's correct. And what was his name? It starts with a J."

"Justin something. No that doesn't sound right. Maybe Julio or something like that. But I don't have time for more questions." He glances at the time on his smart watch. "I've got to get to an important board meeting."

"Thanks, sir; never mind. Here's a lady in a business suit. Ma'am, I'm Leo Marston. Can you tell me your name, what you do for a living and who Julius Caesar is or was?"

"I'm Marie and I am a high school French teacher. Didn't he invent that smoothie they call an Orange Julius?"

Leo suppresses a laugh, and explains, "He was a famous Roman Emperor and something happened to him on the Ides of March."

"Oh, wasn't Julius Caesar the one who was killed on that date?"

"Correct! And when is the Ides of March?"

"March 21? No? March 12?"

"Today, March 15, is the Ides of March, Marie."

The show is interrupted by a loud police siren. Seconds later a squad car pulls up and two officers get out. "Someone called 911 to report a disturbance at this location," exclaims the burly one with red hair.

"No disturbance, officer," interjects Leo Marston's producer. "We are doing some live interviews for the Leo Marston show and we have the proper permits. Here they are."

After carefully reviewing the permits, the police excuse themselves and the show goes on.

"Here's a gentleman who's been standing by. What's your name sir and what do you do?"

"I'm Sam and I'm a bouncer in a local club."

"Okay Sam. What can you tell me about the Ides of March?"

"That's today. A very unlucky day, they tell me."

"Oh, and why do you say that?"

"My boss is a big student of history and very superstitious. He won't go outside his house on the Ides of March. He's Italian you know, and always reminds me that one of his ancestors was stabbed to death outside the Roman Senate on March 15."

"How long ago did that happen?"

"Oh, I don't know. More than a thousand years ago. Maybe two thousand. Back in the days when they rode around in those Roman chariots and dressed in togas."

"Thanks, Sam. Here's a young man passing by. I'm Leo Marston and I'm doing some TV interviews. What's your name and what do you do?"

"I'm Brian and I'm a college student here at UCLA."

"What do you know about today's date, Brian?"

"Today is the Ides of March. Great day for toga parties like my fraternity is having tonight. Should be great fun! You can come if you bring a hot chick with you, Mr. Marston."

"Thanks, I'll pass on that. Here's a hot chick, I mean young woman I'll interview next."

"Hi, I'm Leo Marston from the Leo Marston TV show. "Would you mind telling me your name and what you do?"

"Sure, my name is Tara and I'm an exotic dancer."

Well, Tara, today is March 15, also called the Ides of March. Some people consider it a very unlucky day. How about you?"

"Today is a very lucky day, Mr. Marston. First, because a year ago I got my job dancing at the club. And second, because today I get to be on your TV show. Thanks so much!" she exclaims as she gives him a big hug.

"Thanks, Tara. Well that's about all we have time for. Except here comes Audrey, my secretary."

"Leo, I have a question for YOU. Is today going to be lucky or unlucky for you?"

"Gee, I don't know, Audrey. I feel pretty lucky because I got some great footage for the show. What did you have in mind when you asked?"

"Well, if I hadn't come along it would no longer be a lucky day! I'm here to remind you that today is your wedding anniversary. It would be very unlucky for you if you go home tonight without flowers and chocolates!"

"Oh, crap! How could I have forgotten?"

The I.R.S.

Jessica Morales banged the flat of her hand on the Starbucks table as she exclaimed, "Damn Congress! They are so concerned with getting re-elected that they won't do the right thing on immigration! Did you hear the latest? Ten Senators have announced that they plan to filibuster the bi-partisan Immigration Reform Bill."

"I hadn't heard that. I thought a compromise had been agreed on by the key members of both parties. Not good. But I need to head out for class. Later."

As she watched the blonde leave, Jessica realized her classmate in grad school wasn't as passionate about the issue as she was. Not many of her friends were.

A man in a trench coat in the table behind her got up to leave and handed her a business card. Then he whispered, "If you'd like to do more to right some of these wrongs, give us a call."

The front of the card simply had "I.R.S." in bold blue letters. She turned the card over to see a local D.C. phone number and the words "International Readjustment Society." Intrigued, she put it in her leather wallet, finished her latte, and walked back to her apartment.

Jessica watched the news on CNN after class that evening and decided she had to take some action on this vital issue. Finding the I.R.S. card in her wallet, she dialed the number on her iPhone and soon found herself at the modest offices of the International Readjustment Society about a mile from the Capital.

"Are you the one who called earlier?" queried a geeky looking young man in casual clothes who led her to a conference table with three women and two men dressed in business attire.

"Yes. I'm Jessica Morales, a grad student at Georgetown. Someone gave me your business card today at Starbucks when they heard me complaining about the plans to block a vote on the immigration bill. I want to do something to make sure a vote is taken."

"You came to the right place, Jessica!" A tall red haired woman rose and extended her hand. "Come join us at the table and we'll tell you what we're all about."

"Five years ago twelve of us formed this organization to stand up for social and economic justice. We had all become aware how the Good Old Boys System, major financial firms, and certain world governments had all reached a state of inertia that allowed them to foist their will on the common people. We wanted to readjust this state of inertia, but to do it without violence or threats of violence."

"So how do you do it?" Jessica asked.

The geeky looking young man spoke up, "We work behind the scenes to make minor changes in the balance of power. Do you remember the difficult time the Violence Against Women Act had in getting passed in the U.S. Senate?"

"Sure. But somehow it got past the opposition and was signed into law."

"What you may not remember is that shortly before the decisive vote a video was posted on YouTube of the Good Old Boys in the Senate saying some outrageous things about battered women and rape. As a result none of those Senators voted against the legislation after all. That video was recorded by someone friendly to our organization and we posted it."

An Asian young man with black plastic glasses spoke up next. "In late 2012 a certain major bank in the United Kingdom was ordered to pay nearly $2 billion in fines for money laundering. The whistleblower who testified before the U.S. regulators had been threatened with death before she could give her testimony. We implemented a friendly kidnapping to spirit her away until the day of her testimony, at which time she appeared in disguise."

"However," interjected an older black woman. "Not all of our efforts have been successful. We spearheaded the Occupy Wall Street movement with the hope it would bring about real financial reform, However, when we saw the ways the movement was twisting off, we pulled out our support. And as you know, the banks that were too big to fail at the start of the Great Recession are sadly even bigger and more powerful now."

"So what do you think, Jessica?" asked a blonde woman who seemed to be in charge. "Would you like to join our cause?"

There was no hesitation in Jessica's voice as she answered in the affirmative.

"Fine. We will need to get some information from you first to run a background check. Not that we don't trust you, but to protect everyone. While you are waiting for the background check to be completed, make sure you are watching the news on Friday."

"Oh, why is that?"

"Friday a cloture vote is scheduled to put an end to the filibuster that certain senators are waging against the bill for a federal sales tax on ammunition. You may have heard of the proposal to tax bullets at $1 apiece. We feel that will cut down on drive by shootings and at the same time help pay down the federal deficit."

"So how are you to going to make sure the cloture vote passes?"

"There are five minority party senators who plan to vote against cloture. Each of them takes a limo to the Capital daily from their apartments and we know the route they take. There is going to be a huge traffic tie up Friday morning on that route due to a number of stalled vehicles. By the time the jams are cleared, the Senate will already have voted."

Jessica watched CNN in amazement Friday morning as she saw the prophesied traffic jam take place. That afternoon she got a call that she'd passed the background check and to come in for her first assignment.

"Okay, Jessica. This is a big one and one that seems to be near and dear to your heart. Next Wednesday is the day the Gang of Ten is planning to start their filibuster of the Immigration Reform Bill. They meet for coffee in the Senate dining room each morning. Your job is to put knockout drops in their coffee pot to make sure they miss Wednesday's session. Can you do that?"

Gulping down her fears of being caught, Jessica exclaimed, "Hell yes! I can and will!"

Wednesday morning found Jessica in a waitress uniform in the Senate dining room. She had just poured a little bottle of knock out drops into the coffee pot and was walking toward the table where the Gang of Ten sat conspiring. Suddenly a loud alarm sounded and she was surrounded by Capitol Police.

"Oh, no! I'm going to jail!" Jessica said through gritted teeth. The alarm kept sounding and she suddenly woke up in her own bed in her apartment. It was her alarm clock, awaking her the morning before she'd gone to Starbucks.

"Wow. Thank God, this was all a dream - actually a dream that turned into a nightmare!"

As she got ready to leave for class, she picked up her leather wallet. A business card fell out on the floor. It read "I.R.S." in bold blue letters. She gingerly picked it up and turned it over.

The Long Road Back

The dusty road seemed to go on forever. Herb stopped by a scrub oak beside the way to mop his brow and think. *How long has it been since I traveled this road? Must be close to four years now. But the last time I was headed in the opposite direction and I was speeding along in my new Lexus convertible. Now my shoes are nearly worn through and who knows when I'll be able to get some wheels of any kind, much less a new Lexus?*

With a sigh, Herb stuffed his handkerchief in the back pocket of his road weary jeans and trudged on toward his parent's home. As he did, he recalled the last words he and his dad had just before he drove away.

"Son, you don't have to do this. Your mother and I would love to have you stay and take over the ranch with your older brother when we get too old to live this far out in the country. "

"Damn, Dad. Don't you see that I need to go make my own way in the world? I don't like living away from the city life I enjoyed in college. I want to go make some real money, not raise cattle and sheep. With what I learned in school, I should be able to double the money in my trust fund in a year or two. Soon I'll be independently wealthy and get to travel the world and play with the rich and famous. Maybe I'll even go into politics."

Herb noticed a vulture circling overhead and yelled in frustration, "I'm not that far gone, you stupid bird!" The vulture ignored him and instead swooped down to feast on a dead jackrabbit a hundred yards ahead.

The big black bird reminded him of how his creditors had swooped down upon him soon after his investments took a nose dive in the 2008 financial crash. He'd been riding high for a few months after he left home. By highly leveraging his investments, he'd bought a big house in Las Vegas and made a killing in some financial services stocks. The parties and the beautiful women who had flocked to him had been the talk of of the town.

The road to the ranch seemed more rocky than he remembered. The ache in his feet was almost as painful as the ache in his heart. *I hope that Dad will let me stay in the bunkhouse or the barn, if he won't let me back into the house. Maybe I can pay for my keep by mending fences and feeding the cattle. But based on what my big brother wrote back to me last year, they may not even let me on the property.*

Herb thought back to the prior Christmas season, when he was living on tips he was getting delivering pizza. He'd mailed a Christmas card back home, the first in two years, and told them he'd fallen on hard times. Maybe they'd take pity on him and invite him home for the holidays. Two weeks after he'd sent the card, he got a letter in the mail from his brother, Bob. His hopes were dashed as he read it.

"Brother Herb, how could you even dare to hint that you'd like to come home for Christmas? You never came to Mom's funeral last month even though we tried to call and even wrote you. Dad is heartbroken about Mom and about you cutting off communications with us. We don't want a jerk like you back here! So stay away! Go live the life you've chosen, you selfish bastard!"

Bob couldn't know, of course, that Herb's cell phone contract had expired because he couldn't afford the bills. And he'd moved so many times since his house had been foreclosed on that the post office didn't know where to deliver his mail.

Herb had wept for hours after he read Bob's letter, sad that he hadn't even known his mother had died and angry with himself for all the bad decisions he'd made. But the biggest blow was being rejected by the family he had left. If he'd had more money, he'd have drowned himself in whiskey, but he realized it was good he hadn't.

Since then, things had gone from bad to worse. Herb's old junker of an automobile had blown a head gasket and he couldn't afford to fix it. With no transportation, he lost his pizza delivery job. So, he moved in with one of the few friends who hadn't left him as soon as he lost his trust fund, and got jobs as a day laborer. Last month his friend had moved away, and Herb had started staying in a homeless shelter. The drunks and drug addicts and mentally unstable people he met there encouraged him to try to go back to to the ranch when they heard he was from a wealthy family. As his clothes got more threadbare and the soles on his shoes got thinner, the more he thought they might be right. So here he was, now about a mile from his family home. He'd been rehearsing the speech he'd give his father when he knocked on the massive front door.

Just then, Herb rounded the crest of the last hill before the ranch. He choked up when he saw the big family house with its white picket fence, surrounded by acres of grazing land. It all looked just the same as when he'd left. Only now Mom was dead and his brother hated him. Probably Dad did too.

It looked like someone was sitting on the front porch. Suddenly the figure stood up and started down the path to the front gate. *Was that Dad?* The old man stopped at the gate and shaded his eyes to see him better. Suddenly he broke into a run. *My father, old as he is now, is running? Running toward me? What will he say when we meet?*

"Dad, Dad, is that you? It's so good to see you. I was foolish not to listen to you years ago. Can I stay with you guys awhile while I get back on my feet..."

His speech was interrupted by his father grabbing him in a bear hug and exclaiming, "Why of course, you can, Herb! You are still a member of this family! There, there, you don't have to make any speeches to me and you can wipe those tears away. It's just so good to see you!'

Herb was astounded by the welcome Dad gave him. He didn't cuss him out or even ask him any questions. Instead he pushed him into the house and yelled for the housekeeper to put some soup on. "My son was lost, but now he's not!" exclaimed the old man.

"Dad, when Bob wrote me back after I sent you guys that Christmas card, he told me in no uncertain terms that I wasn't welcome back here."

"What card, Herb? I never saw it. I've prayed every night since you left that you'd come back home!"

"Dad, I wish I'd known a year ago what I know now!"

The Luck of the Irish

I'd become acquainted with Detective Molly Hanrahan when she'd investigated the robbery of my corner grocery store. That was five years ago, before I called it quits and settled into retirement. So it was with interest that I read the story in The Evening Gazette titled, "Irish Cop Always Gets Her Man."

The article described Detective Hanrahan as young, physically fit and attractive, and one of the smartest people in local law enforcement. It seemed that she'd solved every case on which she'd been the lead investigator, beginning with her first case at my grocery store. When asked by the reporter as to the secret to her success, she'd modestly replied, "Just the luck o' the Irish, I guess!"

I had just finished reading the article, when my doorbell rang. Peering through the peephole, I could see it was John, my friendly neighbor who lived across the street. When I threw the door open, I gasped as I got a good look at him in the porch light.

"John, you look like you've been in a war! What happened?"

Wiping the blood away that was dripping down from a head wound, he gasped, "Beats the hell out of me, Gene. I'd just driven into the garage after work when two guys wearing black ski masks stepped out of the shadows and beat the crap out of me. The next thing I remember is coming to on the garage floor."

"Holy crap! What about Lisa? Is she home and is she okay?"

"Oh, she flew to Phoenix yesterday to spend a week with her mother. Gee, I should probably call her."

Realizing John was still in shock, I insisted he come in and lie down while I got a cold rag for his bloody face.

"I assume you haven't even been in the house since this all happened?"

"No, I was afraid to go inside so I came straight over here for help."

I picked up my cell phone and dialed 911. "This is Gene Lee on 911 Capitol Avenue and my neighbor across the street was just beaten by two men as he drove into his garage after work. His name? John Lavelle. We need a squad car over here to check his house. Yes that's right. Probably a burglary, but we don't know that for sure. Less than five minutes? Okay. Thanks."

Sure enough, within four minutes a blue and white police cruiser pulled up and two young male cops came to the door.

After hearing John's account of the incident, the two cops borrowed his keys and advanced on his house. One went around back and the other went in the front door. Soon we saw lights go on in each room of the house. Fifteen minutes later they walked back across the street to talk to us.

"Whoever was there is long gone. Looks like a forced entry through the door that leads from the garage into the utility room.

We didn't notice anything disturbed inside the residence. Would you mind coming with us, Mr. Lavelle, to see if you can spot anything missing?"

About thirty minutes later, John came out of the house with the two police officers. They talked briefly before the cops drove off. Curious to find out what what they'd discovered, I walked across the street.

"So was it a burglary, John?"

"Yeah. But they only took one thing: that big ugly black and gold lamp Lisa bought last week from Overseas Imports. I wouldn't mind that it's gone except that the dang thing cost over $500. What surprises me is that they didn't take any of Lisa's jewelry or the cash sitting on the dresser."

"What did the cops say about it?"

"They just scratched their heads and said they'd write up a report. I don't have much hope they'll find out who attacked me or that they'll locate Lisa's lamp."

"Sorry about that, neighbor. Hope you can get some sleep tonight.

****

Early the next morning I was roused from my morning coffee by the doorbell. I looked out the peephole and there she stood, looking almost the same as when I'd last seen her: medium length black hair tied up in a ponytail and bright blue eyes looking out of a lightly freckled slightly tanned face.

"Detective Hanrahan! To what do I owe the honor?"

"Gene Lee, good to see you again! I was wanting to talk to your neighbor, Mr. Lavelle, and get a look inside his house. But he doesn't seem to be home."

"No, he left for work about twenty minutes ago. Saturday's are a busy day for his bookstore. But come on in and tell me why a famous detective is on this little case."

"Sure, John. I might even take a cup of that coffee I smell."

Settling down at the kitchen table, she began,"to make a long story short, this is the fifth robbery of a lamp bought recently at Overseas Imports. I started getting suspicious after the third lamp was stolen last week."

"Suspicious about what?"

"That there is a sinister connection between these thefts. That's all I am at liberty to tell you at this point. I do want to talk to your neighbor after he gets home. So will you give him my card?"

"Sure. Great to see you again and hope you get to the bottom of this soon. You're my favorite detective, you know." I smiled as she left.

****

Two weeks later, Detective Hanrahan drove up to John's house and returned his wife's lamp. Other than some scratches near the base, it looked intact. I walked over when John called me.

"So, you've solved the mystery of the stolen lamps, Detective?"

"Yes. Since these lamps are imported from Afghanistan, I suspected that they were being used to smuggle heroin into the country. Only certain of the lamps that were sold were stolen, however, so I suspected that the shop owner, Abdul Hussain, must be in on it. A search of his off-site warehouse confirmed that. All of the stolen lamps were in his warehouse and were missing the bottom plate on the base. Obviously something had been hidden inside the lamps. Only it wasn't drugs."

"Really! What was it?"

"When I took the lamps into our crime lab, Marty O'Toole, the technician, happened to check them out with a geiger counter and found very radioactive residue in one of the lamps. So we called in the FBI."

"The FBI!" exclaimed John.

"Yes. Turns out a terrorist cell based in Yemen was smuggling in parts for a dirty bomb inside the base of these lamps. Only one had contained the radioactive material and the others had contained timers, electronic circuits, etc. When we confronted Mr. Hussain, he worked a plea deal and gave us the names of the terrorists."

"Amazing!" John and I uttered in unison.

"Yes. Seems like Mr. Hussain was in it only for the money and hoped to keep his distance from the terrorists by having them steal the lamps after they left his shop."

"Molly; I mean Detective Hanrahan. You've done it again!" I smiled.

"Just the luck o' the Irish, my friends."

The Meeting

Joseph Sampson spotted her as soon as she walked up to the Starbucks counter to order a latte. Tall, brunette, dressed in an Ann Taylor tight black skirt with white blouse, and shaped like a Barbie doll, this thirty-something woman's looks enticed him. He decided to linger before picking up his espresso from the young barista.

"Heidi, grande latte for you," announced the barista. Joseph admired the view offered by Heidi's low-cut blouse as the dark-haired beauty leaned over to pick up her coffee and smiled at him. *It's amazing what fine work plastic surgeons do in this great country*, he thought.

Looking around the coffee shop, Joseph and Heidi each realized that there was only one open table. "Miss, would you mind sharing a table, since there's only one left?"

After giving him an appraising look, she purred, "Certainly, sir. No problem at all."

Joseph smiled to himself that his wavy prematurely gray hair and Richard Gere looks still attracted younger women.

"My name is Joseph Sampson," he stated as he offered his hand. The brunette took it and said, "Heidi Walker. Glad we could share a table together."

The two soon struck up a lively conversation about the unpredictable weather they were having. "Since I'm a buyer for a women's clothing store, I have to do a lot of flying. The stormy weather here and back East has caused me a lot of travel delays. How about you, Mr. Sampson? With your European accent, I assume you are not a native Texan. Do you do a lot of traveling?"

"No, no, Miss Walker. May I call you Heidi? You are correct in that I was born in Geneva, but I've been in Texas ever since I entered The Program."

"The Program?"

"Well, I usually keep quiet about this. But I'm a pretty good judge of people and you seem like a trustworthy person. Can you keep what I tell you confidential?"

"Certainly," she beamed.

"Okay. You've heard of your country's Federal Witness Protection Program, I assume. Interpol has a similar program on a global scale. Five years ago I was an eyewitness to an assassination done by a Ukrainian drug cartel. For testimony that led to some high-level convictions, I was offered a new identity here in your great country. Instead of being a well-known stock broker in my homeland, I am now an accountant in a small local firm."

"Well, that's quite a story, Mr. Sampson."

"Call me Joseph."

"Okay, Joseph. My life story is much more boring. After my nasty divorce, I transferred here last year from Illinois to get away from my ex-husband. Thanks to a nice settlement from the divorce, I was able to buy a little condo overlooking the Riverwalk."

"So do you like being single again?"

"Not really. With the amount of traveling I do, I've not had time to make many friends outside of work. My evenings even here in San Antonio are pretty lonely."

"I'm surprised that a very attractive young woman like yourself isn't surrounded by a number of male suitors that would be happy to keep you company."

Heidi blushed and admitted, "I hate bar hopping. And I'm pretty picky. Most men my age are only interested in themselves or in a brief sexual encounter."

"Well," pronounced Joseph as he touched her hand. "One thing I learned growing up in Switzerland is how to treat a lady. I'm not interested in one-night stands. Would you consent to meet me for dinner this evening?"

Heidi hesitated just a minute, and said. "I'd be delighted. Why don't we meet at Landry's on the Riverwalk about 7?"

That evening Joseph was pleased to see that Heidi was already seated at a quiet table when he arrived at 7 sharp. After an enjoyable conversation, Heidi invited Joseph up to her nearby condo for a nightcap. Joseph's pulse quickened as he immediately accepted and followed her home.

Sitting on a couch in the condo, Joseph enjoyed the rum and coke that Heidi served him and asked for a refill. He admired her firm figure and smiled as she picked up his empty glass and walked into the kitchen.

Soon she called from the kitchen, "I'd like to freshen up, Joseph. I'll just be a minute. Feel free to turn on the TV."

This is got to be my lucky day, he thought. As the minutes ticked by, he allowed his mind to fantasize what living with Heidi would be like. After quite awhile, he looked at his watch and began to wonder what was taking so long. His curiosity was soon answered when she entered the room from behind the couch.

"Joseph, or should I say, Simon Yukovich?"

Startled by her harsh tone and by the name she uttered, Joseph turned to look at Heidi as she approached the couch.

"Yes, Simon. I know who you really are, number ten on my agency's Most Wanted List," she announced as she pointed a Glock 22 at him.

"What? There must be some mistake, Miss Walker. Is that really your name?"

"Yes! Agent Heidi Walker of the FBI," she proclaimed, holding her badge in the other hand. "And there is no mistake. We've been tracking down your whereabouts since you left the Ukraine and I followed you to the Starbucks this morning. I almost laughed when you told me you were in a witness protection program, Mr. Yukovich."

"No! You are wrong about me!" he exclaimed in alarm.

"There's no mistake! To confirm your identity as the notorious Russian Mafia leader and con-man, I lifted your fingerprints off your drink glass. I'm placing you under arrest."

Simon Yukovich, alias Joseph Sampson, considered trying to run for the door. But another look at the gun Heidi held pointed at his chest convinced him to turn around and allow himself to be handcuffed. *There's certainly more to this woman than meets the eye,* he thought with chagrin.

The Ornament

Finally the gray clouds of December gave way to brilliant sunshine. The cold crisp air felt and smelled good as I finished my walk around the park and sat down on a bench to relax and enjoy the outdoor sights. That's when I saw them, sitting on a bench right on the other side of the walkway.

Sitting close together and bundled up from the brisk air sat a white-haired couple, holding hands and talking. Nothing too unusual about that. But what they had with them caught my eye. It was a bright silver Christmas ornament, the kind used for a tree topper. I decided to ask them about it.

"Hi. Nice day for December," I ventured.

"Yes it is, young man," responded the woman with a bright smile. "It's finally nice enough to get out and enjoy the fresh air. My name's Bonnie Schmidt, and this is my husband, George."

"Jack. Jack Wilson. Glad to meet both of you. Is that a Christmas tree ornament you have there?"

"Yes it is," the elderly man spoke up. A grin spread across his wrinkle-creased features as he saw the curious look on my face, and finally he continued, "This is a very special Christmas ornament. It's the tree topper we bought for our very first Christmas tree."

"That was fifty years ago," Bonnie piped up.

"And we've used it on our tree every year since then," George continued.

"Well, it certainly looks bright and shiny for being so old." I puzzled. "What's it made of?"

"Oh, it's just cheap plastic. That's all we could afford for our tree that first Christmas. But every few years I spray on a fresh coat of silver paint," George confided, as he adjusted his glasses to look from the ornament to me.

"But this year, we have no tree to put it on," interjected Bonnie. "This fall George and I moved into a very nice retirement home that has two huge Christmas trees in the dining room and lounge. But there is not space in our little apartment for anything larger than a little tabletop tree. It won't support our tree topper."

"The big Christmas trees in the common areas are very pretty and we don't miss not having our own tree that much. Now that we've reached a new milestone in our lives, it's time to give our tree topper away to someone who will cherish it as much as we do," George smiled sadly as he answered my unasked question.

"Yes, Jack. We are hoping to find a deserving young couple who are just starting life together as we did so long ago and bless them with this ornament," Bonnie explained.

"Okay. I hope you folks do find someone like that here in the park. If you don't mind, I'll do a little reading now," I said as I pulled a book out of my backpack. Soon I was engrossed in the novel.

About an hour went by and a number of couples strolled by laughing or arguing but not paying attention to me or the elderly couple sitting across from me. Finally I saw a young Hispanic couple walk by with a picnic basket and smile at Bonnie. They couldn't have been out of high school more than a couple of years. George and Bonnie called to them and they stopped to visit. *Unusual for such a young couple to be interested in talking to some old folks,* I thought.

"My name is Julio, and this is my fiance, Maria," I heard the young man tell George.

"We are going to be married on Christmas Eve," beamed Maria.

"Do you have a Christmas tree?" queried Bonnie.

"Not yet. I hope to buy one tomorrow when my last unemployment check arrives," said Julio.

"You are unemployed?" asked George.

"Julio lost his job last spring when the plant he was working at closed. He's been looking for a job since then with no luck. I'm a student at San Antonio College and only work part time at a convenience store. But they say that two can live cheaper than one and we're going ahead with the wedding date we set a year ago."

"So we don't have much money for Christmas decorations this year. But Maria and I will be happy just to be together," Julio said with a look that defied anyone to disagree.

"That's the spirit young man. When Bonnie here and I were married, we were both going to college and our only income was what I earned from being a church janitor. Our first Christmas was pretty meager by most people's standards, but we were happy."

"We have something special from our first Christmas that we'd like to give you two as a wedding gift," Bonnie smiled. Seeing the puzzled looks on the young couple's faces, she held up the silver ornament and gave them the same explanation they'd given me earlier.

"That's very kind of you, but we couldn't take this special ornament that means so much to you. You keep it," Julio protested.

"Young man, I promise you if you take our gift and use it every holiday season, it will bless your Christmas celebrations for many years to come. And it will bring you good luck." There was an earnestness in George's voice that caught my attention as I continued to eavesdrop.

"Good luck?" asked Julio with raised eyebrows and a skeptical look as George put the tree topper in his hands.

"Let's take their gift, Julio. We don't have a tree topper yet." Maria looked at him with big pleading eyes.

"Okay. Okay. I do appreciate your generosity. We will take good care of the ornament." Julio relented.

Just then Julio's cell phone rang. He apologized and pulled it out of his pocket. He said hello and listened for a couple of minutes. Then he said, "Yes. That's great! I can come in tomorrow for the drug test. Thank you so very much!" He closed up the phone and put it in his pocket with a surprised look.

"Well?" asked Maria.

"I got that job at Target that I applied for last month! I take the drug test tomorrow and can start next Monday after I sign all the papers."

"See!" George exclaimed. "I told you our ornament would bring you good luck!"

"Merry Christmas to both of you!" Bonnie added.

"It will be a Merry Christmas!" exclaimed Maria as she strolled off arm in arm with her fiance, holding tightly to the old silver ornament.

The Shimmering Sea

The sound of the gentle waves sliding up the beach relieved Dennis' stress after a hectic work day. "Ah, back to the sea! What is it about the ocean that brings me peace? And not only me: a lot of other people?" he mused.

Dennis was fortunate in that his office was only a couple of miles from the Santa Monica Pier, and he often spent the late afternoons at the beach gazing out into the ocean.

The warmth of the sun and the feel of the sand between his toes felt good as he sat down on the beach with his trusty ice chest. Soon he was mesmerized by the shimmering sea, as each wavelet caught a little piece of the late afternoon sunlight. Wave after wave came gliding up the beach, breaking into films of foam at the very edges.

Suddenly Dennis noticed something bobbing out there in the shimmering sea. As he watched it come in with the tide, he saw it catch the sunlight each time it rode the crest of another swell. "What in the heck is that? Why it looks like a bottle. A corked bottle?" he remarked to one of the seagulls flying by. Somehow the seagull wasn't impressed and kept on going.

Soon the bottle was close enough that Dennis could see it contained a small rectangular object. The next wave deposited it on the shore several yards down the beach. The seagulls squawked overhead as Dennis sprinted to scoop it up before the next wave caught it and carried it back out to sea.

Soon he held the clear glass quart bottle and could see its contents. "Strange! It looks like an old pocket transistor radio – the kind my dad told me he had as a teenager. There's the round black mesh speaker grille on front. I can see the Sony logo, the words 'Six Transistor Radio' and the little window to see the station selection. And there on the side is the volume control. Wow!"

Wondering how the radio had gotten into the bottle and why, Dennis picked up his shoes and his trusty ice chest and headed home with his treasure. He called his brother, Ron, on the way and asked him to meet him there.

Soon Ron and Dennis were peering into the bottle and taking pictures of its contents. "Dennis, I have no idea how somebody put this radio inside this bottle, and I'm sure we can't get it out the same way. I think the best thing is to cut the bottle open with your glass cutters so that we can examine this more closely."

Dennis admired his older brother, who was a science teacher at Santa Monica High, and usually took his advice. They soon had the bottle cut in half and each took his turn in picking up the little radio and studying its exterior.

"This is a Sony Model TR 650. I think Sony produced this popular number back in the early 1960's. Say, looks like the owner had his initials etched into the back. SJL." Ron pointed as he handed it back to his brother.

"Wonder if it still works?" asked Dennis as he turned the volume control to 'on' and heard only the click of the mechanical contact.

"Of course it won't work, dummy. The battery inside must be years old. Do you have any nine-volt batteries?"

"Sure. Let me go get one."

A few minutes later they were ready to try it with the new battery inside. Each held their breath as Ron turned the volume wheel on. After the click there was the crackle of static and then a DJ's voice sounded through the speaker, "This is KSURF, 1050 on your dial, playing all the latest hits."

"Wow, it does work! And it picks up a local station!" Dennis exclaimed. Turning the station selector, it soon became apparent that KSURF was the only station the little radio did pick up. " Maybe it's not powerful enough to pick up any stations farther away."

The brothers sat and listened to the music of "California Girls" by the Beach Boys on the little speaker. That had been one of their dad's favorite songs.

"Wish Dad was still around to see this old radio and listen to this song," smiled Ron.

"You're listening to KSURF and that is the Beach Boy's new number one hit, "California Girls."

"What?" asked both brothers in unison. "That was a new hit forty some years ago, but not today."

The next thing they heard really took them aback. "It's another beautiful afternoon here in Santa Monica. Here's the surf report for today, June 17, 1965."

"That's crazy! Is someone at KSURF pulling our leg? Turn on your home stereo, Dennis, and let's listen to KSURF on it."

KSURF was playing 2009 top hits on the home stereo, while the pocket radio strangely kept playing hits from 1965. Then they heard a news flash about a drowning at the beach. More details were promised later and next the radio played "Help Me Rhonda."

The next day Dennis took the radio to his office and turned it on during breaks between conference calls and meetings. Each time he heard music popular the summer of 1965, and several times it repeated the same date, June 17. He called his brother during the lunch hour and tried to puzzle it out.

"Look, Ron. Neither I nor you understand how it keeps broadcasting these old songs and news flashes. But what also puzzles me is what's so significant about June 17, 1965. I'm going to dig through the newspaper office's archives to see what happened that day."

After work, Dennis found a microfilm copy of The Santa Monica Mirror's evening edition for the day in question. There it was on the front page.

College co-ed disappears in Santa Monica surf. Sam J. Lamond, a local surfer, reported that his girl friend ran into the

waves singing and laughing and disappeared from sight. "I kept watching for her head to come above the surface, because she was a good swimmer. But it didn't. It was that damn LSD she took after lunch! She was on some kind of trip," he sobbed to lifeguards. The Santa Monica Search and Rescue team has made an unsuccessful attempt to locate the coed, Ms. Jean Burton.

"Ron, I think the initials on this radio mean it was owned by this surfer, Sam J. Lamond, whose girlfriend drowned on June 17," Dennis reported via his cell phone.

"See if you can find any more news references to this guy."

Using the computer searches in the archives, Dennis found an article dated June 17, 1966 that included photos of Sam Lamond and Jean Burton.

Grief-stricken surfer floats memorial out to sea. Exactly one year ago today, Sam J. Lamond's girlfriend, Ms. Jean Burton, disappeared into the surf while on a bad LSD trip. Mr. Lamond recalled how happy he and Jean had been earlier in the day, listening to KSURF on his transistor radio, and so today had floated a bottle containing the radio out to sea at the spot where he last saw her. "I talked to her guru after she died and he said if I floated the radio out to sea, she might find it and it would bring her good memories. Sounds a little crazy, but on the chance he's right, I had the radio modified and placed in this bottle."

Dennis and Ron met for breakfast the next morning and talked about Dennis' findings. "I wonder if this guy is still alive? Maybe he still lives in the area." Dennis pondered.

"I can check it out," smiled Ron as he pulled out his iPhone and searched the local phone listings. "Sure thing! Sam J. Lamond lives on 3838 Circle Drive. Shall we give him a call?"

A few hours later the brothers were seated in Sam J. Lamond's modest living room. "Looks like you really love surfing, Mr. Lamond," Dennis said as he glanced at all the surfing pictures on the walls.

"I guess it's pretty obvious!" exclaimed the leathery skinned baby boomer. I had to give it up a couple of years ago when I had a knee replacement. But I still go out on weekends to watch the younger set surf. But that's not why you boys are here. You said you found something that might belong to me."

"Yes, sir. I found this floating up on the beach inside a bottle earlier this week." Dennis explained as he pulled the transistor radio out of a bag.

The old surfer's hands trembled as they touched his old radio. "My, my! It came back to me – after all these years!"

"We read the old newspaper articles, Mr. Lamond, about you floating the radio out to sea, and why, but what we don't understand is how the radio got in the bottle."

"And more importantly," Ron chimed in, "how is it that the radio only plays old KSURF broadcasts from the day your girlfriend disappeared."

"That was my friend, Jack Bozniak's handiwork," chuckled Sam. "Jack was an electronics wizard who was way ahead of his time. He told me that sound waves never completely die out. He said he could modify this radio to pick up the signal of the broadcast that my Jean and I listened to on the day she died. And he did it! He showed me before he used an old trick to insert it into that bottle."

"Gee! Whatever happened to Mr. Bozniak?" Ron asked.

"A few years later he told me he'd perfected a time machine. The next week he was doing something inside his lab and the neighbors reported a bright flash of light that engulfed the building. They rushed inside to find Jack gone. He'd disappeared into thin air! I have the newspaper article in a scrapbook if you want to see it."

The brothers read the news clipping and got ready to leave, more puzzled than ever.

"Thanks for the radio, boys! But before you go, let me check for one thing. Jean's guru, the one who told me to float the radio out to sea, told me to put a picture of myself inside it. If the radio ever came back to me and the picture was gone, I'd know that Jean had found it. So I put one of my senior wallet photos underneath the back cover. Let's check it out and see if it's still there."

Dennis and Ron watched carefully as Sam took a little screwdriver and removed the back of the radio. A small photo fell out with the backside up. Sam turned it over and let out a gasp. It was a photo of Jean!

The Stars Above

The cool spring evening was a perfect end to the wonderful afternoon Yuri and Francoise had spent at the beach. The smell of the salt spray mingled with the fragrance of the wild flowers that had somehow taken root in the silty sand. The calls of seagulls filled the air as the orb of the sun sank below the horizon.

"That was a spectacular sunset, Francoise. It looked like the sun's fire was being extinguished as it sunk beneath the waves."

"For a such a serious engineering student, Yuri, you have an artistic side to you that's kinda special." Francoise smiled as she turned from looking at the ocean and gazed at her friend.

Yuri shifted uncomfortably, not used to compliments from such a pretty - and smart - coed. Francoise was the top scholar among her fellow linguistic students and had been a runner-up for Campus Queen.

As the sky turned from light to dark blue, to black, the stars became more visible, looking like bright points of light peeking through holes in a dark velvet cloth.

The view was so spectacular that the two friends gazed in silence for minutes as they sat on the damp sand, with the only sounds being the dark waves crashing against the shore. All the other beach-goers had already gone home.

"Yuri, do you ever look up at the stars above and wonder what they really are?"

"When I was a kid, I used to imagine all sorts of things when I looked at the stars. But as I started studying astronomy, I learned that they're huge balls of fiery gases, much like our sun."

"Yeah, I know. Science has taken all the romance out of the starry night sky. So how many of those stars have planets going around them? Like our sun does?"

"Probably most of them. The question is, though, how many of them have planets that can support intelligent life?"

"How will we ever know?"

"Well, scientists are working on that. You may know that there are special radio telescopes that are trained on some of the closer solar systems, listening for messages from outer space."

"I've heard a little about that, Yuri. Have they learned anything yet?"

"Not that has been announced to the public. But I have an uncle who works with one of those radio telescopes. He recently recorded some sounds from the nearest solar system that he thinks are some sort of message to us."

"Really! What sort of message?"

"I don't really know, but he is busy running all sorts of computer programs on the sounds to try to decode them."

"I wonder if those messages could be related to the sightings of that unidentified flying object that was in the newspaper last week. The one that might be orbiting our planet."

"Good question. I wish our manned space program was further along. So far we've only sent one manned spacecraft into orbit. We don't have the ability yet to intercept something else up in space. But if that unidentified flying object were from the closest solar system, it would have had to travel many years to get here."

"How many years?"

"Lots. It takes light about ten years to reach us from that star. So even if they could travel at half that speed, it'd take twenty years."

"Wow!"

Just then a bright object appeared about thirty degrees above the horizon and seemed to grow in size and brightness as it approached the beach where Yuri and Francoise watched with gaping mouths.

"What is that, Yuri? It looks like some kind of giant metallic cone. Is it going to hit us?"

Francoise's voice rose an octave as the object seemed to fill the sky. She clutched him tightly as the roar of rocket engines almost drowned out her voice.

"Beats the hell out of me. I wish my Uncle Albert was here. Maybe this is the UFO that's been sighted around the world. Too late for us to run. Just cover your ears."

The glowing cone passed just overhead and started to descend to the hillock just behind them. Flames and smoke from rockets on the underside of the cone set fire to some tuffs of wild grass growing in the sandy soil, but soon burned out.

Just as quickly as the rocket roar had started, it subsided as the cone gently settled on the ground. Francoise and Yuri stared at the spacecraft, wondering what would happen next. It didn't take them long to find out.

"Look, Yuri. Some kind of trap door is opening on the side of the cone. Do you think some little green men are going to come out and zap us with their ray guns?"

"Little green men? You've read too many science fiction stories."

No little green creatures came out, but a mechanized vehicle several feet tall lumbered out of the spacecraft and moved slowly toward them. The metallic body was marked with red and white stripes and white stars on a blue background.

"What's that, Yuri?" questioned Francoise, her fingers digging into the side of his arm.

"Looks almost like one of the armored vehicles I've seen in our Independence parades," answered Yuri as he tried to sound calmer than he felt.

The strange contraption stopped a few feet away from them. A mechanical arm appeared out of its side with what appeared to be a glass cylinder with a document rolled up inside. Gingerly Yuri, the engineer, walked over and retrieved the cylinder from the mechanical arm. As soon as he took it, the contraption turned and slowly rolled down the beach scooping up sand samples with the mechanical arm.

"Let's get the hell out of here, Francoise!" exclaimed Yuri as he pulled her away from the beach. "I'm going to take this to Uncle Albert. He needs to see this! Maybe it has something to do with the signals he's been receiving on his radio telescope."

A hour later, Yuri and Francoise were sitting in Uncle Albert's study, amazing him with their story. "This is the glass container I retrieved from the mechanical arm, Uncle Albert. I think there is a document inside."

"Hmm...surely looks like it," Uncle Albert puffed on his pipe as he took the container from Yuri's hands."

"Looks like it's a sealed container. Let's take it to my lab at the observatory and I'll cut it open to examine the contents."

Another hour later, Francoise and Yuri each held their breath as Uncle Albert unrolled the document and began to examine it.

"Looks like plastic-coated paper. There's strange writing and symbols on one side. Looks like some sort of pattern. I'll scan it and feed it into my computers that have been analyzing the messages coming from the solar system nearest us. Then I'll call our project manager to tell him about the spacecraft and mechanical rover you saw."

Later that night Uncle Albert's computers spit out the translation of the strange writing and he read it to Yuri and Francoise.

"To all the inhabitants of the planet we call Epsilon Eridani. The spacecraft that you have seen is from our planet, Earth, which is 10.5 light years away. We come in peace."

The Trip's End

    The blonde young woman shivered in the cold wind as she walked into Central Park with her heavy backpack. "Finally, I'm here!" she sighed. She thought about her bedraggled appearance compared to the way she'd looked when she'd started this trip from San Diego. Four months of chasing leads from one city or town to another, and hitchhiking with truckers, undocumented workers, and whoever else would give her a ride. All to solve a mystery that had troubled her since she was a teenager.

    Her first long stop had been in Phoenix, where she'd lived with her family before 9/11. Before her dad volunteered with the first special forces that went into Afghanistan. Before her mother was killed in a car wreck that left her and her younger brother to fend for themselves. The Army had told them that when her dad's tour was up, he had out-processed at Luke Air Force Base in Arizona. From there, her journey had led to Denver, where there were records that he was in a Veteran's Hospital in Denver for months - before he just walked out one day.

    "Sergeant Hal Wilson? Are you related to him, miss?" asked the kindly white-haired social worker at the VA.

    "Yes. I'm his daughter, Marie Wilson, as you can see here on my California driver's license. I also have my birth certificate with me, that shows the names of my parents."

    After briefly reviewing Marie's documents, the social worker looked up the hospital records. "Your father checked into our facility in July, 2003, suffering from severe headaches. Tests revealed that he still had a small piece of shrapnel lodged in his neck from a wound he'd received while deployed. Surgery here to remove it was successful, but when he awoke from the anesthesia, he seemed to have lost much of his memory. Doctors had him in therapy, hoping that it would cure his amnesia, but one day he left the hospital without checking out and never returned. He'd told his roommate that he was heading to North Dakota to find a job in the oil fields. That's the last we know of his whereabouts."

Marie spent weeks in North Dakota at various oil field offices before she found a crusty old superintendent that recognized her dad's picture. "Yeah, I remember him. Went by the name of Harold White. Said he'd been in the army and needed work. We gave him a chance and he worked for us three years before moving on. He was a really good hand! Hated to see him go, but he said he was tired of North Dakota's cold winters."

"Do you know where he went next?"

"Matter of fact, a couple weeks later I got a postcard from him asking me to mail his last paycheck to a boarding house in Memphis. I might still have the address in my payroll records."

At the boarding house in Memphis, Marie found another clue from the owner. "Honey, I remember your dad. Nice guy and apparently was a good worker. Claimed he had no kin. Got himself a job for Green as Grass Landscapers and worked there for a couple of years before heading down to Pensacola. Seems that he got a job for a big security company there. What was the name of it? Something like TrueBlue. That might have been it. TrueBlue Security."

The office at TrueBlue Security Services was on a main street in Pensacola. At first the supervisor she talked to didn't want to give her any information. Flirting with her big brown eyes and showing some of her shapely thigh finally broke through his defenses.

"Okay, Miss Wilson. I can see that this means a lot to you. Your dad applied for a job with us and in order to do a background check, we fingerprinted him. That's how he learned that his real name was Hal Wilson and it verified some shadowy memories he had of serving in the special forces. He worked for us here in Florida for two years and did a damn fine job. So much so, that when he solved a burglary of a vacation home that belonged to a high ranking officer with the NYPD, he eventually got an offer to go to work for them."

"Did he take it?"

"Hell yes. Great opportunity and he seemed to have the skills they needed. Hated to see him go, though."

"Thanks. You've been very helpful!"

"Before you leave, Miss, do you have time for a drink? There's a nice little lounge just around the corner where I go to blow off steam."

With a firm refusal, Marie hurried out the door and caught a bus to Jacksonville. Having nearly depleted her funds, she hitchhiked the rest of the way up to New York City. At the NYPD headquarters, they wouldn't give her the address for her father, but confirmed that he was currently assigned to a beat in Central Park. A two mile walk had brought her to the park bench where she sat to gather her wits.

"Will I even recognize my dad? And will he be able to remember me? What exactly shall I say to him?" She'd rehearsed possible scenarios for this occasion many times, but that didn't take away the butterflies in her stomach.

Suddenly she saw a tall man in blue, wearing an NYPD badge, walking her way. She was about to call out to him when she saw him stop to talk to a homeless man nearby. When he resumed his rounds suddenly she lost her voice. The tall policeman was about to pass her by, but then stopped to ask her if she was okay. She could see the name on his uniform: Hal Wilson.

"Yes. Yes officer. I am okay for the first time in years. You see, my name is Marie, Marie Wilson."

Taken aback, Officer Wilson stared into her eyes. She saw a momentary flash of recognition and then he said. "They tell me I used to have a daughter named Marie. But when I finally discovered that, no one knew where she lived or even if she was still alive. I was told her momma died in a car crash before I returned from Afghanistan and she and her brother had moved away."

"Maybe you had best sit down beside me, Officer Wilson. Because I want to you to know your long lost daughter and tell you about my brother, who is a rookie police officer back in California. He found out where you were discharged from the Army and gave me some money to go search for you."

The look in her dad's eyes made her four month journey and its hardships all worth it.

The Vice President at Fiesta

"There he is! Walking along Alamo Street, wearing a baseball cap. Follow him!" barked Agent Mike Carrasco. "I need to phone this in!"

Following the homeless man in the crowds leaving The Battle of Flowers Parade wasn't that difficult for Jayne Jones, the FBI Agent at the wheel. After all, the man wasn't trying to evade anyone as he sauntered along with his backpack.

"This is Agent Carrasco. We have spotted the Vice President, dressed like a homeless person. Do you want us to pick him up?"

The FBI had been looking for the Vice President for the three months since the accident took place. He'd been spotted walking away from the scene in a daze, while his Secret Service escort was temporarily trapped in the wreckage of his limousine.

"Okay, Jayne. We've got the go-ahead to pick him up. Pull over to the curb at the Houston Street intersection and I'll handle it."

Mike jumped out as soon as the car rolled to a stop and held out his hand as the homeless man approached. "Mr. Vice President! May I have a word with you?"

Startled, the man in the baseball cap looked up. "What did you say? I was lost in thought."

"Mr. Vice President! We're so glad we found you. The whole country has been worried about you!"

"You must be mistaken. I'm not the Vice President and I'm not anybody important. I'm just down here to enjoy the Fiesta."

After considerable discussion on the busy street corner, the homeless man consented to ride to the San Antonio FBI headquarters in return for a promise of a nice steak dinner.

****

"Your photo ID shows your name as Mr. Jake Goddard. Yet you are a dead ringer for our missing Vice President, Donald Hazelworth. Can you tell us a little about yourself, Mr. Goddard? How long have you been in San Antonio? And what were you doing before?" asked Earl Radcliff,the local FBI field supervisor, in a firm but respectful manner. After all, this might be the Vice President with a case of amnesia. They hadn't yet asked permission to fingerprint him.

"Well, my real name is Jake. Jake Goddard. I used to work for the government myself. I seem to remember that it was something important, but I can't recall the details. But I don't think I was Vice President or anything like that. I've been in San Antonio for quite awhile. I can't say exactly how long, but it seems longer than three months."

Incredulous, Earl Radcliff looked at the homeless man and asked, "Sir, are you kidding me? You don't remember what you used to do for the government? And you don't know how long you've been in San Antonio?"

"Sorry, Mister, Mr. Radcliff, is it? I had a doc at the Salvation Army free clinic tell me I've damaged my brain cells with the mescal bean wine I've been drinking."

"Mescal bean wine?"

"Yeah. You know those Texas Mountain Laurels that grow around here and make those pretty purple blossoms each spring? Well, the Indians used to make a drink from the mescal beans in the seed pods. It gave them visions and spiritual enlightenment. One of my buddies who lives at the shelter with me told us about it. So we made up a drink using the old Indian recipe. We let it ferment and we put some in some old bottles that we keep under our mattresses."

"Go on, Mr. Goddard."

"Well that stuff has quite a kick and it has given my buddies and me quite some rather weird trips, if you catch my drift. The stuff is kind of addicting too. Trouble is, the beans are also poisonous and the doc told me that the toxins in the drink are what's been causing my memory to fade."

The FBI supervisor let out some curses and then calmed down. "So you've been frying your brain by drinking this stuff? You might be the Vice President, and you don't even know it!"

"You can go ahead and finger print me, Mr. FBI man. That should prove something."

****

The FBI's fingerprint database confirmed that the homeless man was indeed Jake Goddard, who had been a NASA scientist in Houston until the last round of budget cuts at the agency. After that he'd dropped out of sight until he'd turned up in San Antonio. That information led to high level discussions with the Administration that lasted several days. Meanwhile Mr. Goddard agreed to be put up at government expense in the Drury Inn with a constant FBI escort. Finally an official with the White House presented Mr. Goddard with a proposition.

"Mr. Goddard. May I call you Jake?" asked the official and then proceeded without waiting for an answer. "You could be the Vice President's identical twin – with your blue eyes, grayish blond hair, build, height, weight, even facial expressions. Even your voice sounds like him. It's amazing! That's why we have a proposition for you."

"And what would that be?" Several days without mescal bean wine had sharpened Jake Goddard's senses somewhat.

"Well, several terrorist organizations around the world have been claiming that they have the Vice President in their custody. Although we don't know where the Vice President is, we're pretty sure that the terrorists don't have him, because they haven't produced any video or photos of him. However, this has been spooking the American public. We need to show the Vice

President on television, and since we can't find him, we want you to stand in for him."

"What? I can't pretend to be the Vice President! I don't have any training in politics! Surely everyone would soon find out I was a fake."

"Not a fake, Mr. Goddard. A temporary stand-in who would be doing a patriotic act for the good of the country. This is the plan. We'll announce you've been found and we'll show photos of you to the press. The next day you will appear in a two minute video on television, getting out of a helicopter and entering Walter Reed Hospital to be examined and treated. A few days later you will appear on TV and give a short statement to the press that you're glad to be back but that you must resign for health reasons. We'll limit any reporter's questions to those asked by a couple of people that we've planted in the press corps. And after that you disappear from the public's view."

"And what will you do for me?"

"We'll put you in the Witness Protection Program and set you up with a new identity in any place of your choosing. Part of that will include a lifetime stipend."

"Better than living at the shelter or under a bridge, I suppose. Okay. I'll do it!"

****

The next week the new resident in Cabo San Lucas saw an announcement in the papers about the return of the Vice President of the United States, complete with a photo of him getting out of a helicopter. Pointing it out to the bikini-clad latina who was sitting by the poolside with him, he said, "its nice to know they'll stop looking for me. Looks like I'm finally out of that rat race for good."

"I think your plan worked, Donald! Why don't you take a stroll with me down to the beach to watch the sunset?"

"Why not?"

The Wall

"Bernd, there is going to be another candlelight prayer vigil at St. Nikolai's tonight. We should go!"

"It's too dangerous, Kerstin! You heard what happened to some of the protestors in Leipzig last week! I don't want to be beaten and arrested by the GDR."

"Coward! The spirit of Gorbachev is blowing across all of East Germany, even here in Berlin! We need to keep protesting until we have free access to West Germany. It's time we stopped being prisoners in the German Democratic Republic! You know what the American President said to Gorbachev: 'Tear Down This Wall!'"

"Sorry, but you know what happened to my cousin, Chris, last winter. Shot by GDR border guards as he tried to defect to West Berlin. Shot dead, Kerstin! I don't want to be next!"

"That's even more reason to press for the freedoms we need. You've seen the banners, Bernd! WE ARE THE PEOPLE."

"Your words are dangerous, Kerstin! Too dangerous to say out loud, even though I partially agree with them."

It was a cold night even for October as Kerstin made her way without her boyfriend, Bernd, to St. Nikolai's Lutheran Church. Christians, non-Christians, all mostly young people, filled the church to overflowing as the weekly prayer vigil for peace began. At the end of the service, Kerstin sprang to the front of the church, grabbed a lit candle from the altar and yelled, "We need to take our prayers and demand for change to the streets. Let's go!"

"Yes!" declared Pastor Christian Fuher. "The time has come to take our prayer vigil to the streets. But we must keep it non-violent, in the spirit of Christ."

Armed with nothing but lighted candles, the crowd burst out of the church and began a march through the streets of East Berlin, gathering on-lookers with them. Historians estimate the number of marchers swelled to 70,000 despite the cold night air. The GDR guards were ready for anything except candles and prayer and could do nothing against the non-violent marchers. Kerstin saw a Trabant parked on the street covered with candle wax and thought that was a sight she'd not forget.

The next morning Kerstin met Bernd for coffee and told him all about it. "You should have been there! I wasn't even cold or afraid! We were all full of such energy and hope! It still gives me shivers to think of it! Change is coming and the Volkspolizei police can't stop it!"

A few short days later, on November 4, Kerstin persuaded Bernd to join her in the Alexanderplatz demonstration, organized by actors and workers in the East German theaters. Over a half million people gathered in the central square of the city with speeches and banners calling for true democracy in East Germany. As they left the demonstration late in the afternoon, Bernd exclaimed, "Did you see that when Markus Wolf, the head of the foreign intelligence service spoke up in opposition to our movement, his hands shook when he heard all the boos?"

"Yes, Bernd! Our peaceful revolution cannot be stopped! It's irreversible!"

Five nights later Bernd and Kerstin gathered around the TV in his flat to hear the 7 p.m. news broadcast from one of the West Berlin TV stations. "At a news conference today, Gunter Schabowski, East Berlin party boss and Politburo spokesman read an announcement that refugees and private parties who wished to cross from East Germany to West Germany, including West Berlin, would be allowed to do so. When asked by a reporter when the new regulations would take effect he said, 'As far as I know effective immediately, without delay.' So there you have it, Berliners, the GDR has opened the border crossings into West Germany for all desiring safe passage. The gates in the Berlin Wall stand open!"

Grabbing her boyfriend, Kristin exclaimed, "Did you hear that, Bernd? We can cross over into West Germany! I'm going to go tonight and see my aunt and uncle in West Berlin. I haven't seen them since I was a little girl. I'm going to call and tell them! Are you going to come with me?"

After some brief stammering and hesitating, Bernd agreed to go with her. They both filled their backpacks with personal items needed for a several day stay and headed out into the dark night toward one of the six border checkpoints. They were surprised by over a thousand East Berliners already at the checkpoint, demanding to be let through. The guards seemed more surprised than Kirsten and Bernd.

"The gates are supposed to be open. Let us through!" chanted the crowd in a chorus that grew louder by the minute as more people gathered in the throng.

"Wait! We know nothing about this! We have to check with headquarters!" After numerous frantic phone calls to their superiors, one of the guards announced, "We can only let those through who are willing to renounce their East German citizenship. Come to the front of the line and we will stamp your passports with a special stamp."

An hour later, those willing to get the special stamp had passed through the gate, but the remaining crowd had grown by several thousand. Kerstin and Bernd were near the front of the line and heard the chief guard slam down the phone and yell, "Damn it, since none of the higher ups will give us orders to start shooting all these people, I'm going to open the gate for them all!"

Kerstin looked at her watch as she and Bernd went through the open gate. It was 10:45 p.m on November 9, 1989. She was surprised how modern and clean West Berlin looked compared to where she lived. As they walked into West Berlin they were overwhelmed by the crowds of West Berliners welcoming them with flowers and champagne. Some of them even started climbing on top of The Wall.

"Bernd, can you believe it? Families are so happy to be reunited. Look, there's my auntie and uncle!"

After several minutes they were able to work their way through the crowd into the arms of Kirsten's relatives, who drove them to their house in West Berlin for a night of visiting and rejoicing.

The next day as they awoke in the free air of West Berlin, Kirsten and Bernd saw pictures on TV of part of The Wall already being torn down. "This week is a week for the history books, Bernd!" she exclaimed, dancing for joy.

And they were amazed to hear that the fall of The Wall was really due to a mistake on the part of Gunter Schabowski. The party boss had misunderstood the new regulations he'd been given just before the news conference. The gates were not supposed to be opened until the next day when instructions had been sent to the guards. Instead there was no way to undo the historic results of his statement to the press. The eventual reunification of Germany had been set in motion. Kirsten and Bernd were now part of what became the new Berlin.

Uncle Herb's Magic Time Machine

"Hey, Uncle Herb. What are you working on now?"

"Hey yourself, young whippersnapper. That's for me to know and you to find out." chuckled the white haired scientist as he looked over his glasses at his twelve-year old nephew.

Jason Greene enjoyed coming to his famous uncle's lab as often as his mother would let him. Uncle Herb was always building a new contraption or conducting experiments that seemed magical to the aspiring scientist.

"How am I going to find out, Uncle? I'm still a kid and I don't understand all the mysteries of the universe like you do!"

"Come back in a couple of weeks, Jason, and I hope that by then I'll be ready to try this machine out. Now run along before you're late for supper."

Exactly two weeks later, Jason knocked on the door to Uncle Herb's lab. When Uncle Herb opened the door, Jason sucked in his breath at the sight of his uncle's strange contraption. There were hundreds of wires and tubes running from a large console with dials and buttons and ending at what looked like a small elevator.

"Wow! You've been busy, Uncle Herb! What is it?"

"That, my young lad, is the world's first time machine."

"Time machine? Like in the movies?"

"Yes indeed. Only the ones in the movies didn't really work. I built this one myself – with the help of my former student, Kathleen Guzman - and I can almost guarantee you it will work!"

"Almost? This isn't going to be like the 3D TV you built that my mother still talks about, is it?" Jason stared with wide eyes at his uncle. "She said it blew up when you turned it on and it almost burned down your house."

"That was when I was much younger, my good man. I've learned a lot since then. But don't take my word for it. Would you like to come and watch Kathleen and me take it on its maiden voyage?"

"Sure! When will that be?"

"If I tell you, you must swear not to tell your mother about it until later. Okay, nephew?"

Saturday morning came and Jason found Uncle Herb and his pretty assistant, Kathleen, doing some final adjustments on the time machine.

Standing back with a smile on his face, Uncle Herb proclaimed the machine ready for its first trial.

"Jason, you come over here behind this Plexiglass screen. Kathleen will operate the controls at the console and I will enter the chrono chamber."

"So where back in time are you planning to go, Uncle Herb?"

"I am planning to go back to 1960, when I was your age. Back then the Riverside Hotel stood on this spot. Hopefully I'll be able to mingle with the other hotel guests without being noticed."

"Is that why you're wearing those retro clothes, Uncle Herb?"

"You've got it lad! Now I must be going," he shouted over his shoulder as the doors to the elevator-like device opened and closed behind him.

"Okay, Jason. Get behind the safety screen like your Uncle said, while I start the five minute countdown," Kathleen instructed.

At each 30 seconds of the countdown, Jason could hear his uncle reporting through a speaker on the console that all was "A-OK."

A blinding flash took Jason by surprise when the countdown clock hit zero. The whole lab shook as though in a minor earthquake and the lights flickered, went out briefly, and came back on.

"Now what Ms. Guzman?" asked Jason as his heart beat wildly.

"Now we open the doors to the chrono chamber. If all worked as expected, it should be empty, as your uncle should be back in 1960."

Before the doors opened, they could hear banging coming from inside the chamber and what sounded like someone yelling.

"What the heck is that?" Kathleen shouted as she pressed the door open button. She and Jason gasped as out tumbled two people – Uncle Herb and a man with long sideburns wearing bell bottom pants and a paisley shirt.

"Where am I?" exclaimed the stranger. "What happened? What did you do with the hotel where I was a minute ago?"

"This is 2011, sir. My name is Professor Herbert McClure, and this is my time machine."

"Sure, dude. What have you been smoking? Can I have some?"

After Uncle Herb had confirmed that the stranger had come from the year 1960 and had showed him that he was indeed now in the year 2011, the man collapsed in a chair and started mumbling to himself. Meanwhile, Jason listened into the conversation between his uncle and his assistant.

"Don't you see, Professor Herb? The machine did the opposite of what we expected. Instead of transporting you back in time, it brought someone from that year here."

"You are correct, my dear. That means there's a major error in my calculations."

Jason came by the lab one day after school the next week and found out that Uncle Herb and Kathleen had done several more experiments, each which resulted in bringing someone from the past into the present. Uncle Herb introduced him to a pirate, one of Cochise's warriors, a Revolutionary War fighter, and a painter from the middle ages. They gathered around Jason and asked him what he knew about the strange magic that his uncle had summoned to bring them there.

"Lad, the sad news is that this seems to be a one-way time machine. It will bring people from the past to the present but not the other way around," explained Uncle Herb with a resigned look on his face.

"How about time travel into the future, Uncle Herb?"

"Well, that's what we're about to find out. I'm going to try to travel to the year 2121, to see what the world will be like then."

"And what if you don't go anywhere, but you bring someone here from the future?"

"Well, at least we'll hopefully be able to communicate with our visitor from the future and learn some fascinating things that lie ahead for mankind."

Jason got behind the Plexiglass screen and watched Kathleen set the machine. There was the blinding flash and shaking that Jason had experienced before. Then his uncle's voice came over the loud speaker.

"Open the doors, Kathleen. It appears that future travel in this machine works like travel into the past. Instead of me being transported in time, a visitor from the future is now in the chrono chamber with me."

Jason and Kathleen looked at each other with great anticipation as she pushed the button to open the doors. At first they saw only Uncle Herb. Then, looking down below his knees, they saw a foot-high robot.

They soon discovered that the robot spoke perfect English and was very smart for its size. It called itself Automan. They found out that it was one of thousands of robots that did all the everyday tasks of life in 2121.

"Well, Automan," queried Uncle Herb. With you robots doing all the regular work, what do humans do?"

"Professor, there are no humans left on earth. They died off years ago."

Unusual Fare

Some days as a cabbie in New York are pretty boring, if you don't count traffic jams and the incessant honking from other cabs when I steer around them. But today was definitely not boring!

About 10 a.m. I was cruising by the First National Bank and the Starbucks next to it. There were a lot of people milling around on the sidewalk and I slowed to see if someone wanted a lift. An ugly looking woman in a baggy blue dress darted out of the bank entrance and flagged me down. *With features like that I wonder if she could ever find a husband,* I thought to myself as I pulled over. She opened the door and pulled her lanky body into the cab along with a huge, heavy-looking shopping bag.

"Thanks Buster," she said in a husky voice that maybe she thought sounded sexy. "Drive."

I stepped on the gas. "Okay, M'am. I'm driving. Where do you want to go?"

"I want to just ride around for awhile. Then I'll decide where to stop. How about driving around Central Park?"

"Sure thing. As long as you've got the cash, I've got the time."

"Don't worry about the cash, buster. I've got plenty of that!" She sounded irritated, like I'd insulted her.

As we drove around the park, she started stripping off her clothes. I've had people do some strange things in my cab before, so it didn't really shock me. But I did keep an eye on her as she unbuttoned her dress and pulled it off. When she undid her bra and I saw her flat, hairy chest, I realized this was a cross-dresser. Next thing I know, she, I mean he, pulled a pair of walking shorts and a polo shirt out of the shopping bag and put them on. Soon he'd wiped his lipstick off and ditched the high heels for some Birkenstocks.

"What are you looking at, Buster?" he asked in a menacing tone. "Do you have a problem with my attire?"

"Not at all, sir. It suits you. Do you want me to keep driving around the park?"

"Nah. Enough of nature. Drive me to the City Bank on Wall Street."

"Sure, buddy."

"You ain't my buddy, buster. You're just my driver!"

"Okay, okay. Whatever!"

Just then I got an NYPD alert on my iPhone. When I heard the bing, I pulled the phone out of my shirt pocket and waited until the cab rolled up to a red light. I did a double take as I read the message: Bank robbery at the First National Bank. Suspect is a woman in a blue dress. Last seen hailing a cab near the scene. Suspect is armed and considered dangerous.

"What was that bing, cabbie?"

I tried to disguise the anxiety in my voice as I replied, "Nothing. Just a text from my girl friend."

"Hell! Don't you know better than to text and drive, buster?"

"I didn't reply to her. Just read the text here at the light. No harm done!"

"Okay. But I don't want any accidents! Today is my big day!"

"Oh, really?" I asked, glancing at him in my mirror."

"Yes. But enough about me. Just drive to my bank, so I can make a deposit."

Looking in the mirror again, it was the first time I'd seen him smile. But it seemed more like a sneer to me.

We both looked out the window when we heard a police siren. I slowed and moved toward the curb, wondering what would happen next. But the police cruiser zipped on past us. We both breathed a sigh of relief, but for different reasons.

Thirty minutes later, we pulled up in front of the Wall Street City Bank and I asked if he wanted me to wait.

"No, that's okay, buster. I can get my own ride from here."
Looking at the meter, I announced, "that will be $74, sir."

The cross dresser peeled off a $100 bill from a roll in his pocket and said, "Keep the change, buster."

As he struggled out of the cab with his heavy bag, I noticed that he'd dropped the high heels in the back seat. "Sir, you left your shoes, I mean your heels."

"Don't need 'em. Consider them a gift. Now scram," he ordered as he closed the cab door and turned toward the bank with another sneer-like smile.

I pulled away from the curb and drove down the street until I was out of sight of the bank entrance. After waiting for my pulse rate to slow down, I pulled out my iPhone and dialed a number in my speed dial.

"Lieutenant Delgado speaking."

"Hey, Lieutenant. This is Joe and I've got a hot tip for you."

Being a CI is a good way to supplement my income as a cabbie and it makes this often boring job more tolerable. But today was definitely not boring. And it was definitely profitable!

We Should Have Warned Her

Looking back now, I should have warned the flight attendant. But how could I have known what havoc my brother-in-law would cause on the flight?

It all started when my wife's younger sister, Mary, suggested the four of us meet in Denver and fly to Seattle for a joint vacation. We'd not spent much time together as couples since Mary had married Doug a few years back, so my wife, Liz, readily agreed.

The fun began when we met up in the Denver airport. Liz and I were already tired since our flight from Jacksonville had been delayed for hours. Mary and Doug lived only 30 minutes from DIA, so, as Doug put it, they were "bright-eyed and bushy-tailed" when they arrived. Doug suggested a drink at the cocktail lounge since our flight didn't board for another hour.

"May I get you folks something to drink?" asked the tired young waitress in her little uniform. Doug and Mary each ordered a gin and tonic while Liz and I got iced tea. When the waitress brought our drinks, I could see Doug ogling her cleavage.

As soon as she left, Doug piped up, "Hey, did you hear what little Johnny said when he came home from school last week?" Not waiting for our reply, he continued, "His dad asked him how he liked the new teacher. Fine, he said, but I think she needs some better clothes. Oh, how's that, his dad asked. Her sweater is like a V in front. And when she bent over to help me with my spelling words, one of her lungs fell out!"

I have to admit that Liz and I did smile at the joke, but Doug and Mary both laughed so loudly that the waitress turned back to look.

Later our iced tea refills needed more ice, so the overworked waitress left us a glass of ice. That was a big mistake. When Doug motioned for the check, she hurried over, with beads of sweat on her forehead from running from customer to customer.

"Miss, you've been a good waitress, but I can see that you're stressed out and hot. Maybe this will cool you off a bit!" Doug stated in a matter of fact tone as he dumped the ice down her bodice. Her face instantly bright red, she threw down the check and stomped off to find the manager.

"You two better head to the gate now, while I try to patch things up here!" Liz could tell by my terse tone how upset I was, but Mary and Doug seemed oblivious.

"Don't get so upset, Ron, " Mary counseled between snickers. "Doug's just a boy at heart and meant no harm!"

Liz and I smoothed things over with the manager and waitress by leaving a $25 tip and hurried to the gate behind Mary and Doug.

Forty minutes later we were seated on the flight, with Doug and Mary sitting in the row just behind Liz and me. Liz had talked to Mary privately and she promised that Doug would behave himself on the flight.

As soon as the seat belt sign was off, Doug hurried to the bathroom at the rear of the plane. Soon I heard a shriek behind us and someone yelled "There's a mouse on the plane!" Sure enough, I saw a little white furry creature scurrying down the aisle past our seat. Suddenly it dawned on me that it looked like one of those windup mice that one of my co-workers brought to the office once. And I realized who it belonged to. But how did he get it past the security check?

The mechanical mouse scampered down the aisle until it bumped the foot of Daisy, the attractive brunette flight attendant who had just passed us with the snack cart. Feeling the impact, she looked behind her and screamed, dropping the coke she was pouring into one of those little plastic cups. It spilled all over her and the passenger on the aisle.

"Somebody capture that creature!" Daisy cried.

Just then Doug appeared from somewhere and picked up his practical joke. "It's not real, sweetheart. See?" He held it up for her inspection.

"Hand that over to me, sir, and get back to your seat!" Daisy barked, regaining her composure. Doug quietly complied. Then she apologized to the soaked passenger and gave her some extra napkins for cleaning up.

I fumed in my seat while Doug and Mary tee-heed behind us. "This is the last trip I take with Doug, even if he is family!" I informed Liz.

Thirty minutes later, Daisy was at the intercom, making the usual announcements about connecting flights. "We'll be landing at SeaTac airport in 50 minutes…"

"Wait, wait! I thought we were on our way to Honolulu!" yelled my brother-in-law as he jumped up. "How many of you would rather go to Honolulu? Raise your hands!" he shouted with a goofy smile on his face.

A group of college students on spring break raised their hands and started chanting, "We want to go to Hawaii!"

Suddenly the pilot's stern voice came over the intercom. "This is your captain speaking. Any passenger who continues to make a public disturbance on this flight will be arrested as soon as we land. And I'll see to it that you're barred from flying on this airline again. Understood?"

Doug stopped shouting and meekly took his seat and the college students ceased their chanting.

Minutes later Daisy came back on the intercom with this announcement: "It appears that SeaTac control is going to put us in a holding pattern for a few minutes. I'll be going through the cabin with the beverage cart one more time. Please have $5 ready for any alcoholic beverages."

"Miss, I'd like a beer. And an extra cup of ice if you don't mind."

As soon as I heard Doug place his request, I knew what he intended to do with the ice. I tried to catch the attention of our well-endowed flight attendant, but to no avail. I cringed, waiting for the inevitable, and turned to watch.

"Sure thing, sir," smiled Daisy, who opened up a can of beer on her cart and filled a cup with ice. The look in her eyes was priceless as she poured the entire can of beer on the crotch of Doug's pants and dumped the ice on top of it. "Oh, excuse me, sir. Let me get you another beer." Everyone around laughed and then clapped as she opened up a second can and also poured it into his lap.

"I think you deserved, that, love," whispered Mary as Doug simmered in his seat. He was strangely quiet the rest of the flight even when we disembarked.

"Believe me, Miss," I told Daisy as I walked past her. "If I'd known he'd pull these practical jokes during the flight, I'd have warned you."

When West Meets East

The rain forest humidity hit me like a wet blanket as I stepped out of the Kuala Lumpur International Airport and hailed a taxi. "Boy, this doesn't look or feel like Houston," I thought to myself. A yellow and black cab screeched to a halt at the curb and the young Malay driver helped me with my bags. "Where to, mister?" he asked in the king's English.

"The Mandarin Oriental, please."

"Sure thing, sir. Nice hotel. Are you from the States? How was your flight?"

I had plenty of time to answer the driver's questions during the fifty kilometer ride into Kuala Lumpur. He proved to be a wealth of information about this city of 1.5 million people.

"I'm from Texas. Yes, this is my first time here in Malaysia, Danial. In fact it's my first time to the Far East. All of my prior business trips have been in the US or Western Europe."

"I think you'll find my country is quite different than Texas, Mr. Wilson. On the other hand, Kuala Lumpur is a very cosmopolitan city and has more similarities to large US cities than many other capital cities in this part of the world."

"Good; maybe that will lessen the culture shock a bit. Have you been to the United States before?"

"Yes. My parents took me to New York City on vacation after I graduated from secondary school. That was before my father lost his job in the Great Recession that started in your country."

"Sorry to hear that. A lot of people have been affected by it."

"Yes. That's why I drive this taxi part-time: to pay expenses while I study at the University of Malaya."

Looking at the scenery as we neared the outskirts of the city, I confided to Danial that the mountains, palm trees, and other tropical plants reminded me of living in Hawaii when I was in the service.

As we neared the hotel entrance, Danial spoke up, "So, Mr. Wilson, will you have any time for sightseeing here this weekend?"

"Well, my first business meeting is Monday morning, so I do have the next two days to get over jet lag and see the sights and sounds. Guess the hotel staff can probably hook me up with a tour guide or something."

"Be careful of some of the tour guides here. Some of them charge way more than they're worth. I have a suggestion. One of my cousins by marriage, Denise Fong, is a travel agent for Sunway Travel. I could have her contact you here at the hotel, if you'd like."

"Sure, that'd be fine. How much do I owe you for the ride?"

Soon I was standing in the magnificent lobby of the Mandarin Oriental, marveling at the marble columns and walls and the huge chandelier hanging from the ceiling. A young lady dressed in western clothes with a scarf around her head warmly greeted me and asked for my Amex card. "You'll be on the tenth floor, Mr. Wilson, with a view overlooking the vanishing edge pool. Do you need any help with your bags?"

"No, that's okay. I can handle them myself. Thanks."

By 4 p.m. I had unpacked and started wandering around the hotel to check out my surroundings. I found one of the dining rooms and had a light dinner. Consulting an app on my iPhone, I realized it was about 3 a.m. back home. No wonder I felt tired.

The message light was on when I returned to my room. I had a voice mail from Danial's cousin, Denise, and called her back.

"Hello, Mr. Wilson. Danial told me a little about you and said you might like me to show you around the city this weekend. I'm sure you'll want to catch up on your sleep this evening. How about meeting for breakfast tomorrow?"

"Sure, how about 9 a.m. here at the hotel? I'll be in the lobby to meet you."

The next morning an attractive Chinese woman wearing a long sheath dress entered the lobby and showed me her business card that identified her as Denise Fong, owner of Sunway Travel. At breakfast, we discussed places I might want to visit.

"The nearby Petronas Towers were the tallest in the world until recently. The view from the upper floors is spectacular and I highly recommend it. If you're interested in shopping, there is the famous KLCC Mall adjacent to the hotel. A lot of Westerners like to go to Pataling Street, where you can buy knock-off watches, DVDs, and jewelry at bargain prices. Then there are some terrific restaurants where you can sample the local cuisine as well as any type of food you can get back in the States."

"All of that sounds fine, Ms. Fong. Is there a tour guide you can fix me up with for the day?"

"Actually, I'm free today and would be glad to take you myself, if that would be acceptable to you. I lived in Houston with my aunt, while attending college at Rice University, and I don't often get to visit with anyone from Houston."

"Rice? That's pretty impressive. What did you study?"

"I got a degree in International Finance, which gave me a good background for the travel agency which I own. How about it? Would you permit me to show you around the city?"

"Well, I'd be glad to pay you. In fact, I wouldn't feel right if I didn't."

"No, I won't take any money from you, Mr. Wilson. But I have an aunt who lives near Rice and I have a gift for her. Perhaps you could take it to her? It's an antique jade letter opener that I'm not comfortable mailing. There have been a lot of thefts with the mails here recently."

The next Thursday, I boarded the long flight back to Houston through Singapore, Tokyo, and Chicago. In my carry-on bag was the gift for Denise Fong's aunt.

It took forty minutes of standing in long lines at Houston Intercontinental to clear customs with my baggage. Breathing a sigh of relief as I was given the go-ahead, I started toward the taxi entrance when a tall man in a dark suit flashed a badge and asked me to follow him. Leaving me in a small office with my mouth gaped open, he said for me to wait there.

Soon, a woman in a business suit entered the office and showed me credentials that identified her as an employee of the CIA.

"Mr. Wilson, I need to see the jade letter opener that you were given in KL."

"What? How did you know about that? Why do you need it?"

"You will see in a minute, sir."

I handed her the letter opener and watched her unscrew the handle, remove a microchip that had been concealed inside, and pocket it. Then she screwed the handle back on and returned the opener to me.

"You have done a service for your country, Mr. Wilson. You are free to go and take the letter opener with you."

That's how I once was a courier for the CIA.

Workin' on the Railroad

Shorty was what they called Sean O'Reilly. Though just five feet tall, he made up for it with a violent temper and down right meanness. Shorty was in charge of a Chinese emigrant labor crew working on the Central Pacific railroad being laid east to meet the Union Pacific railroad coming west. His job was to get the most work possible out of the "Celestials." as they were called in the 1860's. In those days China was known as the Celestial Kingdom.

"Hey Shorty, how has your crew of Celestials been working out?" asked John Spike, the burly track foreman as he walked up to the section of rail bed that Shorty's crew was constructing.

"Better than those white guys I used to ramrod. These guys are small and don't weigh much, but most of them can really work!"

"Would you like some more? The chief engineer says we can get a bunch more where these men came from."

"Why the hell not, John. Bring them on!"

A week later, John Spike brought Shorty a dozen men whose long dark braids hung below their coolie hats. "Shorty, here's some more help. They have assured me they can work, but most of them speak very little English!"

Shorty motioned the dozen over to his tent, where he kept a ledger. "Okay, line up and I'll need you to tell me your names.

Then I will write your name in this here ledger. I expect you to work as hard as you can for six days a week from sunrise to sunset. If you do that, your pay will be $30 a month in gold coins. I'm the boss. So my word is king. If you give me any grief you will regret it. I've been known to beat slackers unconscious with my walking stick. Understood?"

The new men quickly lined up and gave their names one at a time to Shorty. "Hon Chee," said one, "Li Chun," another, and "Kang Phi" yet another.

Finally the last one stood in front of Shorty and said "They call me Dao."

"Dao? Is that all?"

"Yes Mr. Shorty. Just Dao."

The next week John Spike approached and asked, "Shorty, how are the new men working out?"

"Oh. Well enough, I guess. They do know how to put their shoulders to the work, but sometimes I get tired of hearing them jabbering in a language I don't understand."

"Who's that one pounding away at that boulder? He can sure swing that sledge hammer!"

"Calls himself Dao. Speaks pretty good English and he doesn't waste time jabbering with the others. The others seem to look up to him, though."

"Good. We can use more of that type!"

A few days later, Shorty heard one of the men cry out and fall to the ground. Hurrying over, he saw Hon Chee clutching a bloody knee and speaking Chinese.

"What happened?" His question was met by a torrent of words he didn't understand. "Can't anyone talk to me in English?"

Dao came forward and explained, "A chip of granite bounced off someone's hammer and split open Hon Chee's knee. He needs medical care."

"The medical tent is a mile away and I can't spare any of you to carry him there. Wrap it up yourselves and get back to work. Hon Chee can sit out the rest of the afternoon, but he doesn't get back to work tomorrow, there'll be hell to pay. He should have been more careful!" exclaimed Shorty, waving his walking stick menacingly.

The next morning Dao noticed that Hon Chee's knee was swollen and looked bad. When he tried to stand on it, the pain was unbearable. He went to speak to Shorty on Hon Chee's behalf, but Shorty would have none of it.

Striding over to Hon Chee, Shorty demanded, "Stand up and get to work!" When Hon Chee struggled to comply, his leg buckled underneath him.

"Stand up you no-good Chink!" With that command, Shorty started beating Hon Chee mercilessly with his walking stick.

"Stop that!" yelled Dao and caught Shorty's stick in mid-air. Pulling it out of Shorty's hands, he broke it across his knee and tossed it aside.

Shorty stopped for a minute with his mouth agape and then pulled a derringer out of his back pocket. "You can go to hell, Dao!" he screamed as he pointed it at Dao.

Before Shorty could pull the trigger, he fell to the ground gasping for breath. In the blink of an eye, Dao had nearly crushed his windpipe with the edge of his hand.

"I warn you, Mr. Shorty. Next time you try to attack one of these Chinks as you call us, I will kill you before you can cry out. They call me Dao, a nickname that means 'knife.'" My hands are like knife blades and I've been trained to use them in self defense or in defending others. With a single blow, I killed a man in China who tried to rape my sister, and he was much bigger than you. Understand?"

Holding his throat, Shorty stumbled to his feet and mumbled an apology. He never reported the incident to his superiors and he never beat another Chinese laborer. Six months later he and his crew watched the golden spike being driven to officially complete the Transcontinental Railroad.

Would You Buy A Used Car from This Man?

"Hey, Bob, did you see the story in today's newspaper about the arrest of a guy here in Texas who was plotting the assassination of the Saudi Ambassador? It says Iran was behind the scheme and that he was trying to get a Mexican Drug Cartel to do the dirty work for him."

"Is that so, Jill? Why in the hell would he do that?" asked Bob as he finished his wakeup coffee.

"Well, the guy was an Iranian who became a naturalized US Citizen. Maybe he was always a secret agent for his home country."

"Secret agent, huh. What kind of work did he do here in Texas?"

"It says here that he was a businessman of sorts. Let's see, the article is continued on page seven. Here it is. Okay, he used to own a used car dealership down in Corpus. There's a photo of him. Kind of ugly and looks shifty-eyed to me. Gee, would you buy a used car from this man, Bob?"

Setting down his coffee cup, Bob peered over Jill's shoulder at the photo on page seven. "Holy cow, Jill! I did buy a used car from that guy years ago. His name was Jack Arbabsiar and he sold me a real lemon. Biggest piece of junk I ever owned. This guy had given me a written iron clad guarantee that wasn't worth the paper it was printed on."

"Really? Tell me more!"

"Well, it was a yellow Chevy Nova that he sold me for $5000, a little below blue book price. The damn engine froze up about a month after I bought it. The guarantee the guy wrote up was supposed to cover everything on the car for the first 180 days or the first 6,000 miles, which ever came first. So I towed it back to the used car dealership and demanded my money back."

"Then what?"

The shyster had sold the dealership the week before and left town. The new owner wasn't legally bound to honor the other owner's guarantee, so he didn't! I tried to track Arbabsiar down and never could locate him! Makes my blood boil just thinking about it!"

"Hmm. The article says that although this guy called himself Jack, his first name was actually Manssor. Maybe that's why you couldn't track him down. Gee! The article says he has a house right here in Austin!"

"Living here right under my nose! What's his address?"

"Doesn't say."

"Well, I'm going to find out and try to get my money back!"

"Bob, he's been arrested by the FBI. He's being held for arraignment, so he's not at his house."

"Yeah, but somebody has got to be at that house that I can talk to. I'm going to do some searching on the Internet and locate his address!"

"Calm down, honey! You're getting all worked up about this. It's not good for your blood pressure!"

Ignoring his wife's pleas, Bob located the former used-car dealer's Austin address and headed for his jeep.

"Bob, you're not really going there are you? Have you lost all of your common sense? Maybe I should come with you."

"No, stay here, Honey. I know this may be a wild goose chase, but I've got to try!"

Thirty minutes later, Bob pulled up at a two story stucco house that matched the address he'd found on the Internet. There were two Government-issue gray sedans at the curb.

As he strode up to the front door, Jill's cautions echoed in his mind. Maybe this was a waste of time after all. He stood with his finger poised above the doorbell button for minutes as the rational part of him fought with his rage at being cheated so many years ago. Finally he dropped his hand and turned to go. Just then a tall clean-cut man in a dark suit came around the corner of the house.

"Can I help you?" barked the man in the suit.

"Well, y-yes, I guess," stammered Bob. I'm trying to locate Jack Arbabsiar."

"Mr. Arbabsir is not on the premises. Who are you and what do you need?" The suspicion in the man's voice was hard not to miss.

"I'm Bob. Bob Burgin. But before I tell you more, who are you?"

"FBI. Agent Tom Sullivan," stated the man as he showed Bob his credentials.

"Oh. I guess I could have figured that from the cars parked over there. I read about Mr. Arbabsir in the paper and realized that he was the man I have some, some, shall we say, unfinished business with."

The agent's eyebrows went up at that and Bob groaned inwardly. He hadn't worded that very well and started again. "What I meant to say, Agent Sullivan, is that this guy sold me a lemon of a used car years ago back in Corpus and cheated me out of my $5000. I lost track of him until my wife saw the article in the paper. I wanted to see if somehow I could get my money back."

The agent threw back his head and laughed. "Boy, have you got some gall, Mr. Burgin. Ha, ha. Wait till I tell my partner about this."

Suddenly Bob could see how senseless this all was. "I guess, you're right, Agent Sullivan. Guess I'll just have to kiss that $5000 good-bye."

"I'd say so. And consider yourself lucky that you're not a business associate of Mr. Arbabsir. If so, you'd be spending the rest of this week being interrogated behind closed doors."

Backing up, Bob said, "Yeah. Well, I'll be going as I don't want to waste any more of your time." Turning around, Bob walked as fast as he could to his jeep, hoping the agent wouldn't change his mind and call him back for questioning. He jumped in the seat, turned the key, breathed a sigh of relief as the engine started and he drove away.

As he came in their front door, Bob yelled to Jill, "I'm back!"

"That's good honey. Did you get it back?"

"What, my money? No, I didn't."

"Not your money, Bob. I knew that was a lost cause. But did you get your common sense back?"

Chagrined, Bob simply said, "Yes I did"

63186239R00204

Made in the USA
Charleston, SC
29 October 2016